A NEED FOR VIOLENCE

T0014740

A NEED FOR VIOLENCE

THE BATTLING HARRIGANS OF THE FRONTIER

DUSTY RICHARDS

AND MATTHEW P. MAYO

PINNACLE BOOKS
Kensington Publishing Corp.
www.kensingtonbooks.com

PINNACLE BOOKS are published by

Kensington Publishing Corp.
119 West 40th Street
New York, NY 10018

All Kensington titles, imprints, and distributed lines are available at special quantity discounts for bulk purchases for sales promotion, premiums, fund-raising, and educational or institutional use.

Special book excerpts or customized printings can also be created to fit specific needs. For details, write or phone the office of the Kensington Sales Manager: Kensington Publishing Corp., 119 West 40th Street, New York, NY 10018. Attn. Sales Department. Phone: 1-800-221-2647.

PINNACLE BOOKS and the Pinnacle logo Reg. U.S. Pat. & TM Off.

First Printing: December 2023
ISBN-13: 978-0-7860-4923-3
ISBN-13: 978-0-7860-4924-0 (eBook)

10 9 8 7 6 5 4 3 2 1

Printed in the United States of America

CHAPTER 1

A balmy morning in early spring found Mackworth "Mack" Harrigan sitting alone, staring but not seeing the stunning boulder-studded vista before him, a promontory jutting into space holding him as if in a giant, cupped hand, offering him to the world of the West. He had an awful lot to chew on.

He was thinking, *Here I am, late of Harrigan Falls, Ohio, no longer anchored to any one spot, but drifting in the great Western frontier with my family.* He reckoned that, all in all, he could not be happier.

Maybe *happy* was not the best word for it. Maybe it was contentment. Yes, he nodded. He was contented. He knew it could not last, should not last, for nothing got done in life, in his purview, without movement, motion, and effort. To him, those things seemed to be the opposite of contentment.

Nonetheless, he sighed and stretched his lean legs out before him, repositioning work-hardened hands on the cool gray rock behind him as he leaned back. For the moment, contentment ruled.

Having spent the previous hour, rare precious time to spend alone, gazing into the vast purpled place, he knew it teemed with life, though none was visible so early in the morning. He'd gazed at all that glorious nothing.

And yet, with a wry grin, he asked himself, wasn't it everything, too? All at the same time? Seeing none of the splendor of the place, but knowing it was there?

Gradually the vista awakened, and he was treated to a brightening dawn sky cast westward from the rising sun behind him.

His thoughts circled back to land on something of far more import to him—his family. He was still married to the sweetheart of his youth, Elspeth "Ell," and they were blessed with five children. The eldest, strong, thoughtful and curious Kane, was now sixteen; no longer the middle child, Meghan was thirteen; fiery little Fitch was seven; and the twins, Henry and Hattie, were born healthy and well just three months before. His entire brood were all, by the grace of God, in fine fettle.

Mack had never thought he'd be so lucky as to have not only the three wonderful children he'd known for so long, but now, twins! The very idea of it made him smile.

He and Ell enjoyed being parents, though he had to admit the appearance of the twins had rattled him to his boots. Ell had kept the pregnancy hidden from him for quite some time on the trail west. Just as well. They had battled daily to endure life on that ill-chosen wagon train headed by the vile drunkard wagon boss, Ricker Briggs. In the end, Mack had laid him low in a hand-to-hand death match after the brute had attacked Meghan.

Mack's thoughts turned to that time.

Though everyone on the meager little train had benefited from Briggs's unfortunate death, for his pains Mack was thrown to the wolves once they reached the foul stink pit of a trading post in the midst of a blizzard. The others on the wagon train, never fond of the kind, generous Harrigan clan, had told the Northland Fur Company's trading post ruthless, uncouth sluggard managert that Mack had murdered

Briggs without just cause. His companions, leering fellows more curs than men, were fur-wrapped trappers who did more drinking and fighting than trapping. They all spent the winter holed up at the trading post, exploiting the local Indian population in every way possible.

Mack's protests fell on the uncaring ears of braying, drunk men and they had ambushed Mack. In the trading post manager's role as what passed for local white law, he had held a mockery of a trial and found Mack guilty. They beat Mack and locked him, unconscious, in the hide storage shed, a foul, gappy structure with stacks of frozen animal hides awaiting shipment out—in the spring.

As thin luck would have it, the next day an army patrol swung by the trading post on its way back to its home base of Fort Woolsey, several days ride from the trading post. Mack's only thoughts were for his family, and specifically for his wife and daughter. He tried reasoning with the officer in charge of the patrol, a steely young man named Captain Swann, but he would have none of it. Mack railed and fought, but they dragged him out of there and lashed him to a horse, to be tried at Fort Woolsey.

On the way to the fort, they were attacked, pinned down in the open by a rogue band of outlaw Indians the patrol had been tracking for some time, without success.

Through good luck and bold action, Mack, though wounded in the melee, was able to save himself and the wounded Swann. The rest of the soldiers met their maker in that massacre. Mack rode hell for leather, thundering for Fort Woolsey, holding the unconscious young man before him in the saddle.

More dead than alive, Mack and Swann were tended to at the fort and Mack's luck finally turned. The fort commander, Colonel Chase, had been acquainted with the vile wagon boss, Ricker Briggs, and knew it was highly likely Mack was telling the bald truth.

Mack was a lousy patient, and the army had its hands full until he was well enough to depart and reunite with his family. Far too soon, he departed on a fresh mount, with the Army's gratitude for having saved the life of young Swann.

Mack rode not for the trading post but for the wintering grounds of the Shoshone, a band whose chief, Stalks-the-Night, had made their acquaintance at the trading post when Ell had intervened on his behalf. She'd realized he was being taken advantage of by the vile trading post boss.

As the army patrol had led him away from the trading post, Chief Stalks-the-Night had said he would take care of Mack's family and would take them to his wintering grounds northwest of the trading post.

That was all Mack had heard. Despite a brutal storm moving in fast and low, he departed the fort and rode in what he'd hoped was the direction of those wintering grounds.

He'd been roving hard for weeks when he came upon a naked man, greased in honey and dung, lashed tight to a log deep in bear country. The once-burly old fellow with his great cloud of a beard fluttering soon became recognizable to Mack. It was none other than mountain man Bearpaw Jones—the very man who had warned Mack several times back in St. Louis to not join Ricker Briggs's train but instead to wait until spring to head west.

Mack groaned at the memory, but continued thinking of all his family had experienced.

Back in St. Louis, he had felt they could not wait, and so, going against what his gut told him, what Bearpaw had told him, and what Ell had expressed strong concern about, he joined Briggs's wagon train. That poor decision

*had been the beginning of all the bad things the Harrigans
experienced as they roved westward on the frontier.*

Mack smiled. Thanks to the kindness of Chief Stalks-
the-Night, they had some of their possessions, and most
important of all, their lives, including the two new lives of
the twins. The Shoshone had taken their birth as a sign of
good luck and had given them the names Mighty Creek, for
Henry, and Silent Calf, for Hattie.

"What's next, then, Mack?" he said out loud as he continued looking out at the stunning vista before him.

"That's what I was going to ask you, Papa," said a voice
from behind.

Mack turned to see his beautiful daughter, Meghan,
looking down at him. Once more he saw that somehow
without him knowing it, she had become a woman these
past few months with the Shoshone.

She wore an interesting mix of back East clothing and
Indian garb. Her shirt was one her mother had sewn and her
skirt had been made of soft doeskin.

"I didn't hear you, daughter."

"That's good," said Meghan, smiling. "I've been working with Bright Owl on my stalking skills."

"Bright Owl, eh?" Mack watched his daughter's cheeks
redden. *Just like a Harrigan,* he thought. Can never hide
our feelings. *Always betrayed by red cheeks and red ears.*

"Papa, he's just a friend. He's Kane's friend, too."

"I know, I know." Mack winked at her and patted the
stone surface beside him. "I was teasing you."

Well he knew of Bright Owl, the son of Chief Stalks-the-
Night, and a year or so older than Kane. The young men
were blood brothers, having formed a fast, deep bond when
they'd been forced to survive a blizzard together while on
the trail looking for Mack.

Yet if it hadn't been for Mack and Bearpaw Jones, Kane

and Bright Owl might have perished. That the chief had been willing to send his own son to accompany Kane on the dubious rescue mission was yet another reminder of the kindness and matter-of-fact generosity of the Shoshone toward Mack and his family.

Of course it had helped that a very pregnant Ell, assisted by Meghan, had helped nurse the tribe through a sickness that had laid many of their kind low. The Harrigan women had been ably assisted by Red Dove, the Indian woman they had rescued from near-death enslavement to Ricker Briggs.

In an interesting turn of events, during the long winter, the widowed Chief Stalks-the-Night and Red Dove had become close.

Meghan settled beside Mack, stretching out her legs beside his. He noted she had grown taller since they left Ohio, and he sighed. What a long, strange, and unexpected adventure it had been so far.

As with all of them, Mack had spent a busy winter learning new skills shared with them by the Shoshone. In particular, he and Kane were keen to learn as much as they could of the wild world surrounding them—hunting, fishing, and foraging techniques; skills useful in battle, be it with another man or with the not-uncommon fights with bears, mountain lions, and the like.

Of all the Harrigans, it seemed Fitch had taken life among the Shoshone with a relish none of them could match. The fierce, fiery little boy, nearly eight years old, had in recent weeks refused to speak in any tongue but that of the Shoshone, and he refused to respond to requests made to him in English.

It was annoying and frustrating, particularly for Ell when she needed the boy's help. Mack ginned, for it had proven useful in one regard. It had helped all the Harrigans learn the Shoshone language even quicker.

"Did your mother have any luck in getting Fitch to help her with the chores?"

"Oh, you mean the chores you and Kane somehow don't have to do anymore?"

"But—"

"No buts!" Meghan's face was reddening as she looked at her father, holding up her finger just the same way Ell did when Mack stepped in something he should have known to avoid with her. *My word,* he thought. *Mother and daughter are so much alike.*

"Just because I was born a girl doesn't mean I am not as interested in fishing and hunting as you and Kane!"

"You never said so before, Meghan."

"I know." She sighed. "Because I'm not, really. But"—she looked at him again—"it also doesn't mean I shouldn't be asked! Why should I be stuck doing things Kane is perfectly suited to doing? Things like helping Ma clean or tending to the twins or cooking or doing the laundry? It's not fair."

Mack knew better than to say anything. That he didn't really agree with his daughter was something he was not about to say. She could be as frightening as Ell when you got her riled. But that didn't mean he couldn't see her point, either.

"Tell you what," he said, pushing strands of hair out of her face that had slipped free of the rawhide thongs holding her two long braids, as the women of the tribe wore their hair. "I'll talk with Kane and convince him the two of us need to help out more around the teepee. Okay?"

"I guess." She shrugged. "I don't think it'll do any good. You know how he is."

Mack had to agree. Kane was a different sort, always

had been. If something within a hundred yards of him crawled, sniffed, growled, slithered, flew, or hopped, he wanted to know about it. He was always drawing pictures of critters and making notes about them. Mack wasn't certain to what end such notions would lead the boy, but as a pastime it seemed harmless enough.

The moments of quiet rumination alone and then with his eldest daughter jerked to a quick, short halt with the thumping of small feet thudding toward them from the winding trail that led to this spot.

Mack tensed and turned, not expecting much more than children at play. In this he was not surprised, for emerging from out of the low shrubby cover and thin pines leaped the Harrigan's surprisingly resilient hound, Grinner, wearing his perpetual lopsided grin. Right behind scrambled his constant companion, Fitch Harrigan, he of the Shoshone-only lingo.

"Pa! Pa!"

Mack saw the odd look on his son's face and rose to his knees.

The boy did not shout his name again and leaped at him as he often did, but hissed, "Pa!" in a hoarse whisper. His eyes were wide and his color was white on his cheeks, unusual for a Harrigan.

"What's the matter, son?" said Mack, lifting the slight but wiry youth into his arms.

"Pa!" Again the youth whispered the word, then swiveled his head around behind them, back to the trail toward the camp.

"What is all this, Fitch? Tell me now!"

"Pa, quiet! They might hear!"

"Who? said Mack, also glancing up the trail.

"The . . . Indians!"

Mack smiled. "Son, our best friends and hosts are Indians."

"No, the other ones! They're all over the place. Kane and Bright Owl told me to fetch you!"

"Are they friendly?"

Fitch shook his head. "I don't think so. They're shooting arrows. I heard somebody scream." The little, tough child began to shake and weep, and his breath caught in his throat.

Mack stood and looked at Meghan. Her eyes just like Ell's were wide.

"You two stay here . . . down below that ledge. Get into the small caves and overhangs there."

"But Papa!"

"No, Meghan. Do it. I need someone to watch over him."

Fitch had recovered from his moment of tearfulness and growled. "I don't need no woman taking care of me! I'm Shoshone!"

"No," Mac said harshly. "No, Fitch. You are not. You are a Harrigan. And you are my son. Now do as you're told!" Making for the trail, he added, "Besides, not even the Shoshone are fearless."

In a half crouch, he turned. "Meghan, stay hidden and safe." He looked directly into her eyes and she nodded, already beginning to gather in the feisty Fitch.

"And take that dog with you," said Mack, nodding toward Grinner. Though how the girl was going to manage Fitch and the hound, he knew not.

"Stay safe!" were his last words, and then he bolted as fast as he was able back up the trail toward the Shoshone's winter village and the Harrigan home for the past several months, wondering what he would find back at the camp.

It did not take Mack long to find out the situation was not a fanciful notion spun in Fitch's mind—a notion he doubted but hoped would be true.

He heard the crack of a rifle shot and far ahead, shouts, then the chilling scream of a woman. The loud ululating cries of men sounded still far ahead. Their voices were hoarse, high and low, all converging, meeting in shouts and growls—the sounds men make when they come together in battle.

All this he heard as he ran as if Hades hounds were on his heels. His stovepipe boots hammered the worn earth of the trail. All about him springtime in the mountains burgeoned. Aspen were threatening to bud, the sky was blue, but it held the promise of something different from winter skies, something welcome, refreshing and warm. Songbirds had become more active, winging from Ponderosa pine to the safety of thickets of scrub as hunting hawks and eagles winged low.

Mack saw and heard none of it, nothing save for the trail ahead, and the vision of his wife and children in harm's way. The sounds of battle were goads driving him onward.

Before he reached the familiar, comfortable village running at full effort, Mack saw his first evidence the day would not end as he had hoped. A dead man, slumped at the base of a tree, stared ahead at nothing, his hands rested on the earth to either side of him, palms up as if to say, "What else would you ask of me?"

Mack slowed, realizing this man was beyond help, for he wore a red-welling bullet hole in the middle of his forehead. Mack could see the dead man was an Indian, but unfamiliar. The ornamentation and the beading and fringe-work of the man's buckskins was similar to that of clothes worn by the Shoshone, but the way the man wore his hair was odd, bristling upward in a grease-stiffened peak, as if a small porcupine were perched atop his head. Seeing that, Mack knew who the man might be, and thus who the attackers could be.

All this came to him in a sliver of a moment as he bent to snatch up the dead man's rifle. It was a familiar enough weapon, and he hastily slipped free his own sheathed knife, seeing that his hands were trembling as he hacked away a pouch worn around the man's neck. Its flap flopped open to reveal balls and patch and powder horn. It would have to do until Mack could get to his own weapons.

He loosed the pouch from the dead man and shoved off again, the village a hundred yards ahead though the brush. This took mere moments, but they agonized him.

The sounds of battle ahead made him envision his family dying in a fusillade, the last thing they saw leering faces of kill-crazy attackers. He shook off the grim vision with a growl and pounded the trail harder toward screams and billows of black smoke.

As he topped the last slight rise, looking left and right the entire time, any ember of hope of the battle being a minor skirmish winked out as he ran. His view of the village was one of chaos. People swarmed in all directions.

He ducked low and made for the northern edge of the camp where his family's teepee sat. So far it looked not afire. It was a hodge-podge affair of tent and lean-to involving their wagon, parked for the winter alongside their home and yet part of it as well. It was the annex, as Kane called it, a place where they stored what they had as well as where he slept.

Fitch had started out sleeping there, too, but he became untrustworthy, sneaking out in the middle of the night to prowl the camp with Grinner. That set off the other dogs of the camp, and soon Grinner and the boy had to spend their nights in the tent proper with the rest of the family. Kane didn't mind one bit. Fitch had become a burr under the older boy's saddle blanket.

Before he'd made it a dozen strides, Mack heard a low,

growling, bark of a word to his right. Ducking low out of instinct, he held up the rifle and looked that way. Rushing at him was a lean, tall warrior wearing a hair style similar to that of the dead man. Growling, he kept voicing the same word. Nearly unintelligible, it was nothing Mack could pick out, but from the sound and his sneering, grim look, it was obvious the man meant him ill.

He also didn't appear to be carrying a gun. His hands were filled—a small belt ax in one and a wide-bladed knife in the other. And he was closing in fast.

Mack set himself low, legs spread, and pulled the rifle up to his shoulder and thumbed back the hammer. The face of the oncoming brute showed his shock, but it was far too late for change. Mack touched the trigger.

Nothing happened.

The man barreled for him faster, his malice-filled smile wider, his growling words louder.

Mack dropped the gun and raised his own knife.

The attacker had been a solid eight feet away when he launched himself at Mack. He led with his knife, intending to lacerate Mack's face, likely from the neck up.

Mack had other plans.

He dropped low to his knees, and the brute sailed close overhead, his grunting and growling pinching off. Mack used the man's momentum for his own means, whipping up his knife and sliding the honed tip of the broad blade through the man's buckskin tunic and puncturing his muscled gut with a sudden spray of red gore.

The attacker's momentum slowed, and though it carried Mack backward, it soon dwindled. As he began to topple from the weight, he braced himself, throwing his left leg to the side. With a heave and shout he shoved up and back, the knife sinking to his knuckles.

Mack fell over backward as the brute slid from his blade

and writhed, thrashing his buckskin-clad legs and flailing onto his back, his hands clutching at his gut as if he'd been handed a basket of hot coals. His screams soon became a hideous, gurgling sound.

Mack shoved, scooting on his backside away from the flailing fool, only then realizing his knife was still in his hand. *Good. It will have to do.* He was not about to fool with the dead man's rifle any longer.

He left it and the bag on the earth and continued onward. Snatching up his first victim's dropped ax, he fled the scene, leaving the brute still wriggling and flailing, his hands clawing in fury and agony at nothing and everything.

Mack sprinted onward, dodging boulders and trees as he dragged his left sleeve across his eyes to clear the fresh blood. He heard a familiar voice to his right and glanced that way. Bright Owl. And not far from the chief's son stood Kane. Both were set for action, and judging from the bodies fouling the earth about them, they were holding their own.

Mack was torn between his fatherly urge to run to his son, his firstborn, or bolt forward to his wife and babes. As much as it pained him, he told himself, *Kane is a boy no longer, but a man, taking lives and defending lives.* Ell needed Mack.

He made it to the edge of the camp, and spied another warrior astride a small gray horse with black speckling and black legs. The man rode only with a blanket, no saddle, and was making with all haste for the Harrigan tent. In his left hand he held a rifle and in his teeth he held his hide reins. And clutched in his right hand, a sizzling brand waved, hissing flame and spewing smoke. The man was about to set fire to Mack's home.

"Not today." Mack dropped to his right knee, whipped back with the hand ax, and repeated a maneuver he'd worked on all winter in serious play with the men of the village. Everyone had agreed the white man Harrigan had impressive ax-throwing skills.

We'll see if their praise was well earned or not, thought Mack as he let loose with the ax, watching as if time had slowed. The ax whipped toward the man, end for end. Instead of the target being the butt end of a log raised man-height atop other logs, Mack's target was the spot between the man's wing bones, as Bearpaw Jones called the shoulder blades.

The ax sunk true with a fast, hard set. From the way it landed, jamming in without slopping out, Mack knew it had buried deep in bone.

The effect on the man's crouched, determined, shouting body was finger-snap quick. As the ax sunk into his body, his life juices sprayed out to either side of the blade, as if freakish wings. His arms flew upward. As his rifle, freed from his grasp, spun some feet away, Mack noted its location.

The other hand, the right, also whipped skyward. The flickering brand intended to burn Mack's home to cinders spun in the air, end-over-end until it landed flame-first atop a clot of brown grasses that quickly bloomed alight.

Mack rushed to it and stomped at it, sending up flutters of drifting, glowing ash and sparks. He danced a frantic jig atop it a moment longer, then ran for the Harrigan abode.

As he legged it, he caught sight of the pretty gray horse the man had been riding. The ax-wearing man was still astride the bolting beast, but he didn't appear to be long for the saddle. Or in this case, *blanket.*

As Mack ran, the warrior tumbled off the back of the horse, landing, unbelievably, on his back, the small belt ax driving deeper into his body with the savage drop.

Any mewling, high-pitched screechy sounds he'd been

making petered out and his arms flopped to his sides, looking to Mack much the same as the first dead man he'd seen that day. As with that unfortunate fellow with the third eye hole, this man's days were all but over. He might squeak out another few precious moments, but he was, as Bearpaw said, cooked all the way through.

"Ell! Ell!" Mack bellowed his wife's name as he thundered toward the tent, praying in a mash of words and sounds of earnest supplication that she would be well.

He tore at the entrance, but found it tied from within—the only protection to keep people out—scant and ineffective, as the tent was a heavy, solid blend of canvas tarpaulin and layers of skins draped as a covering. It had served them more than well all winter, but of late it had become smelly and close. The residual odors of a winter's worth of human, dog, and smoke had begun to feel baked into the tent's skins.

None of that mattered at that moment as Mack tore at the skins, ripping apart the feeble ties to get at his wife and children. "Ell!" Ell!" He forced his way inside the dark interior. The fire was out and there was no sound. The sounds of the raging battle outside came to him muffled and dull. "Ell!"

"Mack?" The voice came from the back corner, behind stacked trunks and crates containing some of their meager possessions transferred from the wagon months before.

"Ell? Are you all right? Ell?"

Mack heard his own voice, cracked and pleading, howling in the dark space before him.

"Yes! Mack, yes!" Ell stood, holding the two swaddled-tight twins close to her breast. Remarkably, they appeared to be asleep.

"Ell, are you hurt?"

"No, but what's happening? Mack, where are Fitch and Meghan? And Kane?"

"They're okay. You? The twins?"

"Yes, we're okay. Mack, what's going on? I hid in here when I heard the shouting, the screams. I would rather be out there, but the twins . . ."

"I know, Ell." He held her close, feeling the babies between them. He realized the reason they were silent was because they were nursing. Despite the situation, he smiled.

The moment was short-lived because something hard thudded against the side of the tent, then again and again. They watched as the south wall shuddered and swayed under the assault.

"I have to go. Hide, Ell. I'll protect the tent. Stay hidden. There's nothing you can do except protect yourself and the twins!" He kissed her forehead as another savage blow cracked one of the horizontal stays he'd lashed in place himself months before.

Armed only with his knife, he sneaked out with care to catch the intruder unaware and give him a dose of his own attack. Instead of cutting right and confronting the brute head-on, Mack cat walked left, keeping low and scooting around the parked wagon. He hoped to come upon the attacker quickly, as the side of the tent angled out at a point right about where the man was hitting it.

Proved correct in his guess, Mack would have lunged at the man who, in the few moments it took to circle the tent, had managed to hack a rent in the skin wall large enough to jam his head through, which is precisely what he did.

It was not something Mack would have done, had he been the attacker. Who knew who could be in there?

If Ell hadn't had the twins to worry about, he knew she would have brained the brute with a Dutch oven. But since it was up to Mack, and he'd never get a better opportunity, he took it.

Midleap, the thought came to him it might be a Shoshone checking on Ell and the twins until he saw that the back of the man's head was a bristly, odd looking arrangement of hair and sticks and beads. It was an attacker.

The man's left arm clutched a large war club stippled with brass tacks. The long grip was wrapped in rawhide and fringed with dangling beads and other adornments. The club looked sticky with blood and matted with dark hair. He'd killed with that club.

As he leapt upon the man's back, Mack noted they were matched, size-wise. He also saw the man's right hand clutched a pistol and black powder. He kicked at the pistol with his right boot even as he drove his blade deep into the man's left side and angled it upward under the ribcage.

It must have sunk itself right into the man's heart, for the fool had hardly had time to react to feeling a man atop his back before he sagged, his head still poking inside the tent.

"Mack?" It was Ell.

Mack jerked his knife out of the man and slid off him. With difficulty, he snatched the back of the man's head, the shorter hair slick with grease. Unable to jerk the man's head out of the tent, he pulled at the top of the man's buckskin tunic, jerking it upward. It took two attempts before he could lift the man—fully dead and sagging worse than ever—up and out of the hole.

Shoving the body away, Mack shouted into the hole, "Ell? Are you all right?"

"Yes. You?"

"Yes! Stay put! Stay safe! I must go! Stay safe—I love you!"

"Yes!"

She said something else to him, but as long as he knew she and the twins were safe, he could dither no longer. All around him fighting and screams and shouts rose up, mingling with the black smoke of the homes of their friends.

It felt overwhelming to Mack for a moment, then he regained his senses, tried to control his gasping breaths—half out of shock and fear—and dragged the back of his right hand across his eyes. He stopped to snatch up the dead man's fallen club, then on a fleeting thought, grabbed up the pistol, too. *Might be loaded and good for one shot.* If not, he'd beat someone with it.

He'd already bolted away from the tent when he remembered the man he'd axed had dropped a decent-looking rifle. He bent low, looking to his right, toward where the attack had taken place. *There!* Beyond the dead man, he spied the rifle where it had fallen.

"Mack Harrigan!" It was a woman's voice, but not Ell's.

He knew who it was—Red Dove, the Indian woman they'd saved from enslavement by the vile wagon master Ricker Briggs.

Mack looked toward where the voice had come from and saw her fending off the attacks of two strange warriors. She was armed only with the large sheath knife most women carried to use in butchering and cooking.

If Red Dove was asking for help, you could bet your last penny she was in real trouble.

In the many months his family had come to know her and call her friend, Mack had come to learn she was the single most self-reliant woman he'd ever met. Even more so than Ell, and that was saying something. It was also something he'd not mention to Ell. Especially as Red Dove and Ell had become fast friends.

Continuing toward the rifle, he snatched it up and bee-lined for her. Good fortune was with him for the moment, since the mass of the fighting appeared to have shifted southward into the heart of the vast encampment. Here and there hand-to-hand fights were still being waged, but most of the invaders were concentrating their efforts in the Shoshone camp proper, the center of the wintering grounds where socializing and cooking took place. It was also where more of the dwellings were sited.

Because of the divided fight, Mack was able to creep up on Red Dove's attackers. A head shorter than Mack, the nearest of the two was a wide, stout brute with a ring of flab about his middle. He seemed to be holding back . . . as if waiting for his chance to lunge in from her left side, while his partner, also somewhat stout but a pinch taller and carrying less fat, worked closer to Red Dove with each lunge of his lance.

The fatter of the two, Mack's first intended victim, held a wide-bladed knife that looked to have tasted more than its share of Shoshone flesh already. The sight of the big gore-and-hair-slick blade set Mack's teeth tight together, and an all-consuming fire of rage boiled him from within. He rushed at the man, vaguely aware the other had half turned. No doubt he'd seen Mack's movement toward them.

The taller attacker shouted an oath of surprise and shifted his own attack, but it was too late for the fat one to do much more than succumb to Mack's hard-swung club. The blow, a straight shot to the left side of the man's greasy head, appeared to cave in part of the man's skull and dropped the man before he could fully turn his head.

Even as the man dropped, Mack saw Red Dove slamming

her body straight into the taller attacker. Mack swung his club up for a defining second blow to ensure his coup. Just as quickly Red Dove shoved away from the other man, her legs churning beneath the blood-stained layers of cloth and buckskin she wore.

As before, she held her big knife in front of her, rigid and menacing. Wet and shiny, it was slick with fresh blood.

Set to turn his attack on Mack, the tall man instead jerked to a halt and stared wide-eyed at the fallen man, then up at Mack, then somewhat to his left toward where Red Dove stood but five feet away. He shook his head in quick, tight movements, disbelief writ large on his drawn, drained features.

Mack saw why. Red Dove's vicious blade had dealt the beast a death blow, an upward slide just under his rib cage on the left side. It hadn't been a heart strike—the man was still upright—but the wound already gushed thick, red life juice down his tunic and leggings.

Internal organs had been punctured and were useless. The man's chest hitched over and over as if he were caught in a hiccupping fit. Each time, bright wet blood gouted from his mouth and nose.

He looked back down to the man Mack had brained and reached a hand toward him, then his knees buckled and his right hand released the lance. He slammed first to his knees, then pitched facedown across Mack's victim.

Red Dove looked down and muttered hard words at them as she stepped over the second man's legs. "They were brothers," she said, walking to Mack. "I saw it on their faces. They were telling me what they were going to do to me."

Mack's eyebrows rose. "Ell . . . I can't let that—"

Already on the move, Red Dove held up her free hand as she wiped her bloody blade on her skirt. "That is where

I was going before these two slowed me. Thank you for the help, Mack Harrigan. I will go to Ell. You are needed there." She jerked her head to her right, downslope toward the camp proper.

Attackers wheeled and milled on horses, Shoshone mingled with them atop hastily grabbed mounts from their own herd.

Mack turned back to Red Dove—he had questions with no answers—but she was already halfway to the Harrigan home. *Good,* he thought.

That was as much relief as he would be allowed to feel on that day.

Instead of running straight downslope, he cut left, angling toward the sparse copse of trees ringing the eastern edge of the compound. He leapt over the heaped forms of fallen warriors, some of them he recognized as his friends, others their attackers.

CHAPTER 2

After Mack had ducked out of the tent and dealt with
the brute who had jammed his leering face in through the
hole he'd torn in the hide wall, Ell had become embold-
ened and realized the two young bodies she was protecting,
the twins, needed more than a cringing, hiding mother to
keep them safe should it come to a fight.

She had been looking about for something suitable in
the darkened space with which to defend herself when her
gaze had fallen on Mack's felling ax, a slender-handled,
double-headed thing that had always seemed far too big
and heavy to wield for a few minutes, let alone for an entire
day of working in the forest. But Mack did it.

And, she thought as she spied it, so would she.

That decided, from the far northern side of the tent, a
movement and a slight scuffling sound attracted her attention.

But she had to deal with the twins. How to wield an ax
when two babies were clutched to your breasts? They had
finished feeding, so she shifted one to rest beside the other,
jostling them and risking them crying out. But they were
full of milk and sluggish, and for that Ell was thankful.

She moved for the ax with her right hand and saw a face
alongside the base of the hides peering up at her with a

wide toothy grin. It was a stranger, a man with large eyes and dark hair, and a leering grin.

He searched the darkness and then his eyes rested on her, and for a finger snap of a moment she was seized with fear, unable to move. It was an attacker and he'd seen her. No telling how many others were behind him.

She moved for the ax, wrapped her fingers about the long, work-polished handle, and that was as far as she got before he shoved himself manfully inward, into their little home space.

First his shoulders, then one arm emerged wielding a heavy knife. The other arm showed itself—a broad, muscled thing clutching a gun, a pistol. The man worked fast, planting his arms and implements before him and dragging himself forward into the dark space.

All the while he kept his gaze locked on Ell, and his leering grin widened. He said things, words she did not recognize, in a tongue foreign to her. But his tone told her enough. His voice was a low, coarse thing ending in a rasping laugh, as if sand were being dragged over stone.

With the ax in her hand still in shadow and unseen by the intruder, Ell stood roughly six, seven feet from him. It was as if he were mumbling and willing her to stand still.

One of the babies whimpered, and out of instinct she offered it low, shushing sounds and gently bounced the bundle of two babies in her left arm.

All the while she hefted the ax in her firm, nervous grip. She was riled, to be certain, but resolute, especially when reminded by the squirming, fussing babies. *This cannot stand,* she thought. *I will not let this savage tear into our home and—*

She could not continue the thought.

But in action she did continue it. This new one must be her victim, for Mack had bolted away to help what others he might. Ell spun toward the man, using the momentum to raise the ax. It glinted in the scant light cast from the fresh rent in the hides put there by the man she'd heard Mack lay low.

Mindful of the ceiling of the shelter, she raised the tool to the apex of its swing, then brought it down on the up-turned face of the man who was squirming, shouting, and trying to back out of the tent. Somehow he had his clothing on the pegs and ropes and hides securing their floor to the sides of the tent.

He screamed unintelligible words sounding to her an awful lot like pleading. And she did not care. If he was set on ruining their lives, she would do the same to him.

The ax drove down hard and fast, sinking into his neck as he let go of the pistol. His scream squelched out as the blade sought and found something hard to anchor in. It found it with no trouble at all.

The man shuddered and squealed and drummed his hands. Ell could only imagine his backside wriggling as he squirmed and bucked, trying to drag himself out of the tent.

It was, of course, far too late for that. The ax delivered its mighty damage. She tried to walk closer and tug the ax free, but she'd done the job too well. Then she realized that if she didn't free it, she'd have to find something else to use to defend her babies.

And then someone was at the door of the tent.

She grunted and growled, jerking at the ax. Jostling and clutching, she realized she was holding her babies too tight. They began to wail and she, too, whimpered.

The rustling at the flapped skins that made up the door continued to move as a form in the darkness entered, slipping in with ease and stealth.

"Stop right there!" snarled Ell, trying to make her voice

sound hard, which wasn't much of a strain for her, filled with anger as she was. She gave the bone-embedded ax one last tug and it popped free. Using the same motion as moments before, she turned and swung the ax, raising it high and spinning on the newest intruder. But she was too late.

"Ell Harrigan!"

The sound barely sliced through the thick shell of rage Ell had built up. She held the trembling ax aloft, gripped partway up the haft. The deadly blade quivered. A twin squirmed, cried out, and Ell growled and swung the ax down hard at the intruder once more.

The intruder darted to the right, away from the descending weapon, and shouted once more. "Ell! Stop, Ell!"

But Ell Harrigan was a mother, a mother cradling two helpless babies, a mother whose three other children were gone from her sight, somewhere in a raging battle. She would do whatever she had to do to survive and protect her offspring.

As she swung the ax aloft again, the intruder darted close and grabbed hold of the ax handle with two hands, clasping fingers over Ell's own work-hardened grip.

"No!" growled Ell, yanking hard at the offense.

The intruder was stronger and freed the ax from her grasp, then stepped closer as a shaft of light from the rent in the skin wall shone across the face—and it was a face Ell knew. A face that was kind, and spoke kindly but sternly to her. Spoke her name. "Ell Harrigan!"

"Red Dove?"

"Ell Harrigan, come back from your anger! Ell Harrigan, I am your friend. I am here to help."

Ell understood then, and the steel-like rigidity in her body melted and left her feeling as if she had survived a miles-long thrashing in a flooded river. "Red Dove."

The Indian woman dropped the ax and held the silently sobbing woman and her two crying babies. But only for a moment. Then she stepped back, and holding Ell's arms, looked into Ell's eyes. "This place is not safe. The Piegans are too many. We may yet drive them off, but it would not surprise me if they burned all the shelters in the wintering grounds of the Shoshone."

"Oh no!" Ell stifled a sob. She understood all that might mean, but her closest and only real concern was for the babies in her arms.

"Hand me one child and help me to gather what we will need. That satchel." Red Dove nodded toward a large canvas sack Ell and the children used to fetch everything from firewood to roots and other goods they foraged.

"Yes, yes." Ell nodded, shoved her loose dangling blonde hair back away from her face. It did not comply, but she did not care as she rummaged for clothes for the children, two spare sheath knives, foods, and four pair of thick socks she had made with Meghan's help, while teaching her daughter to knit.

The girl had done an acceptable job of it, but it was Kane who had shown an untrained, natural ability for learning the basic techniques.

"But . . . won't they see us?" said Ell once they had filled the sack and hefted the weapons.

Nodding, Red Dove snatched up the ax and held it firmly in a grip just below the gore-slick head. "They might, but if we stay here the chance is greater they will burn the tent. If we try to flee then, they will be near enough to see us. Before we leave, let me look outside." She left the tent for what felt to Ell like long moments.

Slipping back in, Red Bud said, "It is good—the fight is down by the cook fires. If we slice through there"—she nodded at the wall over the man Ell had killed—"we will be able to leave without being seen from below."

Red Dove tugged out her big knife and jammed it through the skins six inches above the prone form of the dead man, looked down and saw that the man had dropped a pistol. "Good. We will take that. But it will not be useful for long." She looked at his other arm, saw the knife beside his clawed fingertip. "That knife is no good. Junk. Mine is better." She shook her head quickly, contempt unmasked on her face. "Let us go before another of them comes here."

"What about the chief?" said Ell, stepping through the slit, planting her leading foot between the legs of the dead man.

"Chief Stalks-the-Night is a good man," said Red Dove. "He will survive or he will die. But he is still a good man. Not like these rogue Piegan. They are thieves."

"At least they didn't attack in the cold months," said Ell, thinking of the hardship being driven out in freezing weather could be.

Red Dove looked at her as if she had sprouted a second head, then led the way up the long, sparsely treed slope behind the tent. It wound up to a path that cut to the west and toward the cliffs overlooking the river valley. Ell suspected the small caves there were what Red Dove had in mind for shelter.

Before leaving the tent each had lashed blankets over their shoulders and tied them with lengths of hempen rope, securing them about their waists. They would need blankets as well as fire and food. These they had provided for, with flint and steel and with as much food as they could carry.

Red Dove held one of the twins, which was whimpering and alternately offering up full-throated cries. This did not bother Ell, for it told her the child, Henry, was well, if hungry. That one always wanted more food. *Just like his father,* she thought, praying that Mack and her other children were not in harm's way.

She held Hattie, a slighter child, but still robust. Hattie appeared to be fighting sleep, giving over to it and then because of the jostling from the brisk walk she was receiving, she would quickly snap awake and utter sharp cries.

"Your babies are strong, Ell," said Red Dove.

"That's because they are Harrigans." Ell knew her friend would find that amusing, as Red Dove thought little of whites, save for the Harrigan family.

Ell could hardly blame her. Red Dove had been treated shamefully by whites, as had most of the Indians Ell had met on the journey from Ohio. Would this unearned hatred ever end? And now they were fighting, tribe against tribe, amongst themselves. Just as white always did amongst themselves.

Humans were little more than warring beasts. Was it this way the world over? She placed one foot before the other, winding up the trail behind her friend, and decided that yes, humans the world over were no different from those she knew. Good, bad, and the rest were somewhere in the middle of those two extremes.

A sound from behind caused Ell too look to their back trail once more, something she had been doing since they began their escape. A strange warrior, caught in the act not twenty yards behind, was sliding from his large brown mount, eyeing them with a half grin, and advancing up the trail.

"Red Dove!" Ell growled the words and her friend jerked to a stop, spinning, low in the trail, her hands already filled with weapons. "Ell, trade places with me. You face up trail. I will face him. We cannot risk a sneak attack from other directions until we have killed this cur."

Ell knew better than to argue. They spun around on the trail and Red Dove slipped the sling holding the baby over her head, helped Ell drape it about herself, then turned around with the pistol in her right hand, her blade in the other. The warrior advancing up the path stopped, jerked upright as if he'd been slapped, then knuckled his eyes and looked at her as if he were in a theater production. He smiled broadly, arched his head back, and laughed a big, deep, voluminous sound.

Ell saw how large the man was. Even downslope of them he was a big fellow, broad of chest and long of leg. And when he raised his hand to his face his arms bunched in muscle beneath his skin tunic.

He lost his smile and spat a word at them.

Red Dove said over her shoulder, "He called us a . . . a bad name for women."

"Oh he did, did he?" said Ell.

Red Dove sneered and raised the pistol. Far enough away and knowing the shot would be a waste of a bullet, the man spread his big arms wide, grinned a big, toothy grin, and exposed his chest.

Red Dove's sneer turned into a half grin as she gently pulled the trigger.

The bullet thunked into the dead center of the big brute's chest and he jerked as if he'd been stung by an irksome bee. He looked down at his chest and slowly lowered his arms. With his pointer finger of his left hand he probed the small puckered hole in his tunic, then looked up at Red Dove and Ell.

Never had Ell seen such anger draw down on a man's face. The big, toothy, sneering grin collapsed into a mask of pure hatred. He bellowed and bolted forward, a cudgel clutched in one hand.

Red Dove tossed the single-shot pistol to the ground and set her stance. Ell nudged the fingers of Red Dove's empty left hand with the ax handle. Without looking, Red Dove grasped it, jerked it up higher in her hand, and readied herself. The last thing she did was to say over her shoulder, "Ell Harrigan, run. Get away from here."

"No way, Red Dove. I'm a Harrigan. We don't run from a fight."

"Foolish friend."

Ell did dash up the trail a dozen feet and with haste unslung the twins and blankets, hers and Red Dove's, and made certain the babes were tucked low and away from the trail. She did not doubt she was doing the right thing, for her gut and her heart told her this was the best way to deal with the bizarre moment.

She tugged free a blade and raced back to help Red Dove.

Almost on top of them, the warrior bellowed like an enraged bull, swinging a huge ham fist in a wide, quick arc from Ell's left. He caught the top of her head with the glancing blow and knocked her staggering toward Red Dove. Ell checked her fall, pivoting to one knee behind her friend.

Red Dove took the moment to swing the still-lowered ax upward. As it was a double-bit blade, it was ready to cleave, upswing or downstroke. The blade dug into the man's swinging forearm, nicking leather and sending a spray of blood spuming outward.

He gasped a cry of shock and became even more enraged. The rifle in his left hand came up, and though he was too close to use it with any aiming effect, he delivered to Red Dove a cracking blow that caught her high under her right arm and glanced across the middle of her chest.

It was a clubbing and not a bullet, but it hurt the woman and she staggered. He advanced and brought his bleeding arm up high to meet the other in a joined pair of fists with the rifle held upright between them as if he were about to sink a fence post. His voice bellowed louder and he brought his great arms down in a clubbing, pummeling motion.

Both women, still staggering from their respective blows, scrambled up trail to get out of his way.

The big warrior's voice cut out and his eyes flew wide. His joined hands were halfway down before him, the rifle still between them. He stiffened, staring at them, then pitched forward, dropping like a felled tree.

Ell felt the ground shake beneath her feet. Red Dove shoved herself upright and held her knife out before her, well aware this might be a trick. She approached the prone brute and jabbed him with the blade tip square on top of the head.

If he is play-acting, thought Ell, he is very good.

But he did not respond to any other pokes or jabs.

"I think your shot finally got to him," said Ell.

Red Dove nodded. "Good. A man that big, things take time to travel to the head. He was already dead I think."

They considered flipping him over to get at his rifle, but decided there was no time. They gathered up their dropped weapons and retrieved the now-crying twins, the blankets, and the gear bags, and hustled up the trail once more.

CHAPTER 3

Hours before, the first thing Kane had felt that morning was a nudging, then a hitting, a pinching feeling in his left shoulder. "Mmff."

It happened again.

"Aww . . . what?"

A hand clamped over his mouth and his eyes snapped wide open. He was, as he usually was, fully awake in that instant. He thrashed and clawed at the arm, at the hand pinning him down. What was happening? He remembered where he was, outside the wagon, sleeping on the earth in his blankets.

"Harrigan, stop!"

The whispered voice was close by his left ear. He jerked his head to the side and the hand lessened its grip on his face. Kane squinted in the gloom of early morning. "Bright Owl?"

A head, silhouetted against the dawning sky, nodded.

Kane sat up, "What are you doing here, Bright Owl? What's happening?"

His friend leaned close once more. "We are being attacked. No stopping. We must go. Leave here."

"Leave? What? And go where?" The young man struggled to stand. When he finally did, he realized he'd been fighting his own blankets, a twisted mass of wool that felt as if it might never let him go.

"Come," said his Shoshone friend. "And bring your gun. Knife, too."

Then Kane heard a shout from afar, and the neighing of agitated horses. He threw back his blankets and, fully dressed, was ready with a few deft moves to snatch up his gear. He had a hundred questions but knew better than to pester Bright Owl with them. All would be revealed.

But no way was he going to leave here. Not without his family. He followed his slightly older friend, son of Chief Stalks-the-Night, who skirted behind the wagon and around to the front of the tent.

Bright Owl knew him well. "I will wait here. We must fight with the warriors. Your mother and the children will be taken care of by the Shoshone women. Meghan, too."

That caught Kane up short. Meghan was one of the children, wasn't she? Then he recalled through the last wispy traces of his sleep-fogged mind, that Bright Owl had been more coy around his pesky sister, Meghan. Maybe his Shoshone friend was sweet on her? Nah, he had more sense than that.

Kane groped at the wall into the tent proper, peeling the overlapping hides that made up the door, and entered. "Pa? Pa?"

"Hush, Kane, you'll wake the twins."

"Ma, where's Pa?"

His mother replied, "Where do you think? He's been slipping out in the mornings to watch the sun dawn over the canyon and river at Sitting Rock."

"Sure, right," said Kane. "I forgot. Where's Fitch?"

"Right here," said a small, angry voice. "I wanted to go with him but Ma said I had to eat first."

"And Meghan?" said Kane.

"She went after your father. Kane, what's wrong?" said Ell, holding one of the twins. The other was sleeping in its swaddles on the low bed behind her. The light was dim as they were running low on lamp oil and trying to conserve it. They had no idea when they might get more, or if they ever would.

Kane hesitated and Ell knew by that slight pause that something was indeed wrong. "Kane? What is it?"

"Bright Owl is outside."

"Then ask him in. We're Harrigans. We leave no one on our doorstep."

"It's not a social call, Ma. He says we're under attack. I don't know to what extent yet. But Pa needs to know."

"I'll go." It was Fitch.

Ell looked confused, worried for a moment, and looked at Kane.

"The camp might not be the best place to be right now. Bright Owl said we should get out of here."

Ell nodded. "Oh dear, oh dear. Fitch, you'll have to be the one to run to Sitting Rock and tell your father. He'll know what to do. Kane, you will stay here and help me get ready."

"But Ma—"

"I can't just up and leave with the twins. There's too much to do first."

Fitch was already moving to the door. Kane grabbed Fitch's shoulder. "You pay attention to Meghan, you hear? She'll be the boss, not you. You do whatever she tells you!"

"I don't have to take orders from you or her. Besides, I'm Shoshone."

Kane sighed. At least he was getting replies in English from the kid. He'd been on his Shoshone-lingo-only run for ages and it was annoying. Mostly because the kid seemed to pick up the language faster than any of them, and Kane swore Fitch was saying nasty things about him. He'd look at Kane and speak, and then giggle.

Kane looked at his mother for help with the kid.

"Mister Fitch Harrigan, your brother is correct. If you do not do whatever Meghan tells you to do, I will hear about it and I will warm your backside, do you hear me?"

Fitch said nothing.

"Fine," said Ell. "Then your father will warm your backside. And you know he's not as gentle as I am on that score, mister!"

"Yes, ma'am."

Kane poked his head back out the door. "Fitch is going to Sitting Rock to get my Pa."

"Good," said Bright Owl, looking past Kane into the tent. "Your mother and the twins should leave, too. Go to safety. It may be no more than a horse raid, but—"

"What?" said Ell, behind Kane. "Bright Owl what is it?"

"Miss Meghan and Fitch should stay at Sitting Rock. Hide there. If it is nothing, I will go for them."

"I see." Ell nodded and grabbed Fitch by the shoulders. With a look at Kane as if to ask if it was really necessary, then knowing it was, she knelt before the boy and looked him in the eyes. "Fitch, honey, you need to find Papa and Meghan. They are at Sitting Rock. Go there straight away, no stopping, and if you see anybody you don't know, you run faster and scream for Papa. He will hear you. It's not that far. But otherwise, be as silent as you can. It's very important."

The boy trembled beneath her loving hands, but he nodded and straightened his shoulders. "Yes, Mama."

"My good man." She hugged him hard and tight, squashing him to her bosom.

After a moment, he squirmed. "Mama, I'm a warrior!"

"I know you are, Fitch. But you're also my little boy.

Now promise me you'll do everything Kane tells you to do. He and Bright Owl are smart young men. They will tell you what to do. We need to find Papa and Meghan. Do you hear me? It's very important. To the whole tribe." This last she said slowly and stared right into his eyes.

"I understand." Fitch walked to Kane and took his hand. "Okay."

Kane looked back to his mother. "He'll be all right, Mama. But we have to go."

As if to accentuate this, a shout, then two more, rose up from downslope to the south, where the tribe had set up its tents ringing the cook fires. Other tents such as those of the Harrigans ranged farther out, but still close to the core of the camp.

Kane ushered the boy outside and Bright Owl laid a hand on his shoulder. "Your mother said what the Shoshone need of you, Mr. Fitch. We will go with you part of the way, then you must run the warrior path to find your father on your own. Can you do this for us all? For the good of the tribe?"

Fitch's face never looked so serious, so grave. He nodded, his shoulders held back. As they departed, circling up on the high side, back behind the wagon, Kane heard his mother moving about in the tent, sobbing quietly.

Already the sound of shouting and horse activity were increasing down below. Something was happening—he and Bright Owl needed to find out what. And soon.

Kane and Fitch and Grinner, who'd emerged from the shadows of the tent when Fitch had stepped outside, crept low. They followed Bright Owl, who walked bent, quickly scurrying up the trail that intersected with the lower trail that led to Sitting Rock, a favorite spot of many in the tribe, particularly Chief Stalks-the-Night.

Bright Owl knew his father loved the Shoshone wintering

grounds more than any other place they traveled through or dwelt. He had once told his son he felt his heart was at peace and he felt his dead wife's presence, when he was overlooking the vast canyon and the river far below.

They reached the intersection of the two paths when Kane whisper shouted, "Bright Owl!"

Instinct forced the young Shoshone to drop to his right knee and pivot. At the same time his left arm swept out and he grabbed Fitch's shirt, as did Kane from behind the boy. The three of them dropped low, the older youths readying their weapons as they flanked the child.

Kane was armed with a sheath knife on his hip and a belt ax, small but keen edged. Over the winter spent with the Shoshone he and his father had become quite adept at throwing it with force and accuracy.

But his primary weapon was the rifle his father had given him on the trip west. It was a fine rifle, and though he was frugal with his use of bullets, Kane was the best shot among the Harrigans, and begrudgingly admitted by his father and many of the other Shoshone men, among most of the tribe. That the young man showed no hint of taking pride in this skill, but rather shared his abilities freely with all who asked for his help in hunting or in improving their own marksman skills was a feather in his cap, to be sure.

Between him and Bright Owl, a rivalry as brothers might feel kept the two young men competing playfully, though with a serious edge of competition and respect. Sometimes begrudging, but still there.

In the midst of this new and strange event—an attack on the Shoshone by some as-yet-unseen force, Kane deferred to Bright Owl, though he had been the one to point out the sounds thundering closer—a clattering of hooves of one, then a second, horse.

"Fitch!" growled Kane. "Down now, behind me. Keep low!"

Bright Owl needed to say nothing. Armed with their rifles, both young men jerked them up snugging the stocks to their shoulders and cheeks, and sighting toward the approaching sounds.

As soon as the mounts and their riders drummed into view, Bright Owl said, "They are Shoshone." He stood, so confident was he of his assessment of them. And he was correct.

The first rider halted behind them in the trail, and behind him the second rider reined left and continued down the other trail back to camp.

Bright Owl and the rider, a man Kane knew as Turtle Eye, talked low and rapidly. Every few seconds, Turtle Eye looked behind them along the trail he'd just ridden up. Then Turtle Eye nodded once and Bright Owl did the same. Turtle Eye nodded to Kane, then tugged the reins left and rode back toward the winter village.

"I told him Fitch will find Mack Harrigan. But Kane and Bright Owl must return. We are needed. The enemy is arriving and are spreading out, surrounding the camp," Bright Owl said.

"Who are they"

"Some are Piegans, but cast outs of their tribe. The others"—Bright Owl shrugged, telling Kane nobody knew who the others were yet—"they want more than horses."

The words and their hidden meaning were not lost on Kane. He bent to Fitch. "Just what Mama said, Fitch. We are depending on you now. You have to find Papa and tell him what Bright Owl said. The Shoshone are being attacked and Pa is needed. But you must stay there, with Meghan, at the cliffs."

"No! I want to help! I'm a warrior."

Kane smiled and hugged the boy quickly. "I know you are, but this is one of the most important tasks you can do today. Do you understand? Now run. Run to Papa. Tell him what you know. Go now!" He turned the boy and shoved up him the trail.

Fitch began running, Grinner at his heels. Then Fitch slowed and looked back. His face held none of the tough, outthrust lip look of previous weeks. Once more he was a sad, frightened little boy.

Kane fought back welling tears and smiled and nodded. Then he held his fist to his heart and extended it to Fitch, who did the same, a small smile on his face. Then he ran for Mack and Meghan, with Grinner tight behind.

"Come, Kane, there is no time to waste. We are needed."

Punctuating the request was the echo of a rifle shot from far off, far beyond the camp, to the east. It hastened their long strides. Neither young man knew what to expect, or when, but they knew the Shoshone and all the Harrigans needed them.

Halfway down the far branch of the trail, making for the camp proper, Kane shouted, "Bright Owl!"

The Shoshone youth halted and turned.

Kane had stopped. "My mother, the twins . . . I can't—"

Even Bright Owl's face showed alarm. He nodded. "Yes! You should go to her. I forgot."

That was all the time they had, for a whooping cry rose up. Two warriors strange to Kane, and with odd hairstyles and clothing, emerged from the rabbit brush to their left.

One swung a nail-studded club, the other held a rifle, but they did not seem intent on shooting anything at that range. Their eyes were white and wide and their mouths showed tight-set teeth behind wide-pulled lips, grinning in their lust for fighting.

"Side by side," said Kane.

Bright Owl nodded once. About eight feet apart, they stood abreast in the trail.

Kane raised his rifle with a quick, calm motion and shot first. His bullet caught the warrior beelining for him high on the left shoulder. It was a poor shot for one so adept at shooting with accuracy.

Bright Owl's gun misfired. He growled and tossed it to the earth, snatching up his belt ax and his wide-blade sheath knife at the same time, one in each hand. He set his stance and waited for the invader to close in on him.

Too late to ready another shot, Kane followed suit just in time, for no sooner had he palmed the handles of each weapon and lifted them free of his belt, than the man was an arm's length from hm.

Before the man landed from his final leap onto the trail, Kane had glanced to his right at Bright Owl, and saw him knocking the intruder's rifle free. Having fought in two other skirmishes Kane knew of, Bright Owl could handle himself in the fight. Kane had no idea if he would fare as well, but had no more time for such thought as he was attacked.

The strange warrior swung his war club from left to right, arching it in a hard, tight swing that brought the head of the blackened club—old, dried blood of former victims guessed the young white fighter—whistling at Kane's head. He jerked back in time and countered with a swing with his left hand wielding the ax.

It was a paltry move, however, easily deflected by his attacker's club arm. It nearly dislodged the ax from Kane's grasp, but he jerked the hand back and at the same time slashed with his knife. It found purchase on the blocking forearm of the man's buckskin sleeve.

Blood welled from the large gash he had caused and Kane was grateful for his father's insistence that he always keep his weapons freakishly sharp. It was something Mack had pushed him to do, even as a young boy with his first knife, a small folding Barlow his grandfather had given him. Mack had said Kane could carry it and use it, but only if it would always be sharp whenever his father asked to see the knife.

Kane knew what the value and the freedom of owning and carrying a knife meant to him, and how grown up it had made him feel, so he always kept it honed with the stone Mack had given him.

Faced with a shrieking, leering man with the most frightening eyes Kane had ever seen on another person, eyes so serious that never left Kane's gaze, he felt certain the man had some mystical qualities about him. As if he were a shaman. The notion caused Kane to falter, to doubt himself in the fight, which gave the aggressive brute an opening.

He pressed forward. His steel grip clamped fingers on Kane's right shoulder and inched toward his neck, the man's frightening gaze but a foot from his.

The stink off the man finally broke Kane's moments-long daze. The man smelled as if he had fouled himself, and as dire as the situation was, the notion seemed comical to Kane, snapping him from his reverie. Seeing the man's tactic, which was to jerk Kane close so he could drive the club down hard on Kane's head and kill him dead right there, he parried another swing of that dried-blood club.

Kane growled, brought a knee up hard, and his lower leg followed. It might not have been an elegant solution, but the result was that his attacker gasped and fell back, one hand clutching at his crotch. He jerked up the club still in his hand and ran at Kane with a growl of his own.

Kane finally saw the man for what he was—*a man,*

nothing more—who'd just been bested in a move in the intricate dance of his own fight.

As the angry warrior charged him, Kane jerked to his left and slashed upward with his big knife. He intended to jam the thing as hard and as fast as he was able into the man's bread basket, but again his arm warred with the reality of the moment, and the blade struck the man's outstretched club arm. But it was enough.

The attacker shrieked a high-pitched scream as his arm flailed, spraying blood on both of them. The brute's club swung up and slipped from his grasp, spinning in the air before thudding to the earth a few feet away. In an effort to get away from Kane, the attacker dashed to his left, toward Bright Owl and the other man. Kane advanced on him, seeing rage in those once-daunting eyes, yes, but also a creeping fear.

The momentary realization gave Kane great confidence and it bloomed in him with finger snap speed. He sneered and growled. With controlled thought and an intention he might end this thing, he drove straight toward the man. Closing in on the man until a couple of feet from the unarmed, wounded brute, he shifted his course and cut to the right one step, which brought him up on the man's left side and in range of Kane's already raised ax.

Thoughts of his mother and the twins drove him on. He had to end this thing now. He had left them unprotected. The camp was likely being overrun with similar beastly men bent on theft and killing. Bright Owl likely knew what the rogue Piegans and others wanted, but Kane had no time for further speculation.

His earlier upward slashing strike had been a severe blow, for the man's wounded right arm hung useless and bloody, his red life juice running down out of the gash in the sleeve and off the ends of his fingers in a steady drizzle.

But the attacker wasn't through. He had freed his sheath knife with his left hand and, as Kane found out, a man who realizes he has nothing to lose is the most dangerous foe another man can have.

The warrior fought like a man possessed by demons. He rounded on Kane and swung the knife, gripped blade down for easy swiping. It whistled over Kane's head as he ducked, jerking his head down like a turtle trying to wedge it between his shoulders.

Seasoned enough in this fracas, he knew turtling up wouldn't do him a bit of good. He rolled with it, dropping to his left to get away from the brute's knife hand.

It seemed as if the man were slashing with more vigor, reckless but relentless, surging forward, stomping closer toward Kane, who felt the opposite of what he'd felt moments before . . . when he had been full of confidence and bold as the aggressor.

Kane jumped up out of his roll, his ax already in motion. A good thing, for the man's knife whiskered in and wedged in the short wooden haft of the ax, less than an inch above Kane's knuckles. More out of instinct than temerity, Kane jerked the ax away, pulling the brute's knife with it, jerking it nearly free of the man's thick fingers.

The attacker surged closer to Kane. Nearly eye to eye, he saw raw brute rage trembling the man's face. Kane wasted no time in driving his knife up hard and fast, thrusting it upward again and again.

With less than a hand's width between their faces, Kane saw the one true thing all creatures share—the light of life—flare in those dark, hate-filled eyes. Then it dimmed, more and more with each passing moment. Kane saw the man's own inner recognition discover the awful truth, that this white boy had taken from him the most valuable thing he would ever have—his life.

The man's rugged, bone-hard body began to soften and sag, his knees bent, and he leaned forward into Kane as his eyes closed. A breath soft as that of a sleeping child wafted close by Kane's right ear as the man breathed his last.

Kane backed up, and keeping a grip on his knife, still lodged up high in the man's chest, he laid the body down with a thump.

The moment's solemnity was broken when he heard a voice growl, "Kane Harrigan!"

It was Bright Owl, still engaged in a brutal fight a half-dozen yards to Kane's right, off trail and in the sparse trees and boulders. The wiry Shoshone was fast losing ground.

The man he fought had somehow conjured up a knife that, wielded by anyone less muscled might look awkward. In that brute's hands the wide, raw-steel, pitted blade looked like something a fellow might savage a tree with. The attacker still held his rifle and used it to dodge and parry and thrust in an awkward counter-rhythm to his deadly, big blade.

The combination of weapons and aggressive attack was similar to what Kane had just faced and seemed to be getting the better of his friend.

Kane wanted to heed his friend's call but was uncertain what he might do in such a dervish attack. Then he raised his rifle to his shoulder—the very weapon he had been forced to lay aside when embroiled in his own close-up fight—tugged it up and snugged its stock to his cheek. He walked uphill, keeping the deadly snout of the rifle aimed at Bright Owl's attacker.

In an effort to escape the swinging, thrashing onslaught, Bright Owl kept moving left and right, getting in the way. Kane cast an eye downslope, making certain no one else was coming up, and to ensure he had a clear path as something slammed into his left side. Jerking to his right out of reflex, and from the impact of the thing, he looked down.

It was an arrow, jutting from his wool jacket. It stuck straight out from his side. He looked up in the direction the arrow had come from. Through the random scatter of pines, bent low but still visible above the waist high clots of rabbit brush and low scrub pines, crouched another odd-haired stranger, readying another arrow.

Kane felt the rush of fear in the sudden realization he'd been wounded. Following on its heels was the flower of rage he'd seen in the face of the man he'd just laid low. Kane used its bursting feeling to full effect in raising his rifle again, sighting on the man who was sighting on him.

Kane wasted no time and touched the trigger. His aim was true. The bullet punched its way into the man's skull in the near-center of his sweaty, broad forehead even as the man let loose the arrow he'd just nocked. Luckily for Kane, arrows travel slower than bullets. Though sent with full power and full intent, it whistled past his right side as he sidestepped and swung his body away.

He lost his footing and collapsed to his left side, causing the arrow stuck in his midsection to bend right over.

And it didn't hurt . . . at all.

For a moment, Kane thought he was already losing the ability to feel anything. He wondered, in fact, if he was going to be able to stand. For some reason his father's voice bubbled up into his mind and spoke, and he heard it clear as a spring bird's call. "Harrigans don't take anything lying down!"

As Kane gritted his teeth and pushed himself upright, he looked down. The arrow that had been stuck in him lay on the ground where he'd fallen. It was whole, its head untainted by blood. He snatched at his side, felt a hole, and realized it had lodged in his journal—his prized possession—

the thing he spent as much time with as he was able, recording his observations, thoughts, and renderings as he rambled, usually alone, in the landscape surrounding the Shoshone wintering grounds. And before that, along the trail west from Ohio, and in similar journals, now filled, he kept tucked away in the modest trunk in which he stored personal possessions.

His notebook, which he knew his father did not understand the need for, but indulged him in nonetheless, had stopped the arrow.

Under his probing fingertips, Kane felt the small, deep, ragged hole the arrowhead had punched in the book. He had never been so relieved in all his sixteen years.

He spun, snugging the rifle to his shoulder once more, knowing he had wasted precious moments that could have been far better spent helping his friend. He would investigate the wonderfully damaged journal later. For there must be a later. He demanded it. Sighting once more on the thick-faced brute attacking Bright Owl, he had not been thus saved to waste his life, his new opportunity.

Kane pulled the trigger and nothing happened. Realizing he'd not reloaded, once more he had to spend precious moments while his friend, still manfully avoiding the mad flailings of his foe, continued losing ground.

With haste, Kane reloaded the rifle and scooted two sidesteps to his left, hoping there wasn't another cursed archer hiding in the trees. Making certain he had a clear view to the man's head and one Bright Owl would not be able to pollute, Kane tickled the trigger.

The familiar crack-and-bang sounded, and the frenzied man shrieked, whipping his head back, his eyes popping wide, his mouth rivaling them with his throat's prominent bump pointed upward as he staggered backward.

Bright Owl stood spraddle legged upslope of the shot

man. Gripping his knife in his right hand, he held it upright as if still waiting for the man to lunge. His left sleeve wore a spatter of blood from a rent high up by the shoulder. His chest worked hard, as if he'd run far and stopped short, but his stance was tight, his face not exhausted but fierce, his jaw muscles jouncing beneath his tight cheek.

Not until the shrieking man dropped to the ground on his knees, his back to Kane and his right side to Bright Owl, did the young Shoshone warrior relax.

Kane's bullet had driven into the man high up on the right side of his chest. At that close range the bullet would have caused terrible damage to the man.

As Kane walked uphill to Bright Owl, he glanced at the shot man, his weapons not quite dropped from his hands, which flexed and heaved as if the fingers themselves had minds of their own and could not decide if they should relax or clutch tighter to the deadly tools.

Blood flowed up and out of the man's slowly gasping mouth. He stared into the nearby copse of poplars, seeing nothing but the filming in his eyes. His wrecked chest heaved, his blood flowed down his chin and on down his front.

Kane stood beside Bright Owl, the two young men transfixed by the awful scene they had helped to create.

In moments, the wounded warrior pulled in a loud, sucking breath, his chest filling with air. His head bent back once more, he stiffened, and his eyes widened, as if afraid of something he'd just seen. He held that pose, tight and rigid, for a long moment, then his weapons dropped to the earth. His left leg, which had been thrust out to the side, stiffened as if trying to brace him, and with a final, quick convulsion, he pitched to his left.

He ended his living days on earth crumpled in a pose no breathing person would choose or maintain—his rump partway in the air, his left leg pinned almost flat, and his right leg somehow buckled in beneath him.

The long silence that followed the man's drawn-out moment of death was finally broken by Bright Owl. "He is gathering himself to leap. But where he is going, it will not be necessary." He walked to the man and looked at his weapons. "They are no good." He looked up at Kane. "Thank you, my brother, Kane Harrigan. You saved my life. Now you are responsible for me."

"The day is young, Bright Owl. We'll even it up before long."

They heard renewed shouts, gunfire, and screams from the direction of the camp, and spied smoke rising up above the treetops downslope of them.

"Come!" said Bright Owl, taking to the trail to the camp once more. And once more Kane paused. "I must go to my mother."

"No, no need, Kane. Your father ran by not long ago on the trail toward your tent. He will take care of your mother and the twin babes."

"My father?" said Kane, falling in line behind Bright Owl, but looking back toward the trail Mack would have taken. "But he didn't stop to help? Didn't shout?"

"He saw that we were busy. A warrior knows never to interrupt a fellow warrior. It could cost him his fellow's life."

Kane mulled this over as he followed Bright Owl toward the Shoshone camp, toward the screams and gunfire and smoke.

CHAPTER 4

Meghan tried to hide the fear in her voice as she sat with Fitch in a natural alcove in the stone below the rim of Sitting Rock. About a dozen feet down from the edge where she had been sitting quietly with her father admiring the pretty view over the valley and the river below, she and Fitch were hiding like frightened rabbits, in fear for their lives.

As for Grinner, he'd tried to follow them down the trail, but had been too afraid of the raw edge of stone and would not commit to descending over it. As he dithered and whimpered, shots from within the forest behind them were followed by a faraway shout, pinched off in a scream. Grinner's long, rangy tail tucked tight beneath him and he bolted for the cover of the forest to the north.

Fitch gathered himself for a shout to the dog, but Meghan clamped a hand over his mouth and shook her head. And so they sat, huddled and waiting.

The sounds of gunshots, screams, and yips, some of them close, far closer than from the village, punctuated stretches of silence.

Despite the unknown situation unfolding above them, Meghan thought it was nice to sit quietly, holding her little brother in her lap, scooched as far into the shallow cave as they were able. They didn't talk much, but when they did it was in a whisper.

For his part, Fitch was not interested in playing the Shoshone warrior just then. He was merely a small boy afraid of the unknown events taking place, events that involved all they held dear.

"Meg?" Fitch's voice was a small whisper, barely audible. "What's happening?"

She realized she knew as little as did Fitch. She also knew that since neither Mama nor Papa, nor for that matter Kane were around, she was now the adult in the situation. She swallowed, licked her lips, and whispered, "Well, some bad people showed up and they want something from the Shoshone and the Shoshone don't want to give it to them." She bent her face closer to his. "Does that sound right? You were with Kane and Bright Owl when they were talking. Did you hear strange sounds or shots?"

He was silent for a few moments, then in a slight voice he said, "Yes. There was a man, somebody I didn't know. I was scared . . . I don't know." He shivered. "I hope Grinner's okay."

Meghan hugged Fitch tight and pulled her shawl closer so it covered him, too. "He'll be just fine. He's very smart." She kissed him on the temple. "We'll be safe here. Papa was wise to tell us to wait here."

Fitch said nothing but nodded. Above them, seemingly right above them, then far off, back toward the camp, the sounds of fighting and anger and battles raged.

Sometime later, Meghan had no idea how long, she noticed the sounds had mostly abated. They were still popping up, here and there, random shouts, rifle cracks, and once, close by, a winded horse running fast.

She half thought it might barrel right off the cliff top and leap out into space. But the sounds of the hooves jerked to a halt—so it was likely not a riderless beast, but someone who was unfamiliar with the terrain and saw the cliff edge in time.

Someone paused there and then Meghan heard a slight scuffing sound and . . . were those whispers? Soon enough whoever it was rode the horse back and forth several times along the cliff's edge before turning the agitated beast.

Had it been a person? A second person whispering to another? What did the other sounds mean? Megan held Fitch close, then he squirmed.

"Too tight!" his voice raised higher than a whisper. He was getting cranky and hadn't heard what she did. He thought it was now safe to speak.

"Hush," she said in his ear.

"No!"

They both heard a scuffing, sliding sound, as if someone had dragged a moccasin-clad foot in the loose dirt up top. The sound was not repeated, but Fitch kept his mouth shut.

She held him close and they scarcely breathed, perking their ears and listening for other strange sounds.

The constant slight breeze in the canyon shifted slightly and they heard the soft rumble and rush of the river far below.

If someone had heard them and were even now skulking around looking for them, whoever it was would surely make another sound, a new scuffing on gravel, scratching, breathing . . . something.

That thought made Meghan think they, too, were breathing too loudly. But she didn't dare tell Fitch to keep quiet. She prayed he stayed silent a bit longer, all the while she strained her ears.

If they just stayed there, quiet, and calm, they would be safe. She had to believe that.

The light from high above shifted slightly and Meghan

glanced up to the rocky rim of the grotto. Fitch looked up, too. And then he screamed. So did Meghan.

Glaring down at them was the face of a demon! The mouth was on top, the eyes below that, and where the head should be was just a spiky clot of weird hair. The thing smiled and hissed and then an arm sprouted from beside it and reached down at them.

Meghan knew what it was—an enemy warrior hanging over the rocky edge of the top of their cave and leering in at them! He must have heard Fitch shouting and crept down maybe the very trail they had taken, useful only by goats and agile folks. Maybe he had been dropped off there by the rider.

Meghan knew she had heard whispers. But none of that mattered any more.

As the hand reached for them, closer and closer, she stopped screaming and scrabbled beside her for something— anything—to grab, a stick, a rock. *Anything.* But all she came up with was a handful of dusty grit and rodent bones and scat.

Fine, she didn't care. She snatched up a big handful of it, the extra spilling all over them, and threw it in the face of the demon man.

He screamed and howled to match Fitch's wailing and jerked his head back.

They heard more scrabbling and scratching and scuffing, but Meghan had regained her frazzled wits and shoved Fitch out the left side of the opening. "Go!" she shouted. "Go down! Make for the river. It will take us back up to the camp eventually."

They slid and groped ahead as quickly as they were able. "If we get separated," she said when their heads were close as they scrambled and scrabbled to find hand- and footholds in the gray rocks, "keep going downstream until you find the camp. You know that, right? You're a Shoshone, Fitch. You can do it!"

"Okay, Meghan!" But he never sounded more needy or tiny or frightened.

Meghan knew she had to look back to see if the demon man was close on their heels, but she was afraid to. It was as if by looking it would make him all the more real. As if he would win this terrible race.

Her chest thudded and thumped with the shock and the effort of scurrying, and then she realized she had been holding her breath. She gasped and kept going. Fitch was faster and had scrambled and slid downslope perhaps twenty feet ahead of her. Then she saw him look back and his eyes bloomed wide.

"Meg—look out!"

As she turned her head upslope, to her left, she saw a flash of something dark, then she was grabbed from behind. He snatched at her hair, her long, foolish hair which she should have worn tied up tight on top of her head like her mother did when she was working. But Meghan had wondered if Bright Owl might come by their tent that morning, which he sometimes did, looking for Kane. And she foolishly wanted to look pretty for him.

The beast was grabbing her hair. She leapt forward down a six-foot drop from one jut of stone to another and freed herself from the brute's grip, but she felt hot pain, as if half of her hair had been ripped right out. Still, she kept running, falling, sobbing, and shouting to Fitch. "Go! Go, Fitch!"

Every time she said it she saw his blondish hair shaggy and creeping down almost to his shoulders, saw the buckskin tunic he wore so proudly, the one Red Dove had made for him over the winter. No way could she let him down.

Supposed to take care of him, she would be hanged first if she didn't follow through on that promise to Papa.

She had scrambled past a long thin line of scree still marked by a narrow cloud of dust where Fitch had run ahead when she dared to chance a look back again. The man was still chasing them. This glimpse was the first time she had seen him in full and he was definitely not any Shoshone she had ever seen.

What she had thought was a demon face was a normal face, but with tight set teeth in a mouth that looked very angry, under a nose flexing with the effort the rough terrain demanded.

But it was his eyes, wide and with arched brows, dark and bulging, that pushed her to move even faster. She gained a few feet in closing the growing distance between herself and Fitch.

They were switchbacking down the raw, rocky face, and every time she grabbed a jutting rock to steady herself, or rounded a cornice, or had to press herself close to the craggy gray surface, feeling crevices and nooks for hand- and footholds, she thought surely she would soon be bitten by an early to awaken rattlesnake.

She had been warned by Kane, who knew much about such things, that the rocky face of this cliff was a favorite haunt of the vipers, and that they would emerge from their long winter sleep any time now.

Somehow, that innate fear of being bitten by a rattler did not tremble her as much as the fear of having that brutal demon warrior get hold of them. She certainly didn't want him to touch her and she most assuredly was not going to let anything happen to Fitch.

No, she growled as she slipped and slid down another length of rock face. She would kill the man with her bare hands first.

And then she remembered she wore a knife. On the suggestion of Chief Stalks-the-Night, her father had insisted she carry the small sheath knife and wear it on her beaded belt, also made by Red Dove.

She had rarely used it, and often felt silly wearing it because the Shoshone women all wore larger knives or had one near-to-hand. But it had been useful in helping her mother prepare meals.

Meghan looked back once more and the man was still a good fifteen feet back there, above and behind them, trying to copy the same route she and Fitch had taken, and finding that his bigger body was not ideal on the narrow ledges and shallow hand- and footholds.

Before her, Fitch jerked to a stop and windmilled his arms. He force himself to sit down and scooted backward a few feet.

"Fitch! Go!" she shouted. "Go!"

"But Meg—" he shouted, looking back at her. "Cliff!"

She hustled up to him. The ledge on which he stood was wide enough to hold them both, but little more. Gazing at the swirling, spring-swollen river still twenty to thirty feet below, she crouched spraddle legged and peered with caution down at the brown flowage, a spray of gravel kicked by her moccasins pelting the water. Her arms, out of instinct, clutched her little brother.

Their chests heaved in time with their gulping, gasping breaths. Meghan looked back up trail, such as it was, little more than an undiscernible path they had traversed down and across, then down again, along a nearly impassable cliff face. How did they ever make it so far?

And yet, not twenty yards behind them, came the warrior. Even at that distance, Meghan could see the freakish mixture of rage and glee on the man's nut-brown face. He had been slowed by the increasing steepness of the route and the growing lack of protruding nubs of rock for gripping, but he was a determined brute. That much was plain to Meghan, and he would reach them very soon.

"What do we do, Meg? He's coming!"

Stroking his head, she held Fitch tight and looked left and right. Neither route was a possibility for them. The uphill ledge right at the drop-off was sheer and impassable, even to a mountain goat.

To the right was another drop-off, also sheer, and though the bottom was a stippled mass of jagged-topped pines, there was no way down. The trees reminded her of looking down at ants working so fiercely and tirelessly dragging the carcasses of other insects, bits of wood, granules of sand, anything and everything, back to their abodes.

Was there, she wondered, a creature larger, greater than humans, looking down at her right now, being chased by another ant in a seemingly endless game of chase and kill, chase and kill?

There is no way off this ledge, unless we are birds. Oh, that we could fly, thought Meg, shaking with a rising snag of fear growing in her with each passing moment. Fitch pleaded with her, glancing back to the savage behind them. The brutal vicious thing had driven them to this awful place and was closing in on them step by step.

"Meg!" Fitch looked up at her with a grimy, tear-streamed face. "What do we do?"

At that moment, the enemy warrior leapt the last distance between them, and like a cat on a cornered mouse, a smug smile of satisfaction leered at them from his homely face.

Meghan looked again at the water, and thought of birds. "We fly," she said, bending low and smiling in Fitch's face. She hugged her brother tight to her chest. And jumped.

CHAPTER 5

As Mack skirted the camp, making his way closer to the fight, he saw more and more bodies heaped, sprawled, collapsed. Many of them were Shoshone he recognized by their clothing and features. Of others he was uncertain. Their heads had been battered in with cudgels, one of which he carried with him.

The thought of being clubbed to death made Mack grit his teeth and move faster.

With increasing frequency, he saw a sight that repulsed him, something he had heard of but had not yet seen for himself—a scalping. On the brittle-grassed ground lay a Shoshone with his bloodied face battered in and his head a gleaming dome of glistening blood where the man's hair should have been. Below the welling mess was a ragged fringe of damp, matted hair.

Mack thought he knew who this warrior had been, though from the beating the man had undertaken, it was difficult to tell. It looked to be Dry Dog, and he had most definitely been scalped.

Even within sight of fighters on both sides, Mack found it difficult to look away from the sad mess that had been a man—a man he had known. It made him think briefly of the men he'd so recently laid to waste, all in fits of frenzy to ensure the safety of his family and their friends. Nonetheless he had killed them.

What was the point of such brute behavior? he wondered. Is there not a better way to solve our difficulties? And just who were those vicious men riding in and attacking what he had come to learn were peace-loving, quiet people?

All time for rumination was gone when an arrow whipped by the left side of his head as he turned back toward the fight. The projectile had been close. Mack swore he could feel a sizzle mark on his bristled cheek.

He spun and growled, instinct driving the sound up his throat. Glancing a last time as he spun away from the slick bloody mess that had once been a man, he ran straight at the intruder with the bow.

Similarly attired as the others, with slicked up hair, greased in that stiff, odd shape, the warrior popped his eyes wide in surprise. Not only was his intended victim rushing at him instead of fleeing in fear, but he was also a white man!

He howled a cry of animalistic rage and excitement. And so did Mack. He doubled his efforts, catching the man by surprise while nocking another arrow. Mack drove forward, and felt the bow collapse in half, snapping between their bodies as he slammed the man to the earth.

Other fights taking place all about him were men engaged in battle with other men. Shoshone women did the same, wielding knives and clubs and the rare gun, be it pistol or rifle, with as much skill as many of the men.

Mack could not help the flicker of random, quick thoughts of his wife and their new babies, and hoped she would be able to stay out of harm's way.

The growling, grunting man beneath him was more riled than the others he'd dealt with. Struggling to gain the upper hand by shoving and kicking, clawing and flailing, the man bellowed strange sounds—part word, part war cry. Mack worked to pin the slithery man, but it was no use. The man was too energetic and Mack was already feeling the effects of the other fights he'd partaken in already.

Suddenly the man did something Mack had not anticipated. With their faces close, the man jerked his head up and bit Mack on the cheek, making Mack quick in drawing back. Though the brute drew blood, he did not come away with what he surely had been after—a hunk of Mack's face flesh.

"You . . . beast." Mack clipped off all the words he wanted to growl at the man. He needed to save his strength and making sounds would only waste breath.

Working to free himself from the man's grasp, for they grappled each other with equal strength in their clamp-like grips, he succeeded enough to free his left arm gripping the enemy cudgel. He raised it high to drive it down at the now-alarmed man's face. But the man whipped his right arm up, stout and postlike, and held Mack's forearm, his teeth set tight behind wide-stretched lips as he strained with the effort.

Both men were forced to relax their efforts at besting the other when a riderless horse thundered at them. Wild-eyed and legs pounding, it showed no sign of slowing. They broke apart, with Mack skittering like a crab around to his right, keeping low and maintaining a claw hold on the neck of his foe's worn buckskin tunic.

"No!" shouted the man flailing his legs to one side as the horse hammered past. His utterance of a word in English shocked Mack and gave the warrior the opportunity to jerk free.

"Yes!" shouted Mack, lunging and swinging the cudgel

with obvious power. It was as if the club had been made for him and him alone.

Although often uncertain if it was good to feel such anger, Mack wondered if it might make him more heartless, if it would erode the kindness and charity he always tried to hold in his head and heart for his fellow humans and critters. Right then he thought of his family, of the innocence of the twins. He brought the club whistling in low and fast, and the foe jerked to his left, rolling out from beneath the blood-stained club.

Shocking him once again, the man smacked him hard across the face with a backhand blow. It rattled Mack's head as if he'd fallen onto a heap of rocks.

Two can play that game. Mack laid off swinging the club in exchange for balling his right hand into a tight ham-like fist. He brought it down hard, and drove a side-swiping blow at the man's left cheek. Something crunched as if he'd collapsed the man's face. His jaw hung slack, the cheek split open in the middle, already bleeding, reddening, and puffing. Though the brute did not appear to have a full set of teeth, Mack's blow had rendered a number of his remaining gnashers snapped, bloodied, and cracked.

Teeth fragments sprayed with blood and meat and little stringy bits were all over the man's chin. Snot dripped as his nostrils worked like small bellows before a smithy's fire. Stunned, he lay dazed. Slowly working his head back and forth, his mouth sagged as it oozed a trail of blood and running snot.

Mack shoved himself back and, gasping for breath, looked at the man a moment.

All about him fights of the same ilk happened. Grim-faced Shoshone fought with howling, snapping, biting, kicking, lunging attackers. Cast-out Piegans someone had said about them.

"Mack Harrigan!" a voice nearby shouted.

Mack looked to his right and upslope toward the voice, happy to see Chief Stalks-the-Night was still very much alive and, if anything, looking younger than he had appeared all last autumn. Most curiously, he wore a half grin on his seamed face.

Uncertain what to make of it, Mack shouted, "Chief! You okay?"

The man nodded with vigor many times, and beckoned to Mack, then his smile slid from his face as he pointed at Mack. Or rather right next to him, for Mack's foe had begun to revive and was rising up and balancing himself on his left arm. Still groggy, his eyes skittered to Mack, who leaned close by, the cudgel poised.

"Mack Harrigan!' shouted the chief. "Finish his days!"

Mack hesitated a heartbeat too long. The man pivoted on his left arm and swung his legs up, scissoring them about Mack's torso and toppling him even as he finally brought down the cudgel. The club rammed harmlessly into the earth beside the man's head. A smug sneer burst through on the broken-jawed face of his foe as Mack writhed once more to get out of the clutches of the enemy.

The brute wasn't playing games. He'd slipped a short-bladed skinning knife free of his belt and slashed at Mack, lashing open a wide, left-to-right gash in Mack's thick shirt and his inner long underwear. Mack saw and felt his own blood leaving him. It was enough to frighten him and at the same time enrage him once more.

As his vision buzzed and blurred, he shook his head. He had lost his grip on the club but still had his own knife. As the man struggled to get in another slash or a jabbing thrust, Mack held the brute's arm by the wrist. Once more they were locked in a close fight, leering and grunting with the effort, holding that tense pose for moments, immobile save for their heavy, ragged breaths.

A gunshot close by boomed—a shotgun. The man Mack been fighting whipped from his grasp and slammed to his back on the dusty earth beside their fighting spot. He jerked and twitched and then ceased, his last breath wheezing from him.

Mack looked to his right and saw the chief but a few yards away, holding his single barrel shotgun, an ancient thing he regarded as a special, almost spiritual weapon.

Mack was not inclined to disagree, especially now.

"Chief . . ." he said, working to untangle his legs from those of the dead man. He staggered, bent over and breathed deeply, trying without much success to look about him for other fights, for anyone who might be looking to do him ill.

The chief, somber once more, walked to him, one arm outstretched. "The Shoshone are victorious. This I know."

Mack shoved his hands up off his knees and straightened his back. He looked down at his bloody shirts and sucked in a breath through close-set teeth.

The chief looked close at the wound then stood upright. "You have been scratched, nothing more. We have much to do, Mack Harrigan."

As the two men stood side by side, with Mack gaining back his wind, and gingerly touching his cut belly, he determined the chief was not wrong. The gash was not a mortal wound, though it did sting like hellfire.

Noticing Mack wincing, the chief gestured at Mack's belly with a gnarled finger. "It will heal, but between now and then, it will not leave you alone." He smiled and looked back to the fighting going on around them.

Horses ran here and there, some of which Mack did not recognize. He saw several young Shoshone men chasing the horses, rounding them up by splitting their forces. All this went on even while random fights still raged.

As if to prove the point, the chief grunted and departed, loading his shotgun as he made for a fresh skirmish between an invader and a Shoshone. Someone tucked into the trees above the camp began shooting down at them.

A Shoshone man yelped not twenty feet from Mack, then spin and snatched at his shoulder before collapsing to the earth. He rose again, with labor, and low-walked as fast as he was able to a nearby tent, something, anything, to put between himself and the shooter.

Mack leaned to his right and made in that direction. As he loped, bending low and doing his level best to ignore the searing rash of hot pain in his belly, he angled wide to get up to the trees above the camp and incapacitate that foul shooter before he shot other of Mack's friends, especially the chief, who was taking no pains to hide himself from any foes.

That seemed foolhardy, but Mack was the one injured and the chief was the one who had lived a long ol' time as leader of his tribe. He must have been through a number of such attacks, perhaps had even led some of his own on other tribes.

Mack gained the trail that provided him with a quicker though more open route to the trees, then worked his way into the trees. Immediately, he regretted not keeping one of the guns he'd used and dropped or passed by on his way. But he had to lay the rogue low.

The man sat atop a boulder, two rifles beside him, and one in his hands. He held it snugged up to his shoulder, the stock tight to his cheek, no doubt taking aim at one of Mack's friends down below.

Though he was no match for a gun, Mack could not stand by and watch the man kill. With no more thought than that, he pulled the club back hard behind his shoulder. As he had done so many times in play throughout the previous winter months with throwing axes, he whipped the club, end for end, at the shooter.

It caught the man square on his near shoulder!

It was not a mortal blow, but it was powerful enough to rattle the man, and half knock him off his perch. More importantly, he lost his grip on the gun and it smacked and rattled across the rock to the ground.

By the time the man shoved himself upright with anger blooming bright on his face, Mack was on him.

The brute looked up at him, a fiendish glare in his eyes. Oddly, his mouth smiled and he snapped his teeth as if he were a cur kept on a too-tight chain. From his knees atop the rock, he lunged. Mack sidestepped, sucked in a breath, and drove the cudgel down hard on the back of the man's neck, collapsing the killer at his feet.

Mack jerked back as if the man were a snake poised to strike. Expecting another lunge, he looked down at the man and saw the odd angle of the man's neck. The quick lump forming between the ragged hairline and the top of the man's buckskin tunic indicated the blow had broken the man's neck.

It had taken Mack a surprisingly swift few moments to usher the man into the ranks of the dead, to keep company with those he had killed moments before.

With no more time to wonder about the odd, violent day dropped upon them, he heard renewed shouts from below and spied the chief in a tight fight with a stranger while others were looking ready to close in.

Mack leapt off the rock and searched the rifles the man had used—all spent save for the last one, and the hammer of that gun had snapped off when the man had dropped it.

He groaned in rage and bolted down the hill, back the way he'd come.

Falling into place beside the stern-faced chief, who was swinging at a lunge of his immediate foe, Mack asked why the foes had attacked. Chief Stalks-the-Night gave him a look that told Mack he truly was not only an outsider, but an ignorant one.

"Because," grunted the chief as he lunged again with his lance, his single barrel shotgun nowhere in sight, "we have had a good year with many horses and food stores. And our women are the finest."

"And fine women," nodded Mack, smiling, "create the finest babies!"

The chief grinned, a rare thing for him. "You know this, Mack Harrigan, because it is the same with the Harrigan tribe, yes?"

"You bet!" Mack flashed a full-on smile and feinted right, then drove forward to his left, slamming a wiry brave with a brutal swing of his cudgel.

As soon as the club connected with the surprised warrior's upper arm, Mack knew he had won the fight, for he heard the man's arm bone snap. The brute folded like a dropped blanket, twisting and jerking his head, his mouth snapping as if he were trying to chew the very air before him.

Mack gave him no quarter, though he did feel a deep-gut twinge for pummeling a downed man. Then he thought of what he'd seen this brute and others doing to his family and the families of the Shoshone, his friends, and he hammered the sidewinder into unconsciousness or death, he knew not which.

When he looked up, Chief Stalks-the-Night had done the same to his foe and was regarding him with a grave but satisfied look that cut through the blood spatters on his seamed face. "Yes," he said. "You have learned well these last moons, my friend." He turned to go, but over his shoulder said, "One day you may yet make a fine warrior. But it is not today."

Drained of strength, Mack shook his head and smiled a weak grin, assuming that passed for humor from the older man. But what if he had been serious?

What will it take to please this man? And why do I care? His thoughts riffled back to a vision of his dead father, burned alive in the foul mill fire. Mack had told the old man time and time again the mill had become a millstone. Now he regretted saying so, and likely would for his entire life . . . however long that might be.

Somehow the chief reminded Mack of his own father. Although younger—indeed he might well be closer to Mack's age—it was difficult to tell exactly how old the chief was. Spending a lifetime in the open air—the sun, the wind, rain, and snow—had made him hard like puckered leather. But there was a kindness in him, too. Mack had seen it over and over again. It was that quality that reminded him of his father, Gideon Harrigan, the finest miller in all of Ohio and a hard-as-stone devil at times, especially if you were his son.

Still, knowing the chief had warmed to him, Mack had unintentionally sought the man's approval since he'd found his way to the Shoshone wintering grounds months before.

"Come along, Mack Harrigan" shouted the chief. "I hear sounds that tell me this fight is not yet won!"

Mack didn't need reminding to get back into the action—his family was there, somewhere. At least Ell and the twins were safe with Red Dove. Of Kane, he only knew he had passed the boy and Bright Owl engaged in fights with the strange warriors. The sight of it had given him pause, and for a brief moment he had not recognized his own son as one of the battling men.

But he trusted Kane was somewhat safe with Bright Owl. He hoped so, anyway. The young warrior was just that, young, and Kane was even younger . . . and far less experienced in the ways of combat and killing. But he would learn, likely had learned that day.

From what Mack had already seen, it was fast becoming a day of quick, hard lessons for them all.

CHAPTER 6

The only thing Meghan heard in the few seconds they dropped to the water was Fitch's screams. If she had told him what they were going to do, there was a chance he would have balked, and that would have slowed them, but as she was stronger than him, it would not have stopped her intention to do this mad thing. She was in charge, and somehow sensed it was the only acceptable choice left to them.

One thing gave her satisfaction. Albeit a cold, quick, fleeting glimpse, the sheer victorious glee on the warrior's face was replaced with shock and growling rage as they jumped. It was the last thing she saw as they dropped below the edge of the cliff on which they had stood.

They plummeted upright, straight into the big river.

The icy flow was the result of hundreds or more melt-water-fed spring freshets coursing down the mountainsides all about them to reach the mighty vein of the river. As soon as their feet entered the freezing river, the coldness sliced into them, through them, enveloping them as they descended through it. It was so cold it felt as if it were burning their bodies.

Trust your belly and your brain, Mack said often as he touched his middle and his head, whenever a decision had to be made. And so Meghan had trusted that her gut and brain were telling her the river was deep enough in this wide spot they weren't going to break their bodies into a hundred pieces each.

That they could end up worse than— No, anything but that. She had heard the stories, and anything would be better than being a prisoner of an enemy tribe of the Shoshone.

As soon as they dropped off the cliff, she doubted her decision. And as the raw cold swallowed them, she regretted that decision. But Mack's other bit of advice about decisions followed the first in her mind, and she recalled him saying, "Once you decide to do a thing, then you are committed and you must follow through."

Never was that notion more appropriate than now, she thought. For there was no changing it, no going back. They were in the water. They had dropped hard and fast, a single plunging thing that sunk fast. She felt the river's bottom, a boulder-riddled mass that wanted to crush them, swallow them. Her feet felt as if they were jamming up and into the rest of her body.

Fitch was still wrapped tight in her arms and wriggled and jerked, as did she. But through it all—the bubbles and brown-green murk and pounding, the deafening chugging, thudding, crashing of it all—she knew she could not lose her grip on Fitch.

But just the same, she did.

And though her legs felt beyond broken and she fought to shove her way to the surface, uncaring for how badly damaged her body was, Meghan's one thought was that she had to find Fitch, had to save him lest he die in the river, alone and afraid.

The thought of this unacceptable idea chilled her far worse than the icy water ever could.

She broke the surface, her brother's name already ripping out of her mouth. She shouted his name over and over, the river jerking her as if it was a great water rope of grasping arms grabbing her and pulling her down.

Fighting the pull of the water time after time, she sputtered and gasped for air, but it seemed she was swallowing the entire river. Finally clawing her way to the surface of the roiling torrent, she stayed there. She blinked hard, trying to spin in the brute flow, looking for Fitch.

It all seemed so different at water level. The riverbanks were treed and rocky, with cliffs here and there giving way to jumbles of fallen-down rock and toppled pines. A clot of them wagged in the current ahead, jutting from a low spot on the same side of the river on which they had been. As the current tugged her downstream, she didn't recognize any of it, and could not see the cliff off which they had jumped.

The river shallowed ahead, and a big brown boulder, still rimmed with ice, looked to be rushing upstream to attack her. Meghan tried to kick toward the near bank but her arms and legs were sodden and ached with the thickness of the river's numbing, deadly cold.

A moment earlier, she'd seen a snag of pines bobbing in the current. Its green branches wagged and bounced with the erratic flow as it sluiced up, around, and over and under them. The pines had slumped into the river when the gravel bank gave way some time in the recent past.

None of that mattered to her. She saw the tree as something she could use to save herself, to haul herself out of the certain death that was the river.

All this time she heard a rasping, wheezing sound and realized it was her voice, still working, still shouting her little brother's name over and over. It was no longer audible above the rush and roar of the river, but she could not stop it.

And then she saw him. In his little buckskin tunic, nearly black and saturated with water. His face so white with cold and fear. He was snagged in the trees. She was carried closer and saw that he was hanging on to the tree. And then he saw her!

She could not hear what he was saying, but his mouth was wide, and his eyes seemed to shout as well. And she knew he was shouting her name, just as she was shouting his.

The most difficult thing Meghan Harrigan had ever done in her life was will her legs and arms to move. They felt weighted by stones, useless things that would never work again. She begged them to flail and kick and grab and reach. Reach toward the tip of the trees.

As she moved, more by the current than by her own effort, she felt an odd sensation beneath her and realized her feet were touching bottom. The rounded cobbles of the river bottom seemed to reach up and shove at her feet, as if resisting her efforts, or perhaps helping her along.

The feeling of solidity after so much water added the barest sliver of possibility—something shy of hope—to her frenzied mien. Meghan grasped it, keeping her little, clinging brother in sight the entire time. One sloppy, slapping movement at a time, she groped forward, lurching and stumbling along. Fighting the will of the spring river to shove her downstream, she cut cross-current toward the trees ten feet before her. Then seven, five . . . all while Fitch shouted.

Something akin to hope began to replace the raw terror that had covered his face moments earlier. In a small, tired voice, he shouted his sister's name over and over, and soon she heard it where before she'd heard only the rush and roar of the river.

And then she was gripping the upstream side of the same treetop he clung to, opposite her. He smiled, fear still keeping its place on his little face, but never had two people ever been so glad to see each other.

"I'm so sorry, Fitch," she blubbered, her lips barely moving. She coughed over and over, snot and drizzle from her mouth mixing with the words she tried to say, but he shook his head.

"We're oaky, Meg." His teeth chattered and she saw that his mouth was blue, as were his gripping fingers. "We're . . . Harrigans."

She smiled at this, their family's own cry of war, though never had it been used to hurt people. She tried to smile, but her mouth had given up movement.

Fitch's hands began to slip and his face began to turn from white to gray.

Again she willed her body to do what it did not want to do. "Fitch! Fitch!" she shouted, and it helped, for a moment.

She looked to her left and through sodden hair and splashing water, she saw the bank was but a dozen feet away. And it was a clear, gravel slope.

She never knew how she was able to do it, but Meghan Harrigan managed to grasp her brother's arm, then tunic. She held him across the thin end of a toppled, river-beaten pine, but she knew there was no way she could get them both to the river bank—so close, yet so far away—without letting go of him.

She reached beneath the tree, felt her nearly useless arm thud against juts of snapped branches, and then felt what she thought was his torso. She grasped it again and again and finally was able to secure a grip on the sodden thing.

She risked letting go of the boy's shirt above the trunk and he stayed there, but began to slip beneath the surface of the roiling water.

Then she did the only thing she could think to do—she ducked herself once more beneath the surface of the water and, using the poking, painful branches to guide her, she worked her way to the downstream side of the tree, to Fitch's side.

She shoved up beside him and gaped once again for air. By then, Fitch's own grip on the tree had slipped away and she forced her legs to slam, one after the other, into the river bottom.

As she held him by his tunic front, his face bobbing in and out of the water, his arms slopping and useless, she used her left hand to slap at and grab the snapped, ice-battered branches, welcoming their painful jabs, not caring if her arms would ever be useful again. She had to get the boy to shore.

The last few feet somehow did not matter. She felt sunlight on them, warmer and warmer in the shallows. And then, with a last mighty heave, she shoved them both up out of the water until only her heels remained in the wet. She flopped her little brother on the gravel and dirt beside her. She'd done it!

For a moment, he did not move, but lay there looking up at the sky.

With a last will of effort, Meghan reached over and pushed his belly, shoved him over on to his left side, and pushed at his little belly again. Water trickled from his mouth. She said his name as if it were a chant over and over, louder and louder. She hit him on the back, then she shook him.

And then he coughed. And he kept coughing, his little body jerking with the efforts.

Then she made a sound that was not a laugh as she intended, but it was close enough.

All was well for many long minutes as they both lay there, big sister and little brother, their chests working, their arms and legs blue and stiff from cold. The sun, though it was still early in the springtime, slowly worked its wonders on them.

How long the stayed that way, Meghan did not know.

But the next thing she sensed was a shadow. She looked up and saw someone looking down at her. "Papa?" Her voice was hoarse, weak, but it was there.

The person shifted and she squinted, and saw who it was. It was not Mack Harrigan.

A swarthy, brute of a man with odd greased hair was looking down at her and saying something to someone else. Soon, she heard two voices, then a third, and they were laughing.

She looked over at Fitch, but he was gone.

CHAPTER 7

As Mack looked about the shattered, ripped-apart Shoshone village, his feeling of relief barely induced the slightest smile on his face. Not until he rounded up his scattered offspring and made darn certain Ell and the twins were all right would he breathe easy.

And even then, he mused, looking about him, it was going to be a darn long time before any of them might smile again.

Already the wailing had commenced as women found the bodies of their mates, their sons, fathers, grandfathers, their children. Other children cried out, wandering, bloodied, and looking for their parents.

Bloodied, battered warriors, some cradling vicious wounds to their limbs, others holding oozing head wounds, limped in no particular direction, crying out for their wives, their children, for help.

Mack could scarcely believe it was the same Shoshone wintering ground camp he'd awakened to. He had gone off so blithely that morning all but whistling a jaunty tune as he made his way, alone, to Sitting Rock to take in the morning sun as it spread its glow and slow warmth over the river valley to the west.

How selfish he had been! How foolish! How—

"Mack! Mack Harrigan!"

He had been making his way through the wreckage back to his family's home, the big skin tent that accommodated them and their wagon and goods, but hearing the voice, a voice he knew, he turned. Something told him he was about to receive unwelcome news.

It was Bright Owl, his son's best friend, and son of the chief.

"What is it?" said Mack, none too gently.

If his tone bothered the young man, Bright Owl showed no sign of surprise or worry.

Before he could speak, Mack said, "Where's Kane? I saw you two fighting together!" He strode up to the youth, who he could just about still look in the eyes. Another season of the growing the youth had done that winter and Mack would look up to him.

"Kane has gone to Sitting Rock to find Meghan and Fitch."

"So he knew I would keep them there."

"That was our hope, yes. But Mack Harrigan."

Mack turned again taking in the youth's serious gaze. "What is it, son?"

"He left some time ago. He should have returned. I was going to find him, but my father needs me."

Mack looked toward the trail leading west to the favored relaxation spot. Then he looked to his right, toward their tent up the rise with a few others in the spot where the camp had begun to expand with new families. He had to find Ell and the twins.

"Mack Harrigan, I must go to my father."

He looked again at Bright Owl. "Yes, son."

The young man nodded once and turned.

"Thank you, Bright Owl. Tell your father I'll be there to help him as soon as I am able." Mack made for the

Harrigan tent, taking in the wrecked camp of mourning, wailing Shoshone, their wounded and dead, the smoke rising up from a half-dozen smoldering teepee fires, a brave chasing down a loose horse. All of it.

It took Mack scant minutes to reach the still-standing Harrigan tent, now a battered mess. The man he'd killed flopped on his back outside. The gaping hole in which he'd stuck his head was still flapping open.

Mack tore past that macabre sight and shoved wide the entry flaps. "Ell! Ell!"

Of a response, he received none. The dim interior was small, open enough that he could take in its entirety in a gaze. He strode forward, upending and shoving away items—a nail cask they used as a seat, a wooden trunk that contained various well-packed family treasures, and stacks of blankets and clothing—and reached the rear of the tent and shoved aside the last lumpy pile of quilts. She wasn't there, hiding as before. Not that he expected Ell Harrigan to cower.

"Ell! Elspeth Harrigan!"

No response.

He spun, his breathing growing raspier, his thoughts skittering, nibbling at rank possibilities as rats might at stale bread and meat. "Ell?" He knew she would not be about the place, so he hoped that meant she had gotten out of there with Red Dove. "Red Dove!"

All this happened in mere moments, and then he saw something foul on the floor to his left. In the dark cleft of shadow where the skins and canvas of the tent floor and wall met lay a man, half-in, half-out of a gash in the tent. His head was a bloodied, dead thing.

Mack's breath left him and he sagged backward, staggering. What had happened? He dropped to his knees, not bothered by the gory mess before him and groped the floor all about the man, searching for what, he knew not.

But his mind tricked him, toyed with him, made him think terrible things about his wife and their twins. Horrific visions of what savages—how he viewed the attackers—might do to a woman and two crying babies.

Once more he found nothing he looked for, shook off the momentary foul thoughts, and pushed his way back outside. Still calling his wife's name, he rounded the tent and saw the bottom half of the dead man he'd just left inside.

He turned his gaze on the Harrigan wagon, nested close by the tent and rigged for the winter as storage and sleeping quarters for Kane. Until his recent refusals to behave like a Harrigan family member, Fitch had shared quarters with Kane in the wagon.

The thought of fiery little Fitch brought the quickest flicker of a smile to Mack's gore-speckled face. He looked beneath the wagon, around it, then quickly heaved himself inside. But all he saw were Kane's things. Left less neat than the boy's usual tidy self allowed, it was quite understandable given the day's events. That was all Mack found out of the ordinary there.

He shouted "Ell!" once more before shoving open the rear flaps of the small wagon and pushing his way out. And what he saw stoppered the breath in his throat.

There stood Ell and Red Dove, looking up at him with wide eyes, each woman holding bloody knives in one hand and cradling a fussing baby in the other.

"Mack!" Ell met him as he dropped to the ground.

He hugged her tight with one arm, his other arm loosely beneath the baby . . . which one it was he could not yet tell. They were alike in nearly every outward way, those new Harrigan twins. Ell was forever mocking him for not being able to tell them apart. For the life of him he could not figure out how she was able to.

Mack said nothing, but teared up, as did Ell. He lifted her off the ground and kissed the top of her beautiful head. His eyes looked up and landed on Red Dove several feet away, who glanced elsewhere, her usual stoic look on her face.

"Red Dove!" growled Mack, and without letting go of Ell, managed to walk with Ell over to the shocked Indian woman. He hugged her as well and she stood, holding the baby and her knife in unmoving arms.

She looked as if she would rather be back in the middle of the fight than be there, enduring a hug by this white man. But Mack and Ell knew differently. She was as close to them as anyone could ever be. They owed their lives to each other so many times over, and for so many months on the long, strange journey. They seemed to understand each other without giving it further thought. They were family. Plain and simple.

Finally, Ell shoved Mack's chest and pushed him away. "Enough! I have to breathe."

"Yes," said Red Dove. "Enough, Mack Harrigan. There is much to do."

Mack nodded. "Of course, of course. I have to go. I have to help Kane find Meghan and Fitch and bring them back."

"Find them?" said Ell. "They're not back yet from Sitting Rock? We could have gone on there . . ." She looked at Red Dove, whose face pinched with guilt.

"No, it's all right. Bright Owl told me Kane just headed that way to fetch them. I told them to hide in the caves there." That was all he had time to say. From the far side of the tent, they heard Bright Owl shout Mack's name once, twice. As Mack rounded the tent he nearly ran into the young warrior.

"Mack Harrigan, come quickly! We have found—" His eyes flicked to something he saw over Mack's shoulder. Ell and Red Dove.

"Bright Owl, son, what is it?" Mack grabbed the young man by the shoulder, turned and looked at Ell.

"Whatever it is," she said, "he can tell me, too.

"Go ahead, Bright Owl," said Mack.

The young man looked as if the very words he spoke were hot coals he could not wait to spit out of his mouth. "Turtle Eye has found tracks on the riverbank, downstream of here." He pointed. "He thinks they are those of Miss Meghan and Shoshone Fitch."

Mack's brows pulled together, then he shook his head. "No, no, that can't be right. I . . . I left the children safe at Sitting Rock. And that's far upstream of here." He pointed toward the spot as if Bright Owl didn't know where it lay.

"This is what I thought." Bright Owl nodded, leaned closer, and lowered his voice. "But Mack Harrigan, he also found hoof prints. And other tracks—those of strange men, not Shoshone. Then they all rode off."

Mack said nothing for a second, then Bright Owl spoke once more. "I am going to Sitting Rock now to help Kane. But . . . Turtle Eye is our best tracker. He knows the moccasin tracks of everyone in camp." He looked past Mack once more. "But he . . . he has been wrong, yes. Yes, that will be it."

Mack looked at Ell as he bolted for the trail. "Don't worry, Ell. I'll find them! I'll bring them back. They're still hiding, that's all." But visions of his two middle children, Meghan and Fitch, adrift somehow downstream, past the Shoshone camp, would not leave him be. And they warred with the look on Ell's face as he departed, the face of a mother on the verge of unknowable grief.

CHAPTER 8

When Mack wanted to, he could cover quite a bit of ground at a quick clip. His speed was especially impressive to Bright Owl, a lean youth still growing, and who was considered one of the quickest runners in camp. But Bright Owl didn't have children in harm's way.

As for Mack, he churned soil digging his way up and across the trail to Sitting Rock, and cursed himself, not for the first time that day, for bringing his family to this hellish impasse in life.

Sure, they had made wonderful friends of the Shoshone, and yes, they had had many adventures, some of them exciting. Among them he knew they all enjoyed the riverboat passage, and it was not just Fitch who got a thrill from the pirate attack during it. And meeting their chum, the crusty mountain man Bearpaw Jones, and his mule, Ol' Gravyfoot, certainly was memorable.

But other episodes, including the grim time on the trail in the small, too-late wagon train, and its vicious wagon master, Ricker Briggs, made for a hellish trip. And then there was the awful situation they found themselves in at the foul trading post.

No, all in all, Mack felt in his bones he had made a decidedly selfish decision in forcing his beloved family to accompany him on this whimsical adventure West, mostly to track down his father's brother, Zeke.

As he neared the final gradual slope that led to Sitting rock, the landscape cleared and the vista opened up before him. Usually it was a moment he enjoyed, and always slowed his pace to take it in, but not that day. He ran faster and began shouting, "Kane! Meghan, Fitch!"

He made it to the spot he'd left Meghan and Fitch hours before, close to the gradual slope that formed the rocky sitting area, worn smooth by generations of Shoshone who came here to think, to peruse the valley below, and to enjoy the sunsets and slow mornings.

Of his children, there was no sign.

"Kane! Kane!"

"Here!"

Hearing the voice of his eldest down below the edge, but to the left, Mack wondered what he was doing down there, that far over. He slid and scrambled down the first few feet to a sizable ledge projecting outward. That was close to where he'd told Meghan and Fitch to seek safety in one of the hidden caves pocking the face of the cliff.

Mack was torn. He wanted to edge his way along there and inspect his two children, but Kane was somewhere in the other direction, toward the river side of the cliff face.

"Pa!" Kane's head appeared around a ledge. He looked rough, his face spattered with blood, his clothes torn. Brown and black stains covered his shirt and coat. And his slouch hat was gone. His hair looked soaked with sweat and hung in his eyes.

"Kane! Where is your sister? Where is Fitch?"

"Pa, I don't know. I've looked everywhere, I've shouted until I'm hoarse." He spoke in a forced, ragged voice as if he'd been without water for days. "Pa, I just can't find them!"

"Did you look in the little caves over this way?" Mack began edging down there.

"Yes, I looked there. I've looked everywhere."

"Mack Harrigan! Kane!" It was Bright Owl, from above them, atop the cliff. "Tracks!"

Mack scrambled back to the top with Kane close behind. They reached Bright Owl hunkered some dozen feet back.

He held his left hand outstretched, his fingers splayed. "Here," he said, without looking up. "Horse prints and men. One man on foot, the other riding. The one on foot—" Bright Owl walked low toward the edge, following the tracks. He stopped and looked up at Kane and Mack. "Ah, you have ruined the prints." His annoyance was obvious, then he resumed on his hands and knees. Every few feet he nodded and grunted, and once he said, "Ha!" and pointed.

Mack and Kane crowded behind, peppering him with questions, but he did not respond. He kept his nose down, and soon he was over the edge, following what appeared to them the barest of scuffs in the gravel.

Mack and Kane waited for a few moments. Then Mack told his son what Bright Owl had said about Turtle Eye finding the prints on the riverbank below camp.

"He's the best tracker in the tribe," said Kane in a low voice, his eyes widening.

Mack nodded. "I thought I should try here first. I'm going back. I have to talk with Turtle Eye. I have to learn everything he discovered. You stay with Bright Owl, see what you can find."

With that, Mack loped back up the trail toward camp. Exhaustion dragged at his heels, but he thought of Meghan and Fitch, and a fire burned anew inside him, urging him on.

By the time he reached camp, he was panting and ragged. The wailing and crying and shouts had dwindled, but random shouts of pain and grief rose up here and there throughout the camp.

Someone brought him a water skin and he downed several long pulls and splashed some over his face. It was a woman who always smiled but never spoke, at least in front of him.

He'd been told she was Chief Stalks-the-Night's sister, and she had lost her husband in a raid some years before. Since then she had kept to herself, but was revered for her knowledge of plants and their uses, and was a respected and valued healer in the tribe.

Mack thanked her and she nodded in return, then pointed toward the trail east of the smoking mess that had been the settlement. Through the smoky scrim hanging low over camp, he saw the chief looking his way.

Graven faced, he beckoned Mack once, then turned and made for the trail leading to the river east of town. Mack followed at a lope and soon caught up with him. The chief seemed to know it was him without looking and continued walking. "Mack Harrigan. Did Bright Owl tell you what was found?"

"Tracks, and that they might be Meghan and Fitch's?"

"Yes. But there is more. Turtle Eye is a good tracker. But he knows it, so I don't tell him so." Chief Stalks-the-Night almost smiled then, but a weariness on his face overrode any attempt at mirth he might have been tempted to make. "We need your help, Mack Harrigan. We have seen this before. The rogue Piegan and the others with them are thieves. Not only do they take food and guns and horses, but they take children. Younger is good for them, for they turn them into Piegan."

What he was saying took a moment for Mack to comprehend, then he grabbed his friend by the shoulder, turning him. The chief allowed this, but it was not something most men would dare do.

"Are you saying they have taken Meghan and Fitch? How can Turtle Eye be sure?"

The chief nodded. "It looks to be so, yes, Mack Harrigan. Turtle Eye knows their tracks. He knows the tracks of all in camp. He is not wrong."

"But how? They were up at Sitting Rock. It can't be."

"They jump in the water to escape Piegans chasing them, maybe. They float downstream, come out here. It is bold. But too many Piegans were still about, watching. They have gone now that they have what they want."

"But surely—"

The chief shook his head. "I have lived many seasons and it has happened several times before. They took other children from the camp, too. Not just Harrigan children."

"But . . . but Meghan. She's not a child. She's too smart to be turned into a Piegan!"

The chief said nothing but stared hard into Mack's quivering eyes. Then the full import of what the chief meant sunk into Mack's mind. They didn't want Meghan to be one of them. They wanted her because she was . . . a woman.

As much as it pained Mack to admit it, Meghan was indeed a woman now. He'd seen the way Bright Owl and she had looked at each other, then looked away. All of it. He let out a low groan and rubbed his face with his hands.

"Mack Harrigan! We need you now, and Kane and Bright Owl, too. A young warrior has been sent to bring our two sons here. They will find us. Other Shoshone men are waiting at the river with horses and weapons and food for us. We must go now while the trail is still with us. We must go after the children."

"But Ell . . . I have to tell Ell."

"She will be told. She will be well. The camp is once again fortified and many warriors are remaining behind."

Walking at a faster pace, Mack questioned the chief. "You said there were others. Other children were taken?"

"Yes. Two girls and a boy. The girls are the daughters of a fine young couple."

"And the boy?"

"He is the son of our good tracker, Turtle Eye."

"I see."

Emerging out of the trees at the riverside, two tied horses were waiting for them.

"Turtle Eye has gone on," said the chief as he swung up onto a horse's back. Mack was about to do the same, wondering for the first time about his own horse, Dainty. She had spent the winter with the tribe's sizable herd. Had she also been stolen?

He saw the trampled muck and brittle vestiges of last year's bankside grasses. "Is this where they found my . . . the tracks?"

"Yes," said the chief.

Mack scrambled down the bank, staying to one side. He had to see for himself. He wasn't much of a hand at tracking, save for a wounded deer in the snow, but he had to see. There they were. The imprints of soft soles, moccasins that clearly belonged to a child and another larger, but not a man's.

"Meghan . . . Fitch." He ran a hand lightly in the indentations and the drying edges crumbled. "I will find you," he whispered. Tears filled his eyes and he let them. "I will find you, and so help me if anything has happened to you, I will tear apart with my own hands anybody who had a hand in hurting you. I promise you."

"Mack Harrigan!"

He stood and pulled in a deep breath. "I'm coming, Chief. Let's find those children."

CHAPTER 9

Meghan could barely speak as she and Fitch ahead of her were dragged up the riverbank by their collars and dropped in the brittle, old grasses and gravel at the top of the bank.

Fitch had put up even less of a struggle than her own weak efforts. But she'd tried, for she knew these men were the enemy. The attackers meant them no good.

She was relieved Fitch was alive, and with each passing minute showed more sign of coming around, if not to his old, fiery self, at least to someone awake and aware of his surroundings.

"Meghan?"

His voice brought her gaze back to his face. He was scratched, still a little blue about the mouth, and his ears were bright red, but he was alert and looking at her with the raw fear only a child can show.

"It's okay, Fitch. It's going to be okay." She looked around, then turned to her left side and looked above them. She recognized the spot. Below the camp where people sometimes fetched water, it was less steep than areas close by the camp.

Their captors were two men on horseback, and two others standing bedside horses. Talking, they looked nervous and kept glancing westward, which Meghan knew was the direction of the Shoshone camp not far away.

Faint wails and shouts from the camp reached her ears through the trees. Maybe she could shout. Or better yet, what if they could crawl back down toward the river and— No, they would surely die if they jumped into the river again. Both had nearly frozen to death or drowned. It was still far too early in the spring to swim and survive it. Papa had explained it was due to all that mountain runoff.

Thoughts of Mack and Ell and the twins and Kane and Bright Owl crowded into her mind. *Oh, what had happened to them all? Were they all . . . dead?* That unthinkable notion rushed upon her and she stifled a sob. But Fitch heard her. And so did one of the warriors.

Before Fitch could scoot closer to her, the warrior strode over and looked down at them. He shouted something she did not understand. She knew she wouldn't, as she barely understood Shoshone, even after spending many months with the tribe.

He shouted again, then shoved her shoulder hard with his foot. She fell over onto her back, half rolling with the shove to avoid another kick.

Fitch smacked the man's legging and shouted, "Leave off my sister!"

His effort was weak, but Meghan was impressed with his spirit, and not surprised.

The man bent low and swung an arm up to backhand the child, but it was Meghan's turn to interfere. She shouted, "No! Don't you dare hit him!"

That somehow halted the brute's intended smack, giving Fitch enough time to shove himself, still wobbly, up onto his knees.

Behind the warrior and up on the path, the other man

laughed, but was hushed by the men on horseback. They continued to look up the rough path toward the camp.

Meghan realized it was now or never, and she shouted, "Here! Help! Help!" She was able to get those three words out, but no more, for the growling man bent low over her, grabbed the back of her head with one hand, and clamped a filthy, greasy, soot-smelling hand over her mouth. She could barely breathe through one uncovered nostril. He pulled her up closer until her face was but inches from his.

Dirt was crusted in the lines on his face. She smelled his rank, sour breath. It was the same man they had seen upside down, and then had fled from. The same man who had chased them without letup all the way to the edge of the cliff.

She saw something else, too—the way he stared at her with unblinking, untrustful eyes. He let them trail down her neck across her chest, and then down the rest of her wet, filthy dress.

He spoke something low and husky that tapered off into a chuckling sound, then nodded his head slightly, as if he had just come to a decision.

Meghan knew what that meant and wanted none of it.

As she struggled to breathe, something distracted him once more. Fitch was shouting and growling, and kicking the man's leg.

The warrior's hand was not stayed. He swung the meaty thing down from Meghan's face and across Fitch's cheeks. One of the men behind him shouted something in a low voice, looked westward, then growled the words again with more insistence.

The warrior snatched Meghan's collar tight behind her neck once more, choking off her wind and did the same to the lolling, sobbing Fitch. He dragged them up to the feet of the other man, dropped them once more, and said something, pointing at Meghan and Fitch.

The younger man looked at both of them, then nodded and retrieved strips of rawhide from his horse. He bound their wrists together in front of them, and set about to do the same with their ankles so Meghan and Fitch could ride horseback. The other man growled in a disgusted tone and he stopped.

She did not want to be taken away from there. She desperately tried to remember what their old friend, the mountain man Bearpaw Jones, had told them about what happened to white captives. But Ell had shushed him before he could finish. What to do?

She did the only thing she could, which was to shout once more. "Help! Help! It's Meghan and Fitch! Help!" She tried to shove herself up onto her knees and then her feet. Her intention was not to leave Fitch, but to position herself in front of him at all times so he would not be harmed. It was the only way she had of defending him.

Again, the man who had tormented them strode back over from talking with the others and clamped his hand over her mouth. Fitch took up the call and shouted as loudly as his waterlogged lungs would allow. The younger, more timid man held a hand over Fitch's mouth.

The little Harrigan proceeded to flail and kick and swing his hands upward, clublike, toward the man who tried to stifle him. Their *tormentor,* for that was what Meghan saw him as, growled something and nodded toward the other men.

The young fellow dragged Fitch along and reached up. Handed down were wadded soft deerskins, which he stuffed into their mouths and then wrapped another thong about their mouths and tied it behind their heads.

The rawhide strips were smelly, not cured, still green, as

she'd heard them called, and were tight, biting into their skin.

Meghan jerked and fought it, twisting her head this way and that, and Fitch tried to bite the younger man's filthy hand, lunging and kicking and flailing the whole while.

The young man barked a sharp, low, "Stop!"

The English word did indeed stop the little dynamo from flailing for a moment. Then he resumed.

By then he was being dragged alongside his sister to the horses. The leering man made to hoist Meghan up on to his own waiting horse, but one of the other men spoke one word in their language and the leering man, while he did not like what he heard, did not say anything to combat the obvious directive.

He none-too-gently hoisted her high up into the waiting hands of the man who'd spoken to him. The man jerked her roughly around and forced her to sit behind him. Her skirts bunched and caught at her knee. She jerked them up a little and the man on the ground touched her long johns-clad left leg. The rider kicked at him with a grimy moccasin.

Breathing was difficult, but she managed. Twisting around as much as she could she located Fitch. He had been hoisted up on to a horse as well, but with the younger warrior who had shouted at him in English.

Meghan had no reason at that moment to feel anything but fear, yet she did feel a twinge of relief. The younger man, while still a brute and frightening, was not as brutal or as frightening as the leering man who, she was quite certain, would soon bother her without ceasing.

Never in her short life had Meghan Harrigan felt anything close to that sort of hopelessness. But she could not show it—not on her face and not to Fitch, who was looking right at her, right in her eyes. His eyes welled with tears and they dripped down his cheeks. Oh, but she had failed him. She should have been able to keep him safe from terrible harm.

Meghan did her best to look cheerful. Not easy in that situation, and not easy with one's mouth stuffed with leather and wrapped with green rawhide. But she raised her eyebrows and tried to smile with her eyes.

Then the horses were whipped and the four riders with their two extra charges, bolted into the forest, cutting north-eastward, angling away from the Shoshone camp where they had spent the winter in peace and happiness.

She and Fitch traveled farther than they had in all that time. The terrain was similar but strange. They rode hard. Then the leering man barked something, and all of the men looked back, then bent low and nudged their horses harder.

Meghan jostled and fought to stay on the horse. She tightened her legs, but they only reached halfway down the horse's big belly.

The man she rode behind reached an arm around and flailed his hand a moment, searching, then grabbed her bound hands and forced them to his belt, where it wrapped around behind him. She gripped there, thankful to have something to hold on to. He pulled his hand forward again and they continued their slamming, jouncing ride.

If they were being chased, she could let go with her hands and legs, fall off the horse, duck and roll to one side, then get up and run! Run back to whoever would be doing the chasing. It had to be a Shoshone or, even better, their father.

She saw Fitch, also jostling, but riding in front of the young man who had taken him on to his horse. She was riding a horse-length behind and to Fitch's left. He was looking back to her, and she knew she could not abandon him. It was a foolish thought, and she could not afford to have any more of those.

Wherever he went, she would go. *Had* to go. She began in that moment to force herself to stop thinking like someone who was in a bad situation and had given up on surviving it. She told herself to *think as a Harrigan.* Harrigans never give up. She looked at Fitch and in that moment he looked back at her. In his eyes was something more than the mere tearful look of a frightened little boy—a spark of determination.

She hoped he saw the same in hers, for she had begun to feel it. She winked at him and he nodded. Since he could not wink, he closed both eyes and opened them again. A double wink. She smiled as best she could around the rawhide lashed about her face.

That gave her the idea of working on the one thing she might be able to control. Although her face had begun to puff and swell from the tightness of the straps, she began to slowly, painfully chew the leather in her mouth. It was disgusting, and she didn't know if it would work, but it was the only thing she could think to do, besides hang on for life.

She worked her teeth at the leather in her mouth, nibbling away like a mouse in the dark. When she had forced it with her tongue to one side of her mouth, then she would work on the hide thongs holding it in her mouth. And then that was through. Who knew?

But already Meghan Harrigan felt better about their nearly hopeless plight. It was not completely hopeless. Just *nearly.* That would have to do.

Meghan guessed they had ridden for half an hour when the man in the lead, riding ahead and out of view for some time, rode back to them. He was the only one she hadn't yet heard make a sound, but he made up for that silence with a quick yip and shout.

From the look on his face, Meghan deduced he was pleased with whatever he had beckoned the others forward to see. Before they made it to the top of the rise before them, she saw on the faces of the others that they, too, were pleased and seemed to be anticipating the thing they were about to see.

The horse on which Fitch rode crested the rise first. Meghan saw by the way Fitch recoiled in place seated before the young warrior, that something shocked or alarmed him.

Meghan's horse thundered up the rise and halted with the others, stamping and chomping. She looked down at an open patch in the trail crowded with what appeared to be more than a dozen riders, all sharing similar hairstyles and clothes. Their horses bore the same peculiar decoration— handprints and lines painted on the flanks, shoulders, necks and heads of the beasts.

Ahead of them rode another six or more riders, driving before them a small but thundering herd of horses. They were Shoshone horses, and for a fleeting moment Meghan thought for certain she caught sight of Dainty, the Harrigans spirited, reliable young horse they had brought with them on the trip west from Ohio. She was recognizable for her light mane, nearly blonde, that contrasted with the color of her rich, darkish body.

Meghan deduced their small group was joining up with the main war party. Some of the other party saw them and held up arms clutching rifles and lances and bows. Yips sounded and soon rippled through the entire small but powerful group. She wondered how powerful they would be feeling right now had they not attacked while the greater group of Shoshone still lay in their blankets in the early dawn.

"Cowards," she tried to say around the sodden, rank hunk of leather scrap in her mouth. It came out sounding like mush. If anybody heard her or cared about her opinion, they showed no sign of it.

Meghan saw something else as they began their switchbacking descent down the short but steep run of trail to get to the wider spot where the larger group ahead was traveling though.

Two children, then a third appeared as the riders weaved in and out, before and after their fellows. Two were girls, perhaps Fitch's age, but from that distance Meghan was uncertain as to who they were. But she knew in her bones they were Shoshone, had to be. They, too, were bound, though not gagged.

Meghan guessed she and Fitch had been too loud—a small slice of cold comfort.

The third child was also bound. A boy, he looked younger than Fitch. Meghan thought she recognized him as Turtle Eye's son. Devoted to his son, the man was raising him without a mother's help, as his wife had died two summers before in an accident. Knowing he was the best stalker and tracker in the tribe gave Meghan a flutter of hopefulness. If Turtle Eye had not been hurt in the raid, he would be relentless in pursuing the abductors of his son, as would her parents.

Meghan spied the distinctive coat of who she felt certain was Dainty, the Harrigan horse, running and harried in the midst of that frenzied herd. Knowing what a gentle soul the horse was, Meghan felt her spirits dip once more. She fought the feeling, telling herself there was always hope. She felt certain Turtle Eye or Mack—someone, anyone— would be on their trail.

As the day wore on, the sun heated the air. Meghan saw Fitch dozing a time or two on his horse, and each time she watched the man who carried him gently seat him upright once more.

Small comforts, thought Meghan.

Perhaps there was some goodness among those brutes after all. Did they not all have families of their own? They could not all feel heartless and crude and cruel like the leering man who rode close behind her.

She'd glanced back a couple of times, and each time he was staring straight at her, a half smile, half sneer on his homely face.

CHAPTER 10

Having explained the situation to Kane, and what Turtle Eye had found at the riverbank, Bright Owl and Kane had raced back to camp from Sitting Rock. It had taken precious minutes to round up mounts, as the horses that were left following the madness of the raid were in no mood to be anywhere near men.

"They could have waited for us!" Kane shouted to Bright Owl as they mounted up on ponies.

Bright Owl said little, knowing Kane's complaint was born of frustration.

Feeling guilty about leaving the camp in such a mess—wounded and dead still strewn about, wailing women and children—the young men rode their horses to a lather before they caught up with the chief, Mack, and Turtle Eye.

Kane hated to admit it, but it was a relief to get out and away from the camp for a while. He wished it wasn't to chase after killers and thieves, but his blood lust was still up after the events of earlier. He'd never killed a man before, but now? Now he knew he could, if pressed. And anyone who stole children deserved no quarter.

They were nearly to the men ahead when Bright Owl emitted a quick, high-pitched call, not quite bird, not quite beast. Two of the men turned, one of them was Mack, and as Kane rode up he could tell his father was pleased to see him and worried anew.

He didn't want that. "Pa, I'm fine. And I know what we're headed for. Don't worry about me."

Mack let out a deep breath, as if he had kept it in all morning. "Kane, when you are a father yourself one day, you can tell me not to worry." He smiled briefly. "By then, you'll know that not worrying is not possible."

Turtle Eye halted the group with a raised arm and slid from his mount. The chief held his reins while the man bent low and lightly touched the trail. He bent even lower and sniffed, then cocked his head to one side as if listening. He sniffed once more, then moved on up the trail, repeating this, then standing and eyeing the distance.

Soon, he returned and swung up on to his horse and spoke in low tones to the chief.

In English, Chief Stalks-the-Night told his son and the two Harrigans that they were following two groups, one was with many horses, though fewer riders.

"The Shoshone herd," said Mack.

The chief nodded and continued. "The second group, smaller, met up with the larger group. Here they all rested for a short time, then the larger group rode ahead. The smaller group did, too, but at a distance."

"Why?" said Kane.

"To watch for us, maybe."

"Are the ones in the second group the people we seek?"

The chief shrugged. "It is likely but not easy to tell." He nudged his horse into a lope to catch up with Turtle Eye who had ridden ahead, not wanting to waste time.

CHAPTER 11

Close to nightfall they halted. Each man could still see the others, but in another half hour, it would be far more difficult. Turtle Eye slid from his mount, led it off trail, and walked with the horse northwestward. The others followed, taking care to make as little sound as possible.

Earlier the chief had explained they were getting closer to the kidnappers, obvious since his group was traveling lighter. He'd also explained they were going to stop well before dark, picket the horses, then proceed on foot. The hope was to catch the abductors unawares, though it was unlikely, since they would be expecting retaliation.

Turtle Eye, the chief, and Mack had agreed to a more tiresome but perhaps unexpected approach in circling wide and coming in on them from a direction different from what the thieves might expect.

It was not much of a plan, but to Mack it sounded solid. The two youths, Bright Owl and Kane, nodded assent, having little say in the matter.

Weapons were plentiful in the small group of five, as they had each made certain to bring along as many as they could scrounge up. The chief had brought a long gun and a pistol for Mack.

In addition to guns, each man wore a belt knife and a

belt ax. Turtle Eye and Bright Owl each had a bow. The two were impressive shots, and the silence of an arrow in a night fight would be valuable.

The horses were hobbled and loosely picketed so they could rove and forage. Each man hoped but did not lend voice to the thought they would be successful in finding and freeing the children. They proceeded with Turtle Eye leading them. Even in the coming dark, he had the skills of discerning the direction.

After ten minutes, it became clear that tracking skills would not be necessary to find their quarry. They heard joyful yips and howls, raised voices. Proceeding slowly since it might well be a trick, they began to see the dim, flickering glimmer and glow of light—a campfire.

The kidnappers certainly don't act like they're being followed, or are trying to keep their presence undetected, thought Mack.

The five men ranged twenty or so feet apart, weapons at the ready, and advanced slowly to avoid cracking tree duff and twigs, dislodging rocks, or walking into a divot or stone that might trip them up.

Over the past few hours, a breeze had stirred up from the northeast but to Kane, it did not smell as if it carried a portent of rain, like Bright Owl had taught him to discern.

Soon, the intermittent breezes became a steady, low-level blow. That proved a benefit to the small band, as they had cut back eastward. The wind carried with it snatches of voices and the nostril-tickling tang of wood smoke.

Soon, Turtle Eye and his companions saw a camp with a small but bright blaze crackling. A half-dozen warriors were seated around it, the firelight dancing on their arms, chests, and smiling faces. The random snatches of words their voices offered to the breeze, though in a tongue unfamiliar to Kane and Mack, sounded proud, manful, and worst of all, boastful.

The rescuers dropped back down below the edge of the slight berm they had crawled up, grouping close to each other. Turtle Eye and the chief conferred in low tones barely audible, the speaker's mouth close to the listener's ear.

The chief repeated the conversation to Mack, in English. The boys crowded close. It seemed to Kane they did not need to take such precautions in masking their voices since they were downwind of the kidnappers, but he said nothing.

Turtle Eye had told the chief, who concurred, that since they could only see a half dozen of the enemy warriors, others must be about. Also, he knew the answer to the only thing Mack wanted to know—where were the children?

"They are out of the firelight, tied nearby in the dark. Turtle Eye tells me he glimpsed one of the men, younger than the others, with the job of attending to the prisoners. He leaves the others for a time, then returns and answers questions."

"I see," said Mack, nodding. But little of it made much difference to him. His children were down there, other children were down there. Bound, perhaps gagged, perhaps worse. "We have to do something." He rose to one knee.

Turtle Eye laid a hand on Mack's arm. "I know. Wait . . . little longer."

Mack felt a twinge of guilt. The tracker was no doubt in turmoil, too, as his son was among the missing. His hesitation was obvious. He had questions. Why had this small band encamped here, with no sign of the larger band of raiders? The group with the horses and loot must surely be camped somewhere close by. Why were these brutes so loud? Perhaps it was a simple explanation—they were confident they had not been followed and were pleased with themselves.

Mack thought about it as they once more crawled upward in a group to spy on the camp from the berm. Turtle Eye jerked as if pinched. He whispered something to the chief, who nodded.

"Turtle Eye says the time has come. At least one of the men appear to be—" He looked at Mack and shook his head. "The older girl, she must be out of our sight. And they are not good men."

"What are you saying?" Mack asked too loud. But the wind was with them and nobody down below seemed to have noticed.

"The time is now, Mack Harrigan. She is in danger."

Already the tracker was gesturing to the others, telling them once again to space themselves out. The plan as Mack could tell through his haze of growing rage, was for Turtle Eye and Bright Owl to creep closest first, Turtle Eye from the northwest and Bright Owl from the southwest. At roughly the same time they would send arrows into as many of the men as they were able. The effect would be immediate.

At first, as much as possible should be done without gunfire, lest they draw the attention of the much larger force of raiders who might not be too far ahead in the dark and wind. If they heard gunfire, they would surely descend from all sides, trapping the rescuers.

Knives and axes were the first weapons of choice, and then guns. The men being attacked would surely use their own weapons, guns among them. The chief had also told Mack that it was possible the kidnappers would attempt to kill the children and flee. It was a difficult thing for Mack to hear, but he respected the chief for telling him plainly.

They could not let that happen.

They also could not let happen what the chief had hinted at regarding Meghan.

Within a couple of minutes, and with the wind still in their favor, the men were in position. They could not see each other, spread out as they were, but they would see the hits of the arrows as they sliced in from either end of their small group.

An arrow whipped in, silent and deadly, from the northwest. With the wind taken into account, Turtle Eye's aim was true. The arrow had barely slid itself into the neck of one of the men seated around the fire when Bright Owl unleashed his first arrow. It, too, found a target, though his aim was off and low. The arrow pierced deep on the thigh of one of the seated men.

Both wounded men jerked upright, but the first, with the arrow sticking through his throat, pitched forward, trying to break his fall but failing. He landed with an arm and a shoulder in the fire.

That was unfortunate. Given the flailing, lurching of the hip-shot man made the camp erupt in a frenzy of shouts from the stomping, running enemy warriors.

Even as the two bowman nocked and released a second round, Mack, the chief, and Kane were on the move, running hell-bent toward the camp.

Mack's target was the younger one who the chief had said was likely tending the captives. Mack wanted that one first. Especially since he had left the ring of men to tend to the children.

The fact that the children might not be there occurred to Mack, but he refused to allow that thought to plant itself in his mind. If it were the case, he would deal with it as he must. For now, he chose to believe he was about to rescue the children.

Though they had wished otherwise, the thing they knew

would happen had begun. Gunshots cracked out from the dark and from the trees ringing the now-scattered fire. Still, as the attackers wormed their way through the near-dark, creeping into the camp with as much speed as each could muster, the bowmen managed to wound another man and, it appeared, to kill yet another.

As they advanced, they spied more figures emerging, then disappearing, at the edge of the weak light of the smoking, damaged fire. Were there others they had not seen?

Mack took it all in, as did the others, but he did not care if he had to hack his way through two dozen men to get to the children. He would do it or die trying. He cut southeast, angling upward to the north, which took him into the trees near the spot where Turtle Eye had assumed the children were being held. Mack saw movement and motion to his right and left toward the fire.

No one knew he was there yet, so he prayed his stealth would continue while he made it to the place he hoped the captives would be.

It did, but they were not there. He dropped to his knees and scrabbled on the ground at the base of trees, hoping for a clue, patting the earth for heel marks, anything that might tell him what he wished to know.

He found nothing.

From the dark to his right, he heard rapid footsteps. He spun around, facing the incomer, and was knocked over backward. The running man hadn't even seen him. He continued on another ten feet, then jerked to a stop and dropped low, crouching and advancing back toward Mack, who had already palmed his blade.

Given that chaos had filled the night, he quickly stuffed

the knife back in its sheath on his belt and tugged free his pistol.

He'd chosen to leave the rifle on the horse, as he'd wanted to travel quickly. He'd had a vague idea of being the one in their group most able to rush in and cut the children free, somehow lead them to safety while the others provided covering fire.

Now he saw this rescue mission would not likely work that way, and regretted leaving the rifle on the horse.

Realizing the slow advance of the man who'd all-but tripped over him could not see him, Mack kept low and wished he had skittered to one side. He could see the rogue, though barely but if he moved he would be seen. He heard a muffled sound off to his right as if someone were screaming with a hand over his or her mouth.

Mack could wait no longer for the fool in front of him to attack. He shot at the shape, a little alarmed at the harsh sound the gun made so close to his ears, especially after the silence they had traveled in.

The shot did what he hoped. He heard a gasp and a long, drawn-out groan as the man dropped from the scant outlined view Mack had of him.

Wasting no time to see if the man was in pursuit, Mack bolted to his right as other shapes moved in the purpling night. The wind came at him from the right, bringing a chill he appreciated. He welcomed anything to keep him unsettled and alert. It had been a long day and showed no signs of slowing in that regard. He needed to be wide-eyed.

Tall shapes were visible ahead, perhaps ten yards, when something whistled in from his left and he felt a brutal, sharp pain in his arm below the elbow. Whatever it was knocked him to his right and he staggered, slamming against the rigid, unmoving bulk of a sizable tree.

His cheek slammed against it for a brief moment and the word pine bloomed in his mind. *Yes, fine, rough, craggy bark,* but he did not care. He reached for his left arm and felt nothing there that should not be . . . except a gash and stickiness. It was his own blood. He'd been grazed by something—a bullet? A knife? And by luck. He couldn't count on it happening again.

He prayed it was nothing that would slow him down. He had to find the children.

Where was Kane? A flash of frustration and anger at all of them, his friends, the attackers, all of them, worked itself out in a growl. Mack flexed his left hand, felt the fingers move without pain and resumed his run.

It had truly been a lucky shot. Someone had seen him and had thrown something at him. He didn't think it was a bullet wound, as he didn't recall hearing a gun at that moment. It felt more like a gash a thrown blade or maybe an arrow might leave behind.

And ahead were the large, hunched shapes he'd seen. Horses with riders.

Mack cut to his right, debating whether to use a knife or pistol, but it was too soon to know. Let the situation dictate the weapon.

They were maneuvering through the trees, one horse in the lead and two others following. The first appeared to have one, perhaps two riders. The others he could not see so well.

Upwind of them, his smells and sounds would carry to whoever was on the horses. If they knew what they were doing, and he had no reason to think otherwise, they would soon look his way and see him loping alongside, just yards away.

CHAPTER 12

Fitch Harrigan had never felt so afraid in all his life, and by his reckoning that was a mighty long time. He kept trying to keep in mind everything the Shoshone had taught him all winter long when the rest of the Harrigan clan, as his father called them all, were so busy with the things they thought were important.

Notions and more flitted in and out of Fitch's mind as they rode for what felt like days and weeks.

Mostly it was those babies. At first, he had been annoyed. They were always crying and howling and making bad smells and needing so much attention. Mama kept telling him he'd been the same way, but now that there were two of them at once, Henry and Hattie, there was twice the work for her and no time for him. Most of that time, that suited Fitch right down to the ground, as Bearpaw Jones would say.

Still, Mama used to sing to him at night in a quiet, soft voice and the next thing he knew he'd be waking up the following morning. It always seemed like a magical trick. He'd asked her about it once, long before they loaded up all their stuff on the wagon and headed west. She had nodded and said that's what it was. She called it "mother's magic." He liked that idea but reckoned the twins were getting all that magic. Actually double the amount.

That was all right, especially when he began learning things from the Shoshone. At first he'd snuck around and pretended to ambush them . . . but without the ambush part. He just watched them, learned and listened. Then some of the warriors and even some of the other kids noticed him and started to show him things like how to sneak up properly on someone. Or how to pretend you were a bird, which had worked pretty well, except for the flying part. And he learned some words in Shoshone, too. More than any other Harrigan, he reckoned.

That felt pretty good.

Of course, Grinner was always with him. But that day was not like anything that had ever happened to any Harrigan, ever. Grinner knew it, too, and he'd done what all animals should do when they got scared. He ran.

Fitch wished he had paid attention and had gone after him. They could have run and hid together. Maybe then he wouldn't have gotten Meg in trouble. Now he was stolen by the smelly men with bad tempers, and Meghan was, too. He knew it was his fault for talking too loud in their little hidey hole.

When they jumped in the river, that was Meg's fault, and they almost drowned. But they didn't. He kept looking for her in the water and finally saw her. He also kept looking at the riverbank, hoping to see Grinner running along there like he always did when Fitch was playing in the water.

Grinner liked water, but only after Fitch got in first and started splashing. To get Grinner in there was a tough job. He had chucked the dog in the water and then jumped in with him plenty of times.

As he rode, Fitch's mind wandered, and he kept falling asleep. The man he rode in front of seemed to know when it was happening and pushed him back upright again. That woke him and he looked around as if that scary man was coming after him all over again. To get the man's ugly face out of his mind, he continued thinking.

He had Meg to worry about, too. She seemed to be look-ing at him for help. Fitch reckoned that was because she was a girl. He figured the only help he could give her was to look strong, like a Shoshone warrior, which is really what he was. He wanted to be one, so he was one. That was all there was to it.

And since he was a Shoshone warrior, he had to figure out a way to get them away from the raiders. That would be tricky being they were in the saddle.

Fitch jerked. The rawhide tied around his wrists and face hurt something awful. As it dried, it got tighter and tighter. He'd stopped looking at his hands. They were puffy, bigger than his hands had ever been. They looked bad. He figured his face looked like that, too, because Meg's did and it worried him.

Every time he looked to find her he saw her looking back at him. It seemed like she was trying to smile, or maybe say something to him. He wanted to tell her to save her strength for a fight. As soon as they could, they had to fight with all their strength. It's what Harrigans did. *And Shoshones.*

About that time, the larger group of raiders that had been riding way far in front of them had slowed. Some of the men on horses dropped back and talked in their lan-guage. It was something like Shoshone, that much Fitch could tell. He tried to listen to them, but it was no good. They talked too fast and too low.

Nobody talked much to the younger man Fitch was riding with. Pretty soon he saw another thing that surprised him, and that was saying something on a day like that. Three more riders dropped back, and they weren't alone on their horses. They also carried children with them. And they were trussed up just like him and Meghan.

As they rode by, taking places in line at the back Fitch saw they also had puffy faces from tight ties, but he knew who they were! The boy was the son of Turtle Eye. If there was one Shoshone who Fitch wished was his pa—if he didn't have Mack Harrigan as his pa, that is—it would be Turtle Eye.

The man never smiled, so he was a little scary, but Fitch had learned that was how a true warrior behaved. At least he thought so. Turtle Eye wasn't like Mack who smiled all the time, joshing and singing little silly songs and sneaking up behind Ell and tickling her when she was busy cooking.

She always shrieked and rounded on Pa with a big wooden spoon dripping with soup or something, and she always threatened to give him a good hiding.

And Pa always said the same thing. He'd dance away a few feet and say, "Promises promises."

Thinking like that made Fitch feel bad, but he forgot it soon enough. Two other horses walked by close enough that the knee of the warrior on the first horse knocked against Fitch's.

The man looked at Fitch and Fitch looked right back at him, trying to give him what Bearpaw Jones called "the hard stare." The old mountain man had said that if done right, it was a crippling sort of look. Fitch was still working on that.

Even though he was afraid to make the warrior angry enough to hit him or push him off the horse, the man glared right back at him, then squinted his eyes and nodded once.

From his many months with the Shoshone, Fitch knew getting a nod like that was as good as a handshake. At least that's what he chose to believe. He reckoned he had done something important in staring down that warrior. Even if the man was a child-stealing thief.

The child on the horse was another one he recognized. It was a Shoshone girl, and she was as surprised and as fearful looking as the boy had been when he passed by. Fitch didn't have time to think on it. The next horse came along, and what do you know? Another Shoshone girl was on that one, too. But the warrior she rode with looked angry or bored or both. He kept jerking his horse's reins when he didn't need to and looking all around him. It seemed he looked just about everywhere except at Fitch, which was too bad. He was going to practice his hard stare again.

Anything to keep his mind off the pain he was in. His face hurt like mad and his hands throbbed so much he wasn't sure if he could last another minute more.

But he had to. As soon as the new horses with children had fallen into line with them, the big group far ahead kept on going. His group advanced, too, but at its usual pace, which was not quite a trot. He reckoned that was a good thing. No way he would be able to stand any more thrashing and bumping. His face and hands hurt so.

Fitch looked back at Meghan and for the first time in a long time she wasn't looking toward him. It looked to him as if she wanted to cry.

The steady breeze that had been puffing at them since they took to the trail had become a more forceful beast, gusting and sometimes clawing at them. It came from Fitch's right side—he thought it might be the east—which was something Kane kept trying to teach him. He said Fitch had to know the four directions, whatever that meant, in case he ever got lost.

It hadn't seemed to matter to Kane that since Fitch was a Shoshone now, there was no way he could get lost. Kane had shaken his head and walked off. Fitch had long ago decided big brothers were silly like that.

CHAPTER 13

Mack knew he had to get a closer look at those shapes, indistinct in the near dark, lit by the purple-blue glow of the night sky above and beyond them all. He was thankful it had been a cloudless day, which in turn gave way to the brightness of the coming night. He'd take any leg up at that moment.

His right leg slammed hard into the projecting jag of stone sticking out of a boulder. It jerked a gasp and groan from him. Almost as soon as it escaped his lips he jammed the knuckles of his left hand into his mouth to stifle the sound he made, but it was too late.

He heard the horses to his left come to a shambling stop, heard whispers and saw the first two, no, three riders hold up their fists, signing to those behind them to stop.

They had been traveling at a pretty good pace considering the darkness, and Mack had been matching them stride for stride, trying to figure out how to do what he knew needed doing. He had to stop them and fight the warriors riding the horses and rescue the kids, if those were kids with them.

All the riders by then had stopped and held, but their arms were not still. They were bringing their weapons to bear in his general direction. And he bet most of them were carrying guns of some sort. Likely long guns.

Mack held, keeping to the crouched position he'd dropped to once he rammed his knee. It wasn't an injury that would prevent him from doing what he needed to, but it sure wouldn't help him any.

And then, as the man on the lead horse slid from atop his mount, Mack saw his faint silhouette disappear. The rider on the horse to the left and back a bit steadied the man's horse.

Like it or not, Mack Harrigan, the fight is coming to you once more. Would this day ever get better? Maybe, Mack thought. *But not just yet.*

The man appeared not ten feet before him. A slight scuffing of gravel, then a twig snap, and there he was. Each man saw the other, but Mack was the first to move.

It was either take first action or lose his balance. He'd landed in an awkward pose when he'd whacked his knee and had to move with it. Which he did. He tucked and rolled his body to his right, angling behind the big rock he'd moments before come to blows with.

The man advancing on him cut to his own left, bent low, and dashed forward, covering the space between himself and the rock in near silence. Mack saw the man carried some sort of weapon, not a long gun, but something short handled, more likely a knife or belt ax.

Mack used the few seconds to set his low stance, no avoiding the collision now, and ready his pistol. Then the man was on him, covering the last few feet in a dive. As the man dropped on him, Mack pulled the trigger—and nothing happened but a quick, dull click. His surprise lasted a second too long, and the man's thigh knocked the gun from his grasp.

Mack collapsed beneath the man, who was already flailing

hard, raising high what Mack saw was a big, wide-bladed knife, but not much more than the outline of the upraised arm, the angled knife gripped to slash, and drive downward hard and deep.

He jerked his head to the left, jamming his bum knee upward hard at the same time. It was enough to land a lucky blow to the enemy's groin. The brute gasped and folded over Mack like a snapped branch succumbing to a knee. His big knife slipped from his grasp and turned over in its drop, the blunt handle clunking harmlessly against Mack's gut before dropping to the earth.

His wheeze was a sound that only men can make when they've been the victim of such a blow. Even as Mack jerked to his left to get out from beneath the temporarily wounded man, he felt a twinge of sympathy for the fool. That was all he'd give the man who was no doubt still bent on killing him.

His torso inched to the left as the man's wheezing turned to gasping and his limbs began to scrabble once more. As his arms became free, Mack felt the wide blade of the man's knife beneath his fingers on the ground. Still obviously in pain by the gasping, sucking sounds he made, the man landed a punch to Mack's right temple, buzzing his head like a rattler was set loose in there.

The brute clamped his other hand about Mack's exposed throat and squeezed hard and fast, collapsing Mack's windpipe.

Mack's right hand thrashed and grabbed, but the man felt it and moved his grunting, heaving body over, pinning it so Mack could not move his arm. He clawed at the graveled earth with his left hand fingers and felt the keen edge of the knife blade cut his fingertips. The pain gave him renewed alertness and strength.

He snatched at the thing, heedless of the damage it

might be doing to his fingers, and felt the thick handle, vaguely aware it was made of antler, for it bore the nubs that grow at the base of a deer's rack as it emerges from the beast's head.

His fingers closed tight over it as his breath left him. Even though it was night, the sky, at least within his own mind, burst apart with brilliant knife pricks of light. He was fading out, fading away, a few more moments and this man would win. Mack would never rescue Meghan and Fitch and the other children, all small and frightened. Kane might well find him, if the boy survived the night himself. He would never see Ell and the babies . . .

Those thoughts wracked through his diminishing mind and, with a last, growling, surging snag of strength, Mack Harrigan whipped the warrior's own blade upward and drove it straight into the side of the sinewy man's rib cage.

Mack felt the thick steel tool gouge its own path, not the easy route sliding between ribs and into the man's precious innards, but vertically. It rammed into the man's ribs, powered by the might of a man so desperate he would do anything, anything at all on earth and beyond, to live another day, to live to see his family whole and well and safe and through this mess.

The blade sunk deep, severing three rib bones on its journey into the man's struggling body. The effect of its arrival where it never should have ventured was finger-snap quick. The warrior gasped once more, but it was the last time.

He stiffened, his back arching, and his head whipping farther back, so he stared straight upward at the sky. The hand wrapped tight about Mack's neck weakened.

Mack's hand was still on the knife's handle and in a gasping whisper he said, "Sorry," then cranked hard on the handle, twisting it inside the man's already ruined chest.

He heard another gasp and then, as he tried to edge farther to his left, the warrior spurted a gout of blood from his mouth, spraying it outward. It drizzled down on Mack's cheek even as he shoved the weakening brute from atop him.

He made it out from beneath the man with the big knife in his hand and slid it out of the man's chest with a sickening wet sound. Mack clunked into the cursed boulder.

That little moment of slow down enabled a second warrior to continue his creeping path toward Mack. The brute appeared above the big rock as if out of nowhere. For a moment Mack thought it was the man he'd just stabbed. The impossibility of that vanished quickly as the man descended toward him.

Pinned as his left side was against the boulder, Mack jammed hard with his heels against the earth in an effort to churn himself head first away from the new attacker. It did no good for the man was poised. Mack hoped the man did not have a gun as he swapped the knife to his right hand from his half-pinned left and continued digging with his heels.

The man skirted the boulder and kept coming, swinging a cudgel in one hand. If there was something else in the other, Mack could not see it.

Mack had shoved himself far enough from the boulder that he could pivot his hips. Making himself a narrower target, he swung the big, heavy knife, still slick with gore from his previous victim, at the attacker's straddling legs. It struck the man's left leg about six inches above the ankle.

The cudgel whistled down.

Darker than ever at ground level, Mack fought more out of instinct, relying on sound and smell rather than sight.

The club slammed into the earth so close to the left side of Mack's face he felt it singe his whiskers.

Once more, as if copying the maneuvers of his fellow moments before, the warrior dropped down on Mack, one hand grasping for his throat while the other lifted the brute club for another strike. Mack's right hand was still free and still holding the big knife, he jerked it forward and up in another slashing move, but it struck the man's leather tunic and did not penetrate. The man's hand mashed against Mack's face, smearing his mouth and nose as if he were trying to wipe tears from Mack's face.

Once more his airway was becoming constricted. He swung the knife again and again, hoping to land a blow that would penetrate the man's buckskins.

The savage tried to land a solid blow with the club and maintain a grip on Mack at the same time. Realizing he was still awkwardly close to the rock that prevented the attacker from swinging his arm with full freedom, he heard what sounded like a girl's voice, half-muffled, but still as pretty as daylight.

"Papa! Papa! We're here! We're here, Papa! Papa, we—"

The voice was clipped off short by something Mack did not like to think about. He had no time to dwell on it. The sound of Meghan's voice and the fact that she'd said "we" was a powerful remedy for pulling Mack out of the slowly sagging, losing end of his second fight in as many minutes.

He growled and bucked and struck a solid blow, then another, feeling the club-wielding savage wince. He cursed the man, spitting out words that if he had ever heard any of his children using them, no matter their age, he would dose their mouths with lye soap.

The man landed a jarring blow to Mack's left shoulder and he felt something crack deep inside his upper arm. His left arm jolted, and hot lances of pain raced down and up his arm once more. He sucked air in through tight-set teeth and rammed harder than ever with the knife, kicking upward and driving his right knee toward what he hoped might be another successful blow. But in that he failed.

The knife, however, did not.

The attacker's strength flagged and his blows, which still came, were less frequent, less powerful, less accurate, and he wobbled.

A good thing, as Mack didn't think his shoulder or his arm could sustain another blow. The second attacker leaned to Mack's right side, and Mack still held on to the knife handle, but the blade was halfway in, lodged in the man's side. As the man slumped, gasping and lolling more with each moment, the knife became more lodged, pinched somehow between the man's gut and his ribs.

Mack let go of the handle and the man finished his drop.

Before Mack could get himself fully out from beneath the failing man, another warrior appeared. Holding a rifle, he looked down at them.

Mack could see the man's head and shoulders outlined against the lighter purple of the night sky. He was aware of other sounds, voices rushing closer, then far off, from back by the horses. He wanted to shout to Meghan but wasn't certain this new fiend knew his location. Mack kept his mouth shut, inched his right hand close to his own belt, and grasped the weapon that rode there—his belt ax.

What he heard were the sounds of battle, hand-to-hand fighting, close in and hard pitched on both sides.

He hoped the children, including Kane, were out of harm's way. It was something he wished he could extend to his eldest son, but he was a man now, and had taken lives this day. And if he was still among the living, he would likely take more.

Those thoughts kept Mack's sight focused on the dark

to the side of him. In that way he was assured of seeing as much as possible. *Would that he had the eyesight of a cat. But he was stuck with who he was.* More such annoying, silly thoughts flicked in and out of his mind as he waited, unable to do anything more, lest he give himself away.

He heard a strange sound, far off, coming from the south, from the direction they'd traveled that day. Coming in fast. It was the baying of a dog. A hound. And it was long, loud, and growing louder.

Best of all, it was familiar.

It was Grinner, the Harrigan family hound. His sole boon companion in the world was Fitch. No way would Grinner let anything more happen to the boy without trying to give his very life to prevent it. Never had Mack seen a bond between a person and an animal so strong. Save, perhaps, for the odd but steel-clad bond between their chum, the crotchety mountain man, Bearpaw Jones, and his trusty mule, Ol' Gravyfoot. But he reckoned they were a special case. Or at least that's how Bearpaw would have it believed.

Mack did not ruminate on the dog's barking and what it meant for long, for he had to figure out how to get to his children before one of those brutes rode off with them again.

CHAPTER 14

As soon as Bright Owl departed from the group, Kane had received low, heartfelt words from his father.

"Son, act with boldness, yes, but boldness bowing to caution. Take no needless risks, and come back to your mother and me. You are loved beyond measure." Those last words came out pinched. Then Mack had squeezed his shoulder and quietly slipped into the dark. Kane saw the chief and Turtle Eye do the same.

Part of him wanted to shout to his father there had been some oversight. Kane was still a boy, not a man. He was too young to die in a senseless fight with people he hadn't even known existed. And then, just as quickly, he remembered what those brutes had done to the peaceful Shoshone camp and all the lives he'd come to know, lives clubbed and bludgeoned, scalped and peeled apart.

He thought of his mother and father, Meghan and Fitch, and the newborn twins. He thought of all the fights he'd been in just that day—all the near misses he'd endured, and how none of those men he'd fought and killed had seemed to regard him as anything but another man to fight . . . to death.

He pulled in a deep breath of nippy springtime air. It reminded him of ample snow not that far away in the foothills and high peaks surrounding the pretty country. Winter had been long, spring was slow in coming, but somehow it invigorated him like no other place he'd ever been. *He loved it.* With that hopeful thought in mind, he bent low, shoving through the rabbit brush, low-walking in the general direction he had been assigned when they'd been forming their vague plans.

Arriving at the spot he figured was close enough, he was about to await the archers to unleash their missiles when that very thing happened.

The men encamped below stiffened in the finger-snap moment of stunned silence that precedes howling panic, and the night erupted in yowling, angry shouts and gun shots. The handful of men scurried in all directions before one of them kicked soil over the small fire, deadening the dim, light-giving coals. Then his foot scattered them, making the night a whole lot darker than it had been.

Kane bolted for the scene, hoping he could find the children, any children, without fighting one of the thieves. They were a brutal, horrifying bunch.

He'd not kidded himself the Shoshone were incapable of such behavior. He'd asked bright Owl in a lull earlier if his people had ever done such a thing. His friend had looked at him with a glance that seemed filled with so much meaning, and then Bright Owl looked down. For the briefest of moments Kane was reminded of Fitch's face when the little rogue was caught in the midst of an act of trickery or mischief of some sort peculiar to Fitch. Then Bright Owl looked away and that had been that.

Sure, we are all capable of shameful behavior, but stealing other people's property? And worst of all, their children? With those thoughts, Kane continued down to the edge where he'd seen the men hunkered and chatting low, occasionally one of them emitting a quick, low bray of laughter. *Had they thought they wouldn't be followed?*

Any thoughts of sneaking in and out again with the children in tow were quashed when a quick rustling sound to his left caused him to turn that way out of instinct. A solid fist slammed into the right side of his head, between the ear and the eye. The dark night became the opposite in that moment after the fist met his face. Kane's head snapped to the left, and his world exploded in light as if he'd emerged from a hole in the ground at noon on a cloudless day in August. Just as quickly, it winked out and he dropped to the earth like a sack of corn meal and knew little more.

Fortunately Bright Owl had bolted down the long, low slope at about the same time as Kane. The now-vanished vision of the man he'd marked as his first victim was ghosted into the young Shoshone warrior's mind as he made for that spot and met no one on the quick path down. He had guessed the man's direction, moving to the right, once the fire's light was deadened.

The chief's son did not wait to verify if he was knifing a compatriot by mistake, for he was confident in his guess. He leapt aboard the man's back, and before his prey could react with more than a shocked raising of arms, Bright Owl drove his big hip dagger into the soft hollow between the shoulder and the neck of the man. Once, twice, thrice his brute blade found purchase deep inside the enemy's body. He fancied the tip tickled the man's lungs. Good.

Bright Owl wore the look he'd always pulled on when he found himself in the midst of a difficult or dicey task—his top lip pulled back flat against his teeth, and his mouth clamped shut, tight, his bottom lips pulled downward in a leer, as if he were a little disappointed in himself.

Despite the gushing knife wounds, the man remained upright, spinning in a ragged, jerky fashion with the whipcord muscled, lean body of Bright Owl perched on his back.

The Shoshone youth slashed at the man's flailing arms, ignoring the savage shrieks and cries of pure pain leaking out of the man's gabbling mouth. Soon this behavior dwindled and Bright Owl rode the man down to the ground. Certain the warrior posed no further risk, ever, he left him there, his forehead on the earth, his slumped, twitching body leaking out its life juices at a place he was certain the man had never intended to die.

Looking to his left in time to see a dark shape barreling toward him, Bright Owl once more dropped low, set his stance, and waited for the figure to come to him. He did not have long to wait. The shape was one of the thieving warriors, as Bright Owl knew it would be. He was not bowled over, but received a hard hit to the left side of his head.

Dizzied a moment, he held up his right arm, blade whipping and gashing the man's gut enough that he dropped back and eyed Bright Owl. The two men circled each other, chests heaving with exertion. The stranger barked something at Bright Owl, who did not respond. The man spat at him. Again, Bright Owl did not react.

Gunshots and shouts sounded in the darkness behind the man. Bright Owl barely heard them, so intent was he on laying low this thief.

The glow of the emerging half moon lit the barest edges of the scene enough to show each man the other, enough to grapple and fight fully, no longer blinded by darkness.

A gunshot to Bright Owl's left, close by, jerked him from his single-minded concentration. The man he sought to make his victim also flinched, and then stiffened and dropped to his knees. His wide eyes stared at Bright Owl in shock and wonder.

The young Shoshone realized someone had shot the man

he'd been fighting. He glanced to his left, saw a familiar face on the figure loping toward him, and realized he was safe. It had not been a misfired shot intended for him.

He dashed forward and slammed the butt of his knife's horn handle into the side of the shot man's head. In a quick blink of time, the warrior gasped and his eyes looked up, showed white, and he groaned and dropped, unconscious or dead. Bright Owl did not care.

He spun and caught Kane as he staggered into him. "What has happened to you, Kane?" Bright Owl guided his white friend to the earth and sat him down.

"Punched me. Knocked me cold for a few seconds." He rubbed the side of his head. "Came to and saw two men fighting, then the moon shined a little, just enough to let me see that one of them was you . . . and the other wasn't."

"And you shot him."

"Tried to," he gestured with a wag of his hand. "I guess I slowed him enough for you to get your licks in."

"No," said Bright Owl, glancing about them, still hearing the random, low sounds of fighting in the dark, none too close. "It was your shot that laid him low."

"I think we're even then. Because you were fighting with someone else, I'll wager that distracted him from finishing me off when I was out."

Bright Owl shrugged. "It makes no difference. I must find the children. I'll leave you here."

"Not on your life. I'm going, too."

"But you cannot walk straight."

"Don't need to," said Kane, shoving back upright to his feet. "I'm going to run." He did just that, keeping low and leading the way as the two youths took advantage of the moon's meager light to show them where they might travel in the woods.

"The horses were there," said Bright Owl. "To your right. Deeper in. But they will have gone."

Kane didn't respond but made for the spot. He fought a niggling wave of dizziness that made him want to throw up the meager provisions he'd eaten that day—a couple of strips of jerky and a handful of hard tack rounds. His mother had made him take them with him only the day before when he'd been heading out into the deeper forest to the northwest of the Shoshone camp. He'd shared them with Bright Owl on the ride.

About to become part of the forest, Kane was afraid of making such noise as throwing up brought with it. He kept it all down, but had to stop and lean against a craggy pine. His vision still speckled in and out with needle points of stars he knew were only in his head. He gulped in two, three deep breaths and the sudden wave of dizziness began to recede.

"You stay here, Kane. I will go."

"No. They're my family."

"And mine," said Bright Owl.

For a moment, Kane was confused and thought Bright Owl and Meghan had come to some sort of secret understanding. It came to him then that Turtle Eye's son and the other two children were all Bright Owl's cousins. "Yes, of course. Okay then, let's go save our families."

Reading to move on, they heard the far-off but closing in baying of a hound dog. The sound was so jarring and odd for a brief moment it sounded to Kane as if all of the participants in the small melee were stilled, listening. No doubt many of the Indians had never heard a hound dog's peculiar baying and were wondering what it might be, but after a few strange moments, Kane knew.

In all the hubbub of the day, he'd forgotten Grinner, Fitch's constant companion. The dog was a natural-born tracker with a nose for following a scent trail that could not be denied. Kane also knew the flop-eared fellow would tear apart anything or anyone who might harm Fitch.

"Come, Kane. The children are this way."

"You've see them?"

"The horses carrying them, yes. Something has stopped them not far from here. Perhaps my father and yours. Turtle Eye may have gotten there first."

They crouched and loped ahead, cutting a trail through clawing, snagging brush and rocks. Kane held one hand before him, as he had seen Bright Owl do, in an effort to avoid slamming into undetected trees.

They were nearly to the spot, for Bright Owl had slowed and motioned to Kane with a nod, when low night clouds parted to reveal the moon at half steam, as Kane's dead grandfather back in Ohio used to say. It was enough light to show Kane the horses ahead. Several of them appeared to be mounted by men on the small side.

Kane thought the riders, small as they seemed, might be held up or waiting for somebody to do something. It appeared their fellow warriors were fighting.

Bright Owl advanced and motioned Kane to follow. A man standing rear guard by the horses closest to them watched something to his right. He looked agitated and moved from his spot, pacing toward the front of the short line of horses, then the horses began moving forward, obviously being led by the agitated fellow.

Neither youth spoke, but they continued to creep closer. Once they had reached less than ten feet behind the rear horse, they saw the beasts for what they were—horses topped with bound and gagged children.

Bright Owl crept to the left of the horses with Kane making for the right. He noticed a fight taking place off trail and to his right. Then he heard a quick, rushing, stomping of light footsteps up ahead, beyond Bright Owl. They stopped suddenly, a man's shocked voice yipped loud, and commotion followed at ground level. At the same time the short string of horses began fidgeting and jerking.

Using all that as an opportunity, Kane reached the rear horse and looked up, his knife drawn in case it wasn't who he'd hoped was up there. Enough moonlight showed him it was a child. Although not Meghan or Fitch, it had to be Turtle Eye's son. Kane reached up and lifted the lad down. He wasn't very big at all.

Working fast, trying to keep his senses alert to anyone who might creep up on him from any direction, Kane patted up and down the boy's short body, felt the bound wrists and the swollen hands beyond, rawhide thongs all-but buried in there. He found a clear slight space between the thongs and slipped his knife tip in. Feeling all around it with his fingers to ensure he did not slice the child needlessly, he gently sawed at the straps.

Up ahead, it was plain someone or something had attacked the thief who'd been agitated and had finally begun leading the horses forward once more. From the growling, savage sounds rising up from the lead horse, it sounded as if it was a dog. Kane would bet money he knew which one, hoping the dog didn't get himself killed.

Kane worked like a demon until finally the child was free. He felt the kid's face, finding more wraps buried beneath puffed flesh. "Easy, now, easy. We are here. Your father is here, too. Easy, we will get you out of this." He hoped Bright Owl was up to more of the same as he advanced on the second horse.

"You stay with me, all right?" He remembered the little boy didn't speak English and Kane's Shoshone was pitiful, though he had been telling the boy as much as he could in his own tongue. He was confident he got out the correct words for *father* and *home* and *friend*.

The yelp of a struck or wounded dog sounded somewhere ahead, beyond the small string of ponies. He hoped it didn't mean the worst for Grinner.

From the way the boy held up a throbbing hand trying to hold on to Kane's trousers, he was not leaving Kane's side any time soon. Fine with Kane, as he didn't want the boy to wander off and be lost in the fighting mess as he moved to the next horse. Rewarded with the feel of a child's leg, he looked up and saw outlined in the dim moonlight one face, then another. Indeed a second child was there. Okay, they were the two little Shoshone girls.

He repeated the act of lifting them down, slicing them free of their horrendous green hide wrappings, all the while doing his best to explain to them in a whisper, who he was and that they were safe, even though he knew he could not promise it.

They clustered and clung to him as he moved ahead to the next horse. But when he reached up, no one was there. He gripped the beast's back and felt nothing but a tattered blanket. Fear crawled up his gullet as he hustled forward to the last horse in line, the lead horse, barely aware the sounds of the savage dog attack had ceased. He did hear muffled whispers, then a shushing sound. Something compelled him to make for those sounds as the children clustered by his left leg, hugging him and each other in sloppy, pained grips.

Their swollen hands and faces were aching terribly, yet they did not offer a peep of complaint.

Reaching the head of the lead horse, Kane saw why the string of horses did not stray or run off—the reins were hastily looped about something on the ground. He traced them down and at their end, felt a leg wearing deer hide leggings. "Bright Owl?" he said in a low voice, his heart thudding harder. He bent low and felt the body, patting with his free left hand while his right held his knife.

He felt halfway up the chest before he realized it was not his friend. Who, then? Likely it was the thief who had seemed agitated, and he guessed had also been the one to suffer Grinner's rage. *Speaking of,* he thought as he continued to lean close, looking at the man's face in the moonlight, *where was that dog?*

And then he heard a familiar voice a few feet away, no more than ten, ahead and to the left.

"Hang on there, boy, hang on."

It was Fitch! Kane knew that small, tight voice anywhere. Just then the man he had been inspecting coughed and groaned. Kane looked down at him, the moonlight once more gracing them with a fleeting stab at vision.

The face was not what he'd expected to see. It was one of the attackers, yes, but he was young, no older than he or Bright Owl. He also appeared to be in a bad way. His throat had been savaged, as had his right cheek, and his right arm and hand, with which he defended himself. In short, the youth was a bloody, bleeding mess. His breath came in a wheeze, but he looked at Kane and tried to speak. A blood bubble formed between his lips. Then it popped. He coughed again and this time a whisper came out.

Although he could not help feeling awful it had happened, Kane was angry it had happened at all. A rustling to his left moved closer and he drew back, shuffling the three children behind him and waving the knife with menace.

Whoever it was moved closer. And then he saw it was Grinner.

The dog was clearly wounded, but he was limping, staggering forward. He seemed to recognize Kane, for he let out a soft crying sound then laid down on the other side of the man he'd so recently savaged.

Before Kane could move to the dog, another creature scurried in. It was short, moved quickly, and shouted, "Grinner!" Fitch grabbed the big dog about the neck and hugged him with ferocity. The dog's bony tail thumped the loose earth and he licked at the boy's face.

"Fitch!" Kane said in a low voice. "Fitch, it's me, Kane!"

The little boy looked up. "Kane? We thought we'd never see you again."

Typical of Fitch, thought Kane. Though he detected warmth and relief in the boy's voice, he did not leave his wounded dog's side. "Is Meg okay?"

"Yeah, she's with Bright Owl over there."

The two moved over to Kane and Fitch, and Meg knelt beside the boy.

"Meg! It's me, Kane! You're okay?"

She gave out a little cry, stepped over the wounded man's legs, and hugged Kane as if she hadn't seen him in years. He hugged her back with his free arm.

"We're not out of danger yet," he said, pulling her arms from him. "Can you look after these three?" He guided her hand to the three little ones behind him.

"I will help," said Bright Owl, who had been crouched beyond the dog and Fitch. "Come, we must hurry. Our fathers and Turtle Eye need our help."

Before they could gather and retreat back the way they'd come, Fitch knelt by the warrior at Kane's feet. "You . . . you hurt my dog!"

The man slowly turned his head and looked at Fitch. Then he smiled, and in a hoarse voice, louder than a whisper, he said, "You . . . wildcat." He patted the boy's arm then his hand slid from Fitch's arm to the earth. The man's head slipped to the side, and his raspy, gurgling breath pinched out, and he lay still.

Fitch stared at him a moment longer then touched the man's still hand. "He was the one I rode with."

"He was not so cruel as the others," said Meghan, then ushered the three small children before her, and followed Bright Owl.

"Come on, Fitch," said Kane. "We have to go."

"What about Grinner?"

"What about him?" said Kane, nodding to indicate the dog.

Fitch looked behind him and saw the big hound standing a bit wobbly, but he was upright. He walked over the dead man and growled. Kane thought for a brief moment the dog might be about to lift a leg on the fellow, so he steered Fitch away and Grinner followed.

"Kane?"

"Yes, Fitch?"

The boy grabbed his older brother's trouser leg as they walked. "If Grinner can't walk far—"

"Don't worry," said Kane, stroking the boy's head. "If he can't walk, I'll carry him. Don't you worry."

"I knew you'd say that," said Fitch, holding tight to Kane's leg.

They followed Bright Owl, Meghan, and the three little ones back the way Kane had come down to the campsite.

Moving in silence halfway up the slope, Bright Owl paused at the rear of the single-file column. Kane noticed the absence of his friend's light footfalls behind him and he, too, stopped.

"What is it?" he said in a quiet whisper.

Bright Owl stepped once, bringing himself alongside his friend. "I heard something. We may be followed."

Kane began to mimic his friend's pose, lowering himself

and readying his weapons as they looked into the dark below partially concealed by the brush and boulders and random pines dotting the slope.

"No, Kane, you must continue with the children. Get to the horses."

"I'm not leaving you to fight alone."

"Kane, the children are more important. And they have no warrior with them now."

"That's not true!" said a small, loud voice right behind them.

Both young men turned their heads upslope to see the raw-faced Fitch, lightly rubbing his wrists where the rawhide straps had chafed.

"Fitch, quiet!" Kane's voice came out in a harsh whisper.

"Why?"

"Because if I've told you once, I've told you a hundred times, Fitch Harrigan, to mind your elders." The new voice emerged from out of the dark just below them, along with less cautious, hurried footfalls.

"Pa?" said Kane, still tense as he and Bright Owl continued to shoulder their guns.

The figure emerged about ten feet below them. Mack Harrigan trudged forward, hands held up as if in surrender.

"Papa!" shouted Fitch and rushed down the slope toward the man.

"Hush now," said Mack, scooping the boy up in his arms. "We have to keep quiet. We're not out of danger, children." It took him several long minutes to make the rounds among the children, his own and the three Shoshone tots.

"Where were you?" said Kane.

"I was not too far from you, but I didn't dare call out for fear of alerting the brute I was fighting to your presence. He was angry and ready to kill anything that came near him. But I could tell, or hoped I could, from the sounds you all made that you were getting the upper hand." Mack stroked the hound as he spoke.

The dog bent his head and wore that funny smile as his tail worked like a sideways pump handle.

"I'm so happy you are all right. I was in the middle of that fight, but hearing you gave me the strength I needed."

"Have you seen my father? Or Turtle Eye?" said Bright Owl.

"Not yet." Mack shook his head, looking around in the dark. "It would be foolhardy for us to go looking for them in the dark." He began walking upslope, Fitch on one side of him, while Meghan walked ahead with the three smaller children. She kept looking back at Mack as if he might disappear.

"We should stay true to our plan and get back to the horses." Mack said to Kane. "Which way, son? In the dark, I'm afraid I'm a little turned around."

"We get to the top and then make westward."

"Ah good, yes."

They walked slowly and as silently as possible, and were able to find where they'd left the horses. Bright Owl and Kane roved ahead to scout the scene.

Mack had to keep himself from telling Kane to stay back, that he would go. It helped that he was near exhaustion. The only thing keeping him plodding forward was the fact that he had found his children, safe and whole, at last. He could picture Ell's face when they finally made it back to her.

The horses were all there, and Bright Owl scouted the edges of the place for sign of enemies hiding. He found none and returned.

"What do we do now?" said Meghan.

"We wait for Chief Stalks-the-Night and Turtle Eye," said Mack.

In this they did not have long to wait, for the two men made their way together back to the horses, approaching from the northwest.

The first sign anyone had of them was a thin, high whistle, as of a lonely night bird.

Bright Owl stood erect and listened. The sound repeated. He replied with the same call. It repeated once more, and then he said, "Father comes."

Sure enough, within a few moments the chief and Turtle Eye emerged from the darkness.

Mack could not help but notice the meeting of the chief and his son was quiet but tender in their own subdued way.

More of the same transpired between Turtle Eye and his young son. The man held his boy close to him, let the boy hug his leg, while he rested a hand on the boy's back and looked skyward as if communing with an unseen entity.

"Homeward," said Mack.

"No, not all of us," said the chief. "Turtle Eye and I must track them. The enemy have taken much from us this day and we must retrieve the most valuable of it."

"What could be more important, more valuable than the children?" said Mack.

"You are right Mack Harrigan, yes, but scalps were taken. We cannot allow them to boast of such a taking and not do anything about it."

"But—" said Mack.

The chief shook his head. "You are not Shoshone, Mack Harrigan. You do not know our ways."

Mack nodded, but said nothing.

Bright Owl stepped forward. "I will go with you, father. To avenge our people."

The chief regarded his son for a long moment, then shook his head. "No, my son. This is not the time. One day soon, but not now."

The young Shoshone warrior suddenly looked to Mack like a big child, so much weight did the chief's words seem to drape over him. He remained standing, facing his father, but his gaze was directed at the earth between them.

Other than the slivers of moonlight still angling through the pine branches, there was precious little light, but enough for Mack to see the discouragement on Kane's face.

"Son, no. Not you."

"But—"

Mack realized how much his son had grown in the last months, and yet how young he still was.

Turtle Eye held his son at arm's length, one big hand on each of the small boy's shoulders. His gaze was pinned on the boy's, who looked back, tears brimming in his dark eyes. They said nothing but remained that way for long moments, then Turtle Eye nodded once and stood, walking to the chief's side.

Mack spoke first, cracking the brief moment of awkward silence. "Kane and Bright Owl will be able to take the children back to the camp. I will, of course, go with you, Chief and Turtle Eye."

"No, Mack Harrigan." The chief held up a hand, palm forward, as if to stop Mack. "You must return to the Shoshone camp with your children. Your wife will worry about you."

"But I can be of use to you. I have a stake in this, too, you know."

The chief almost smiled, a rarity for him. "Your words show the man you are. That is good. But the Shoshone need you, too, back at the village. It is Shoshone who must avenge those wronged by the enemy on this day."

Turtle Eye spoke low to the chief. Then Chief Stalks-the-Night once more looked at Mack. "Turtle Eye wants you to take his son safely back to our people. He trusts you with this most sacred of tasks."

Mack was tempted again to argue, but he realized what the chief said was right—the safety of the tracker's son was of the most importance to the man. He nodded. "Yes, this I will do."

Turtle Eye, a man of few words and a quiet, steely demeanor, offered Mack a slight bow, his gaze penetrating Mack's. Each man nodded once, then it was done.

The chief nodded once more, glanced at his son for a long moment, then said, "We have waited long enough. We must go."

As all present knew it was not an invitation, but rather the Shoshone man's quiet way of telling his son everything he needed to in such a moment. That it was likely they would never again see each other in this life. But that this task had to be completed.

Turtle Eye and the chief made to depart, to descend once more toward the enemy's wrecked camp, Turtle Eye on foot, the chief riding the horse he had ridden earlier.

"You should take two horses, chief," said Mack. "We can manage on three."

"No, we shall take another horse from those they left behind."

"There are four down below," said Bright Owl. "Where we found the children."

"They will still be there?"

Bright Owl nodded to his father. "Yes, I think so. They are tired, but good horses. Their riders are all dead."

"Good," said the chief.

With that, the two men left. Within moments, all sight and sound of them vanished into the dark of the middle of the night hours.

Mack helped load the bone-weary children onto three

horses. Meghan rode one and held the two young girls in front of her. Mack lifted Turtle Eye's son in front of Kane and loaded Fitch onto the third, then mounted behind him. Bright Owl rode the forth horse alone.

"We'll switch it around in a while," said Mack, in case anyone wondered at the configuration.

They rode southward at a plodding pace, everyone fighting sleep, each night noise sounding like a threat somehow. Each scuff and crunch and nick of a hoof causing them to eye the dark searching for leering, fiendish attackers.

Sometime later Mack jerked his head upright. Forcing his eyes wide, he noticed he could see more of his surroundings. Morning was on its way. Though that might also mean they would be visible to whoever might still be out there tracking them, with each minute that brought them closer to the Shoshone wintering grounds, he felt that threat lessen.

"Pa!"

More out of instinct than anything else, Mack pulled back on the reins, taking care not to rouse Fitch, who had slipped against his right arm and slept the sleep of an exhausted child.

"Kane?"

His son rode up alongside, also cradling a sleeping young boy. "It's Bright Owl, Pa." Kane looked behind them. "I didn't notice until just now."

"What?" said Mack, looking behind them into the gray landscape.

"He's gone."

Mack watched for a moment, then said, "He's defied his father."

"What do you mean?"

"I mean he's gone against his father's wishes, against his chief's orders, and he's riding back to help his father and Turtle Eye. That's something few sons would do. But a man might."

If his comment stung Kane, the young man did not show it. But neither did he forget it.

"I'd say that's a sign," said Mack.

"Of what?"

"Of Bright Owl becoming a true Shoshone warrior."

"I'd say he already is one. He certainly fights like one."

"As do you, son, but there's more to being a warrior than making war." Mack tugged the reins and rode back toward Meghan, who had held up and looked beyond him at their back trail.

She wore a look of fear, the same look he had seen on Ell's face when he had left the Shoshone camp the day before.

"Let him go, son," he said to Kane. "It's his place to be with his father." Mack faced forward and heeled his mount, urging the tired mount to resume its plodding walk. "Come what may."

CHAPTER 15

Homecomings are often sweet, but the return of the Shoshone and Harrigan children to the Shoshone's wintering grounds caused widespread elation. Though Mack and the others had only been gone from the camp for a day, it felt to him as if he had been wandering distant lands, fighting wild beasts, and never certain if he was going to survive from one moment to the next.

He knew it was the result of fatigue and pain from his various wounds, slashes and gashes. They would heal, unless some sort of sleeping sickness crept into them. Time would tell. But even if he were the sort to give voice to complaint, he did not consider doing so. For the camp was filled with people—good people, his friends—who were mired deep in mourning.

When he'd left the day before, he had seen a number of dead Shoshone, some with their scalps hacked away. The sight was a vision he would carry with him for the rest of his life. It would serve as a harsh but necessary reminder to always be on guard. Life in the West was not much like life had been back in their quiet little mill town of Harrigan Falls, Ohio.

Despite the brutality of the previous day, if given the opportunity to reconsider the trip west and all it had brought his family—good, bad, and otherwise—he didn't think he would change his mind. They'd had difficulties, to be sure, but, he reasoned, if a man didn't take a chance in life, he would have to live with the worst of all niggling feelings worming away in his mind his whole life long. The notion that he might have done something more, something different, something better with his life—would be unbearable.

As Mack Harrigan hugged his family close to him late that afternoon upon their arrival, they were whole and alive and together, and that was all that mattered.

"And . . . Chief Stalks-the-Night?" said Red Dove in a low, quiet voice.

Mack knew what she was thinking, that the chief had been killed on the rescue mission. "He is alive, Red Dove." He saw the relief on her face.

Though she was very good at maintaining her stony mask, her eyes told him she wanted, needed to hear more.

"He and Turtle Eye were fine when we parted from them. They chose to continue on, to avenge the Shoshone deaths." Mack did not mention that he had tried to go along as well.

"And Bright Owl," said Ell. "What of the boy?"

"He made the choice to stay with his father."

A sob, quickly stifled, escaped from Meghan's bruised mouth. She looked away from them and no one said anything for a moment.

"I don't know when they will return, but, they will return. Of that I am certain. I have a feeling a strong feeling about this. And you know my feelings, right Ell?" Mack eyed his wife with a hard stare. "They're rarely wrong."

"Oh, oh that's right," she said, nodding.

Red Dove looked at Mack, then Ell. "You cannot know

such things. The only way to know if they will return is when they return. But it is kind of you to say otherwise." With that, Red Dove left the site and made her way toward the trail that led to Sitting Rock.

"She's exhausted," said Ell. "We all are. She fought like a man. No, better than a man, because half the time she helped me with the twins."

"She is an amazing woman," said Mack. "And a good friend to the Harrigans."

"I can't imagine what she's been through. She keeps it all inside." Ell looked toward the north. "Oh, that chief, those men. So foolish. Avenging the dead won't bring them back!"

Mack rested a scarred hand on her shoulder. "No, but it's their way, Ell, and we have to respect that."

"I know, I know." She wiped her eyes. "But I don't have to like it."

Four days later—four days spent dealing with and honoring the dead; four days filled with wailing and impotent anger at enemies no longer there, but seen nonetheless; four days of waiting and cleaning up the camp and repairing and tending the wounded and helping the suffering—a sound came from the north. Approaching fast, it brought a fresh wave of alarm and anger and attentiveness to the Shoshone camp.

Weapons, all now easy to hand, were snatched, horses were mounted, children and the elderly were hidden away as the sounds increased. A wave of dust rose up, clouding anything solid within. Horses could be made out, running fast enough it was obvious something chased them. Some were familiar.

Among them Mack recognized Dainty, the Harrigan's sweet young mare. Others among the fifteen or so thundering beasts were unfamiliar to him. Before anyone could take in much more, two mounted figures appeared, driving the small herd forward from behind. Everyone recognized the familiar, erect, trim figure of their leader, Chief Stalks-the-Night. Beside him rode a younger, larger version of himself. It was of course, Bright Owl.

Behind them trotted a horse on a lead line. It bore a flopping body draped and lashed down over the big mount's back. The head and arms jostled with each trotting step.

The initial mood of excitement at the return of the chief and his worthy son ushering in many of their stolen horses quelled when the camp caught site of the dead body of their greatest tracker, the much respected Turtle Eye. Lamentations renewed.

Though he was not close enough to hug the boy, Mack felt and saw the grief Turtle Eye's son had instantly succumbed to.

Having no sons of their own, his aunt—his dead mother's sister—and her husband, a kind if lazy man named Stone in Water, had taken in the boy, waiting until his father's return. They would now have a son, though not in a way any could have hoped for.

The chief did not wish to speak of the journey right away. He limped through the people, a matted, bloody wound on his head.

Red Dove stood a little off to the side of the other women, a place she was used to, not being of this tribe. But she regarded the chief and he her. He made for his teepee and lifted the flap, then looked at her and nodded. She followed the limping, broken warrior inside.

Those two firm, but kind souls, who had each suffered untold losses in life, were meant for each other, thought

Mack. He had seen no scalps, and for a brief moment wondered what the point of the venture was, but again he had to remind himself he was not Shoshone.

Bright Owl stood before his horse and looked over the heads of the people of his tribe. They were quietly praising him, patting his arm as they walked by to relieve the rear horse of its burden. His gaze landed on the Harrigan family standing in a cluster away from the tribe and relaxed.

Mack looked to his left, to the other side of Ell. Meghan had returned Bright Owl's look, then blushed and looked down. She was crying tears of relief.

Mack felt a quick stab of anger that the young man had somehow won the heart of his own dear daughter. At the same time he felt a twinge of pity, for such a match was not destined to be. *It cannot be,* he thought. *For so many reasons.*

Ell laid a hand on his chest and looked into his eyes. "You worry too much." Then, smiling, she handed him a twin. "Your son has soiled himself again."

Mack looked at the baby. "Are you sure it's not Hattie?"

"It?" said Ell, rolling her eyes and shaking her head. Walking to the Harrigan home, she felt humble but whole. At least for the time being.

CHAPTER 16

By the first of June, or thereabouts, according to Kane's reckoning, it seemed to all in camp that spring had finally come to their high country haven. The Shoshone prepared to move to another favored spot lower in a valley in the range the chief had said was fertile with game, and a river with fish. The tribe's preparations would see them depart later than usual because of the attack a month ago.

That was just fine with Mack, for he had been having trouble with their wagon, and he needed the time to hew and carve new parts for a damaged wheel. While he was at it, he made multiple spares, just in case.

After his return, Fitch had been quick to resume his previous role as a self-appointed Shoshone warrior. Nobody in the family had the heart to dissuade him from his pursuit, given that he still screamed each night in his sleep.

Meghan slept poorly, too. Even in the midst of her day's duties, she would slip into a reverie, staring at nothing for minutes on end. When asked, she would startle and say, "Oh, nothing, nothing."

But Ell and Mack knew differently, and watched her and worried over her.

On the night he finished repairing the wheel, Mack

walked with Ell alone, leaving the sleeping twins in Meghan's care. "It looks like we're just about set, Ell."

She said nothing.

"Now now. You knew there would come a day when we had to take our leave of the Shoshone. You haven't lost sight of our dream, have you?"

"Whose dream, Mack?"

"I thought you wanted to get to California as much as I did?"

"Maybe not as much, but yes, it was true. I admit it."

"Good," he said. "We can leave when the tribe does."

"But that's in two days!"

"Well, you didn't think we were going to travel with them forever did you?"

"No. But there's so much to do. Friends . . ."

"It's not like we'll never see them again, Ell. We live out here now, you know."

"Yes, but out here is a pretty big place, Mack."

"We'll find a way, Ell." He looked westward, off past the tree tops.

"Mack Harrigan, you never change."

"Can't," he said, smiling. "I'm an old married fellow, remember?"

"Yep. And you'd better keep that in mind, mister."

Two days later, after their clothes and goods had been winnowed down or offered to members of the tribe as gifts, found all the Harrigans resuming their journey westward. They were given offerings in kind from their tribal friends.

"Where are we going, anyway, Pa?" said Kane, looking lively despite the departure from his friends.

Mack patted his inner coat pocket. "Got a whole list of mine camps here that Uncle Zeke mentioned in his letters.

We'll try the last one first and work our way backward. He'll turn up."

"Not likely," said Ell.

"What do you mean?"

"He's a Harrigan, Mack. And he's the one you got your fiddle-footedness from. I bet cash money that is one character trait he has not lost."

They were interrupted by a series of snarling shouts from behind Ell inside the wagon. It was Fitch. "Let me outta here! I'm a Shoshone warrior and this ain't right!"

As if to concur with him, Grinner set up a long, plaintive baying wail that all-but drowned out everyone else's shouts.

"Good thing I tied him in," said Mack.

"You did what to my baby boy?"

"Just until we get far enough away that he can't make a run for it."

Ell shook her head. "Oh my stars. What has my family come to?"

As for Meghan, she had taken the decision to leave the Shoshone people behind rather quietly and rather well.

Mack was pleased, of course, but he had not yet figured out how to talk with Ell about it, or if he wanted to. Something wasn't right with his daughter. Why wasn't she pining for Bright Owl? Maybe she was. Girls and women were something he could not figure out. And now there were three in the family. Still, he smiled, riding ahead on Dainty, scouting the vista before them. At least there were still more Harrigan men in the clan than women.

He chuckled and vowed to never say that sort of thing out loud . . . at least not in front of Ell.

* * *

Fitch made his first escape sometime in the middle of that first morning back on the trail.

No one quite knew the moment it happened, but gradually Mack, Ell, Meghan, and Kane, realized they were enjoying the sounds of the trail—the wagon wheels creaking along, clunking over rocks not steered around, the blowing snorts of horses—and not the growling and wailing of the irate little wildcat they loved, but at the moment could not stand.

"It's too quiet," said Ell, when Mack dropped back to see how they were getting on. She drove the wagon and Meghan sat beside her, each enjoying the soft, warm spring day, each holding a napping twin.

Mack and Kane, who rode a Shoshone horse gifted to him, had agreed to trade leading and trailing duties. Kane rode forward and they chatted for a few minutes, then he moved to the front.

"I know, and it's a relief—" Mack saw his wife's raised eyebrows and the first flush of motherly controlled panic creeping onto her pretty face.

"Hold up!" he said to her and the wagon rumbled to a halt.

Kane heard it and trotted his mount back to meet them. "What's wrong?"

"Maybe nothing," said Mack, sliding down out of the saddle and handing Dainty's reins to Ell.

As he circled around to the rear of the wagon, he heard Kane sigh and say to his mother, "It's Fitch, isn't it?"

Mack tugged the bottom of the canvas cover free and lifted it to peer inside at the usual orderly jumble of crates and bundles, barrels and bedding. But no Fitch.

But there was the rope Mack had tied to the seething child's trousers and looped over his shoulders, in braces-like fashion. He'd realized Fitch could wriggle out of it but had trusted the boy would heed the somewhat symbolic nature of the effort at restraining him. At that point Mack had hoped the child would resign himself to the fact that he was once more a full-blooded Harrigan and not a Shoshone.

That had obviously not worked. On the floor of the wagon in a heap sat the rope, still attached to the boy's often-mended trousers. One end of the rope was still tied to a ring bolt in the wagon.

Mack sighed and answered Kane. "Unless the boy has shrunk or grown thinner than we thought, yeah, it's Fitch."

Not only was there no Fitch, there was also no Grinner, who'd been only too happy for the opportunity to ride in the wagon. Since his brave action on the rescue raid, as Mack had come to think of the night they retrieved the children from the attackers, Grinner had been showing his age, limping and groaning softly when he rose. He'd been clubbed and lightly grazed with a knife in his fight with that young enemy warrior.

And now Grinner was gone. For Mack that was the surest indication Fitch had flown their rolling home. No doubt about it, he had made fast tracks back to the Shoshone. The trouble was, the tribe was also on the move, making for its summer grounds.

Mack doubted Fitch knew in what direction . . . but they would be easy to track and would be moving much slower than were the Harrigans. He returned to the front of the wagon and told them the news.

"Aw, let them raise him, then." Kane shook his head.

"Kane Harrigan!" Ell's bottom jaw thrust out and she held a pointed finger in his face. "You will not give such thoughts voice, do you hear me?"

The boy turned red and hung his head. "Yes, Mama."

While Mack agreed with Ell, he had to admit he'd given the thought fleeting, if non-serious, consideration himself.

Fitch was a challenge, had been since he was born. Never satisfied, always nosing around elsewhere.

Mack set off, straight back the way they had come, putting into use the few but effective tracking skills Turtle Eye had shown him throughout their time with the tribe. He missed the Shoshone, and he thought it a true shame, for many reasons, that Turtle Eye had been killed.

As he rode, Mack ruminated, his mind half on the task at hand of following the boy and his dog, and half on his family. It was interesting to see Kane, a nearly grown youth who stood a head and a half over his mother, looking down at her, yet cowed by her. The power of mothers is a curious thing. Mack felt blessed Ell wielded it with grace and prudence. He'd met others who trampled their offspring and left them bitter, only to pass the same attitudes on to their own children.

He also noticed that Meghan, who normally would not let an opportunity such as Kane's chastisement pass without slipping her older brother a smug smile, was quiet throughout this latest Harrigan headache. He and Ell had talked some, and he'd agreed they should leave Meghan alone following the raid and her rescue.

Ell had shaken her head and calmed him, as always, with a gentling hand on his sleeve. "Give her time. She'll tell us what she wants to when it's time."

But he really needed to chat more with Ell. He sorely wanted to ask Meghan if the vicious brutes had . . . done anything wrong to her.

They'd also noticed that following the raid and Bright Owl's return with his father, something between Meghan and the chief's son had changed somehow. It was as if they had both undergone experiences that had forced them into adulthood, changing them forever. Perhaps there was no return to, what days before had been, a more innocent, kinder time in their lives.

Mack shook off these heady thoughts and concentrated on the task at hand. He was on horseback and Fitch was afoot. That was a card in Mack's favor. Yet because the boy was on foot and wily, for a seven-year-old, Mack had to be prepared for whatever evasive measures Fitch might take should he hear Mack's approach.

At least there was Grinner, which would also make the pursuit much easier. A year ago Mack never would have thought he would be tracking a rangy, limping hound and a half-naked boy, beelining, no doubt, for the Shoshone camp and beyond. Despite the potential dangers his son might face before he could find him, Mack could not help but be amazed at the wonders of life.

Far ahead he caught sight of something dark and slender poking up above the tops of sparse gray brush flecking with the green leaves of spring, It waved casually back and forth. Mack grinned. If he were a betting man, and he was not, at least not in the standard money-wager sense, he'd bet the thing he saw was Grinner's tail.

Urging the horse forward a few yards, he thought of how annoyed he was with the boy . . . then tamped down that feeling. Instead of riding in on the boy and shouting him down, which was his initial inclination, he'd have a little fun with the situation. He cut southward and down a slope, masking him for the time being from the boy and dog. When he felt he had ridden a sufficient enough distance, he angled Dainty northward, guessing at the spot where he might intercept the boy's course.

He could do nothing to hide the height of the horse from Fitch and Grinner, but he didn't much care. Within moments he heard a familiar sound—Fitch speaking in Shoshone, or rather a blend of Shoshone and English. Peppered throughout were the sounds of whistling and short bursts of the boy's imitations of various wild beasts, among them bears and lions.

Fitch walked into view, his head popping up above the brush and snagged grass stalked of the previous winter. So intent was he on his private conversation, and so earnest did Grinner seem to be paying attention that he drew within a dozen feet of Mack before he looked up. Fitch halted, his little mouth formed into a long O and his eyes followed suit. He held like that, his words halted in midsentence, then realizing what his father was doing there, he spun and raced southward.

He didn't get more than a couple of dozen feet before Mack and Dainty thundered up and once more stood before him. They repeated the silly game twice more, with Grinner lolling away behind Fitch. Finally Mack slid from the horse, held the reins in his right hand, and snatched up the wheezing, red-faced boy. Tucking him under his powerful left arm, Mack prepared for a long journey back to the rest of his family.

Fitch caught his breath and once more began to shout in a mix of words strange and not so strange. Such was the choice phrase, "I don't want to be a Harrigan! Harrigans are stupid!"

That was all Mack wanted to hear on the subject. In life he'd rarely ever shouted at his children, and hardly ever raised a hand in violence toward them. In his view, not only was it not necessary, it was savage, and told more about the poor job the parent was doing than it did the child. But on that day, a long one already with many miles to cover yet, Mack decided enough was enough.

He pulled in a big breath and bellowed like he'd never bellowed before. "Shut your mouth now!"

It worked like a magical charm. Mack adjusted the

silent, sobbing boy around in front of him in the saddle and placed Fitch's hands atop the saddle horn. Then he clicked the horse into a trot and they made their way back to the wagon.

It took the better part of half an hour to reach the wagon. By then the sun was nearly overhead.

Kane had set up the shade tarpaulin off the long left side of the wagon, had tended the stock, and roved ahead to scare up game for supper. Meghan had laid on a picnic spread of bread, biscuits, dried meats and fruits, and cool water. Ell was nursing the babies in the shade, and on Mack's approach shielded her eyes to the sun, nodded once at seeing his success, and looked back to the bairns.

Mack slid down off the saddle and lugged the silent but still fuming boy over to his mother. He stood Fitch before her and left to tend his horse.

After a moment, Ell looked at Fitch. "I'm disappointed in you, Fitch. Never more so than now."

If she had hoped that might make him feel awful and guilty, she was mistaken. "I don't care! I want to be with the Shoshone. They're my real family I—"

Meghan stepped in front of him, knelt down and held him by the shoulders. In a soft voice she said, "Fitch do you remember how scared you felt when we were taken by those rogue Piegans? How scared you were when you thought you'd never see Mama and Papa again?"

His eyes widened and he nodded.

"That's how we all felt when you left." She turned away and went back to laying out the noonday meal.

The little boy stood in silence, thinking. His eyes brimmed with tears and he sat down close to Ell, who wrapped her arm around his little muscled body. "I'm sorry, Mama. Don't be scared."

"Okay, I won't. You, too?"

He nodded and buried his face in her blouse.

When Mack returned, he looked at Fitch and raised his eyebrows, not daring to speak. Ell smiled at him, then looked at Meghan, who had turned from them and looked to be tending to something at the front of the wagon. Ell nodded toward her while looking at Mack.

He walked to his daughter and gave her a hug.

A while later, Kane rode back with a brace of rabbits. While Meghan tended to his horse, he and Mack tended to the rabbits. "I see Chief Pain in the Backside has returned."

Mack gave him a quick look, and Kane said, "Okay, okay."

A couple of moments later, Mack said, "In my mind, I've been calling him something worse." He winked and they both suppressed chuckles as they finished dressing the rabbits.

CHAPTER 17

Other than occasional bursts of howling from Fitch, which lessened the farther west the family roved, the Harrigan trek to the promised land, as Mack had discerned from his uncle Zeke's letters, was surprisingly enjoyable. While not uneventful, it was peppered only with episodes of laughter and wonder at seeing fresh vistas of far-off mountains that never seemed to become larger no matter how long they traveled toward them.

And then one day, there were those mountains.

Several weeks into the trip found the Harrigan wagon train—one of many—encamped along the banks of what Mack had identified, according to his scanty maps and trusty travel guide, as the Jewel River.

Thumbing through his brutally worn copy of *Maitland's Overlander's Handbook,* Mack said, "And if that's the case, that puts us about here"—he tapped the map—"or somewhere thereabouts. That means, at the speed at which we've been traveling, we ought to see California by . . . a week or so from today." He smiled at his family and expected shouts of hurrah all around. What he received were looks of, if anything, disappointment.

"Does that mean once we get there we'll be done traveling?" said Meghan.

"Well, sort of, yes," said Mack. Again he surveyed the faces of his family. "I thought you'd all like that."

Kane, in a mannerism that reminded Mack of his own father, rested one hand on his hip and rubbed the back of his neck with the other. "It's just that, well, I can't speak for anyone else, but I sort of like being out here."

"Yeah, me, too," said Meghan, nodding.

Mack was shocked. The girl hardly ever agreed with her older brother.

"Me, three!" said Fitch, performing a small rain dance in a tight circle, his hands waving above his tousled, sun-bleached head.

"Ell?" said Mack.

She smiled. "Me four." She wiggled each of the babies. "And five and six."

"Wow, that surprises me. Well, then the good news is that my estimate might well have been a bit too optimistic. It'll likely be a few weeks yet until we're somewhere where we feel at home."

"And maybe longer?" said Kane.

Mack nodded. "Sure, maybe longer."

"And the bad news, Mr. Harrigan?" said Ell.

"The bad news is that the trip has to come to an end at some point. It's the reason we set out in the first place, correct?" He received a round of weak agreement. "Well, okay then. We'll worry about that when we get there. Right now"—he smacked his hands together—"who wants to bathe in the river?"

Over the next two weeks of travel, increasingly they met other wagons. They'd seen no full trains yet, but plenty of single and double teams of families from back East, some from farther east than Ohio. Most were pleasant and friendly, often rolling within hailing distance and camping nearby each other in the evenings. The company was welcome and the Harrigans were able to catch up on news from the larger world.

They received not a few askance glances when they met folks, though. At first, Mack was confused as to why people looked at them with wariness.

Finally, one fellow nodded at Mack. "That injun gear you and your family wears—that mean you folks are half-breeds, or some such? I don't mind. I'm just curious to know. The missus, she's particularly worried about run-ins with the savages." He gave the surrounding foothills a hard squint and let loose a stream of chaw.

"No, we're no more Indian than you, but to make a long, exciting story short, the lives of my family were saved by a tribe of the kindest people I've ever met. We spent the winter with them, in fact. A band of Shoshone."

"Kindly, you say?"

"Yep."

"Huh. Well now, that's something you don't hear about, nor read in the newspapers of back East. It's all scalpings and killings and flaming arrows and such. I often wondered on the trustworthiness of those report, to be honest," said the man, warming to his topic. "They look like men and women, right? Just a little different, speak different, live a little different. But they are humans, got offspring. I guess they love them like we do our own children. So what makes them different?" He leaned an elbow on his saddle horn and looked at Mack.

It seemed as if the man wasn't spoiling for a fight or coming at one around the back door so to speak. Mack said, "From our experience, there's nothing, absolutely nothing different about them, really. We're all the same where it counts." He tapped his head and then his chest. "And that's what matters, I reckon."

"Amen to that." The man leaned over, smiling, and held out his hand. "I'm Judd Newcomb. My wife's Ethel, and the loud, small ones yonder are Hester, Harold, and Howie. Lord help me." He shook his head at the sight of his offspring running a ring in the earth around their parked wagon. But he was smiling, too.

The two families encamped and traveled together for two days, until the Newcombs departed on a northward trail that would lead them to land a relative had bought for them the year before in Oregon Territory. They were eager and excited and Mack envied them.

But a little of him pitied them, too. He didn't want to tell Ell, not yet, anyway. He liked very much the feeling of freedom from a homestead and owned land the trip had afforded them. It was impractical, he knew, to spend their lives traveling, wandering like they were, but he'd enjoy it while they were at it, while they were able. For if he had learned anything in his life, it was that nothing is permanent.

Everything was changing all the time. The kids were growing and changing. He and Ell, too, were different from how they used to be. The seasons rolled on, one spring different from the previous. It did no good to expect permanence. Instead smile at the constant state of change and see where it took them. He had plenty of time to think such thoughts as they rolled closer to the state of California.

One overcast, steel-gray day in mid-July they reached it by way of a passage through the Sierra Nevada Range. Descending from the mountain pass, the long, curving road looked to have been well traveled.

Judging from the increase in the number of wagons and such in recent days, it was a surprise to see they had the pass to themselves for much of the day. Reaching the state had been his goal for so long Mack wondered if the other members of his family still felt the same creeping stain of dread their journey might somehow come to an end. He said nothing and did his best to remain smiling and cheerful, but inside he felt otherwise.

Less than a day later, they followed the roadway and rolled right into the heart of their first mine camp without realizing it. He noted the place was named Sugartown, as a poorly chiseled hunk of scrap planking propped atop a boulder informed them as they squeaked their way in. It was a harsh place with hard, suspicious stares from the haggard inhabitants.

Mack doubted Sugartown had been offering its residents much in the way of promising ore for some time, but he offered a nod, a smile, and a touch to his hat brim to the first stranger they rode by. "Good day."

The only response he received was "Town's full up." The stranger spat chaw juice, spraying a sloppy mess down his already caked chin whiskers, beard, and shirt front.

As they rolled slowly, creaking and squawking through the rutted, dust-dry track that served as a trail in and out of camp, Mack prayed one of their horses didn't lose a shoe or their wagon snap a spoke. He kept an eye on their backtrail where Grinner was tagging along. The old dog could take only so much rumbling and creaking inside the wagon before he hopped down.

Fortunately, Fitch had stayed in the wagon. This Mack knew because he'd checked with Ell when sign of the first tents and shanties appeared to either side of them.

They made it through, even Grinner, though he, too, received surly glances and the threats of two ribby camp curs that had rushed out at him. To the hound's credit, he stood his ground, lock limbed, and the only thing on him that moved was his upper lip. It flashed a fierce big tooth and the rumble from way down deep in his chest matched it.

The strange dogs folded like a bad hand of cards, tucked their tails and slinked back to their sad lives in the dusty, rocky, depressing place that was Sugartown.

Mack, for one, had no desire to ever see the place again. In Ell's eyes he saw the same worry he felt—and wondered if all mine camps were the same. If so, the list in Mack's pocket, which he'd copied from his uncle Zeke's various letters, concerned him.

About a mile from the camp's last tent, they passed another shelter, a tidy little shanty with an old, skinny, bearded man sitting out front on a stone most likely rolled there for just that purpose. The fellow smiled and nodded and puffed a cob pipe as they moved slowly along.

Mack decided to risk a conversation. "Good day, sir," he said, again touching the brim of his brown felt slouch hat.

The old man nodded again, his eyes smiling and his pipe sending up a cloud of blue smoke. "Still above ground, so yep, I reckon it is." His beard split and a cackle burst out of his mouth, as he smacked his leg and shook his head. "You ought to see your own face, mister! Why, if I was thinking what you're thinking about me, I'd be downright embarrassed." His laughter sputtered out and he sat there smiling and shaking his head.

"I promise you, sir, I meant no offense. I—"

"Naw, naw, I'm only joshing you. Don't you worry. Not everybody hereabouts is like those sour-faced folks up in Sugartown. You'd think they didn't realize the wonders of this world, right smack in front of them!" He waved an arm wide at the sandy, rocky landscape.

Mack smiled and nodded. "Well, in that case, let me introduce myself. I'm Mack Harrigan. And this fellow here"—he indicated Kane on the other horse—"is my son, Kane. Driving the wagon is my wife and daughter, Ell and Meghan. And—"

"And I'm Fitch!" shouted a smaller voice from the back of the wagon. He slipped out from beneath the tarpaulin, followed by Grinner, and made his way forward, with very little caution displayed.

As he drew alongside Mack's horse, Mack snapped a finger and pointed at Fitch, who sighed and stopped walking forward. But he did not stop talking. "Do you know my friend, Bearpaw Jones?"

"No, no, can't say as I do. But the West is a mighty big place, young fella. He could be anywhere and I could be somewhere else in anywhere and we might never come across each other. You ever think on that?"

"No. But you remind me of him."

"Oh, well, I hope I can take that as a compliment." The old man looked to Mack with raised eyebrows.

"You can," said Mack. "Fitch, back to the wagon. You, too, Grinner."

The boy complained but the dog stood behind him with his head lowered and looked to be nudging the youth in the backside . . . toward the wagon.

"Let me guess, let me guess!" the old man smacked his knee. "You got a letter from a friend or relation or some such telling you there was more gold out here than a man could stand! And all ripe for the plucking! Huh?"

Mack's raised eyebrows told the fellow what he was thinking, for the codger giggled and smacked his knee again. "Knew it, I knew it!" He shook his head.

"So, it's not true, then. I mean to say—" Mack felt himself growing red about the ears. "I know the gold isn't everywhere, but—"

"Oh, there's gold all right, gold enough for you, me, them." The old man nodded toward the wagon behind Mack. "And everyone else in the States, besides."

"There is?" said Kane, inching his horse closer.

"Sure there is! The old man craned his neck forward. "You want to know the secret to finding it?"

Kane and Mack both nodded.

"Me, too!" Again, the old man roared, his half toothless mouth chortling away, and collapsing back into a hairy shape around his pipe stem. "What I mean is, it's there, all right, but finding it's the trick. Nothing's easy, save for them who get lucky. The rest of us have to grub for it." He nodded toward the wagon again. "It looks like you've come set with a whole brood of diggers! You'll do all right, sure you will."

That bit heartened Mack and he pulled out his short list of camp names. "Do you happen to know of a mine camp named Digby?"

The old man thought, then shook his head no.

"How about Silverton?"

Again, no.

That happened three more times, then Mack came to the last name. "Devil's Creek?" Expecting another sorry head shake, he was rewarded with a smile and a nodding head.

"Yep, yep. Been there myself, I have. It's yonder." The old man pointed northward. "I'd say a good three, maybe four days ride with the wagon. Yeh, good camp. Early on it was, anyway. That where your relative waits?"

Mack folded the paper and tucked it away. "I doubt it. He's . . . fiddle-footed." He glanced at Ell, who did her best not to smile. "I'm sure he's moved on by now."

"That's a trait I know well, being of that nature myself.

Seeing as how my diggins are all played out, I am inclined to think—living hereabouts you tend to get long stretches of time to do just that—men are more prone to wandering than are women. And I'll tell you why." He leaned forward, his brow furrowed, warming to his topic.

Mack did not have the heart to interrupt him, though he sorely wanted to make it to Devil's Creek as soon as possible.

"It's because women are more satisfied in life. They make decisions and they stick with them. Good or bad, they ride out the storms, stay put, and take care of their bairns because they have that nurturing side. Maybe that's where all their smarts come from. Men, on the other hand"—he winked at Mack and Kane—"are fools. Fiddle-footed, wandering fools!" He smacked his leg again and cackled.

"I expect that's about right, yes," said Mack, finding himself in large agreement with the strange but likeable man.

"What our new friend said about men," said Ell, "would certainly account for your uncle's behavior, Mack."

"Ha!" The old codger smacked his leg again. "Well, what's his name? Maybe I've crossed his trail, or he mine."

"Zeke. Ezekiel Harrigan."

"Zeke, Zeke, Zeke Harrigan." The old man scratched his beard with work stiff, bent fingers. "Nope, no recollection of such in my head."

"Well, I hate to say it, but we had better be getting along if we want to make it to Devil's Creek sooner than later."

The old man nodded but leaned forward. "You take my advice, son. Arrive there when you're fresh. Make tracks today, sure, but camp up before you get there. Been a while since I've taken the measure of that town. Might be things have changed. Womenfolks are scarce in these parts and when men get liquored up, they'll act poorly under cover of the night. You hear my meaning?"

"I do, indeed. And it's sound advice. I appreciate it Mr. . . ." Mack realized they had not gotten the man's name.

"Ned Winkler. Folks who know me call me Digger. But the name's Winkler. Just like what your eyes get up to when you see a pretty lady, if you've lived as long as I have, that is." That seemed to strike the man as humorous and he was about to continue when he said, "Now then, you Harrigans had best get rolling."

Fitch darted away from the wagon, where he'd been standing near his mother. He grabbed Digger's hand and shook it. The old man laughed again.

"Now, Mister Fitch, you be sure to give ol' Zeke and Bearpaw my best when you see them, you hear?"

"I thought you said you didn't know them!"

"I don't. But that doesn't mean I might not meet up with them someday!"

As the Harrigans departed from Digger Winkler's little rocky paradise, they were smiling, in large part because Digger was still cackling and waving.

"Pa?"

"Yes, Kane."

"Why didn't we just stay the night there? He was friendly enough."

"Because as friendly as he is, I think Digger values his privacy even more. Otherwise, he would have invited us to camp there for the night."

Kane nodded. "I guess that's why Bearpaw goes off on his own for long stretches and then spends a night or two in a town. He said he gets the creeping willies and he has to get out by himself again."

Mack smiled. "Yep, that sounds about right." He was

thinking, though, of the terrible state their old mountain man friend had been in when Mack found him some months back. Naked and smeared with honey and dung and lashed to a log, he'd been left to die after having been robbed by two brigands. It was by mere chance Mack found him. The old mountain man had taken it as a matter of course, and said that's the way life was out there on the frontier.

Mack looked to the trail ahead and once again wondered what sort of adventures he was about to lead his family into.

They found an ideal spot to camp that night, and another the next.

Midday on the following day, something told Mack they would make it to Devil's Creek before nightfall if they kept pushing as they had been. He considered Digger's advice and decided the old man might well be a whole lot of things, but he seemed honest.

Ever since the hellish experience of the wagon train they'd joined late in St. Louis, when he'd ignored Bearpaw Jones's voice to steer clear of the wagon master, Ricker Briggs, and his ill-formed, paltry train, Mack had vowed to trust his gut. And to weigh the sage advice of others.

He gladly, willingly opted to appease the small voice in his head that agreed with Digger Winkler, and the larger, roiling sound in his gut that told him the sooner they called it a day, the sooner Ell might have something tasty to eat bubbling or crackling over a warming blaze.

Besides, he told himself as he rode forward to tell Ell and Kane to scout a camping spot, it would give him and Kane a chance to do a little hunting.

It didn't take long before Kane found a decent spot for them to spend the night. There was even a small supply of dried branches and a fire ring—signs that it was used by other travelers, though from the lack of prints, it looked to Mack to have been some time, perhaps weeks, maybe even months, since anyone had used it.

There's just one problem," said Ell, climbing down from the wagon and stretching her back.

"Oh." Mack looked around, worried that he'd over-looked something obvious.

"You, mister, and Kane, get to traipse off and do a little hunting. Something that has brought smiles to both your faces, I see. But Meghan and I get to stay here, watch over the animals, watch over Fitch— " They all looked to see where the little rascal had gotten to.

He'd scaled a wagon-sized boulder, trying to coax poor Grinner to join him.

"And tend the twins," said Meghan.

Ell nodded. "Yes, and, to top it all off, we get the honor of making supper for everyone. From scratch, because we've been pushing so hard to get to this Devil's Creek place to find Uncle Zeke, who won't be there anyway, that I haven't had a proper day of no travel in more than a week in order to bake, so we can have food to keep on moving forward, to wherever it is you feel we have to get to so blamed quickly!"

She had begun the diatribe, Mack noted, calmly enough that he thought it might turn humorous, but by the time she'd finished, her color was up and so was his, and every-one else's. And the twins had begun whimpering.

She turned and stomped off beyond the wagon.

Mack said, "Kane, tend the horses. Meg, you tend the twins, please. I'll be back."

As Mack passed the base of Fitch's rock, the boy said, "Hey, where's Mama going?"

"Not now, Fitch. Mind your sister and brother."

"Aw, that's not fair!"

Mack held up a finger toward the boy and kept walking, following Ell. "He caught up with her, uncertain if he should follow her, but knowing, too, that it was strange country to them. "Ell, honey, why didn't you say something sooner?"

"I shouldn't have to," she said, turning on him.

She'd been crying and the sight of it made Mack wince inside. She was the toughest woman he'd ever met, but it seemed he alone had the power to make her cry, and he hated that. He'd do anything to stop her from feeling so low.

"All right, then," he said, "From now on, I'll help you with the cooking."

She laughed. "You? Mack Harrigan, you are quite capable of a good many things, but cooking is not one of them."

"Then I'll tend the twins. And . . . Kane and I can pitch in more . . . with Fitch, sure, but with other chores. You're right, Ell, I've been ignoring all the things you do and it's not right."

"Mack, I'm just tired. We've been at this a long time and I am tired. Tired of it all. I need a home place again. Even if it's just for more than a night somewhere."

"Okay, then. We'll make it to Devil's Creek tomorrow and if it's anything like what Digger Winkler recalls, we'll hang our hats there . . . for a while, anyway. See what we can turn up."

"No, it's okay. If it's not what we're looking for, we can keep moving on."

Mack held Ell by the shoulders. "My dear, we are in California. We made it already. And it's early enough in the season that we can take some time to figure out where it is we might want to settle."

Even saying the word settle gave Mack a quick, cold feeling, but he hugged her close.

CHAPTER 18

Midmorning the next day, just after the Harrigan wagon rolled in to Devil's Creek, Mack was surprised to find a large man peppering him with a question in a foreign lingo.

"You jehu?"

"Huh?" said Mack, uncertain what the man said. "Me? No, I'm Mack. Mack Harrigan." He proffered a hand to shake.

The man shook his head, but knuckled onto Mack's hand and looked him in the eye. "I said do you jehu? Do you drive? A team?"

Mack still looked confused.

The man sighed and still jerking Mack's hand in his own big mitt, pulled him close. "You a drinker?"

"What? No!" Mack shook him off. "Now look, I don't know what this is all about, but I just got here to Devil's Creek with my family."

"Uh-huh, well, look." The man rasped a big hand across his stubbled face. "I own a teamster outfit. Well, one wagon just now, but I aim to get bigger. Big plans, I tell ya. Anyway, I'm down a man. My old pard, small quiet fella by the name of Howell or some such, he up and got killed in a cave-in a few days back."

"Oh, I'm sorry to hear that."

"You ain't just whistlin'! Left me high and dry, I don't mind saying."

"Oh, I see." Mack was beginning to wonder about this fellow's mind, but the man kept talking.

"Look, I freight all manner of goods from one camp to another, here and there and over yonder and back again. Make a circuit through all the camps and towns hereabouts, and farther out, too. Why, there's nowhere I won't go with my wagon. That's why folks hire me!"

"That's nice for you," said Mack. "Look, maybe we can talk another time? As I said, we just got here and we need to settle in. Say, you wouldn't happen to know if anyone hereabouts is hiring, would you?"

"Good gosh a mighty!" bellowed the man, his head thrown back as if in disgust. He looked at Mack with a weary cast to is eyes. "That's what I been doing here for the last ten minutes, ain't it?"

"What's that?" said Mack, beyond confused.

"Offering you work, man! Work! Paying work! I got contracts and daylight's wasting! You in or not? I got time to make up!"

"You want to hire me?"

The man sighed, closed his eyes, and nodded.

"To do what, exactly?" Even as he said it he knew the man's response would be one of exasperation. And it was.

"Jehu, son. Jehu, driving a team. You and me, we'll be swapping off driving duties in favor of the shotgun. Lots of thieves and rascals hereabouts who'd love to get their claws on the good of my customers. Shotgun comes in mighty handy. You do own a shotgun, don't you?"

"Yeah, I do." Mack had finally gained a sense of what the man was on about, and he wasn't so certain he liked the fellow, though the offer of work was unexpected and not unwelcome.

"Good. Bring it and shells. We leave in fifteen." The man spun and stomped off.

"Hey!" shouted Mack. "What's the pay?"

The big man returned, looking left and right. "Ain't anyone tell you it ain't polite to talk money out in the open? He shook his head and scratched his chin. "Seems to me, since you're unproven, I'll have to start you out at seven dollars a week."

"How often do we make it back to Devil's Creek?"

"Oh, every week, week and a half. It's a home of sorts for me. Generally spend the night here then light out first thing again."

"I'll do it."

The man smiled and made to speak, but Mack held up a hand. "But I'll need ten dollars a week, and found."

"Ten dollars? A week? Man, that's more than I make! I'll go belly up! I'll starve! Just who do you think you are, anyway?"

"I'm the man you came to, remember? I didn't go looking for you."

The big teamster regarded him through narrowed eyes for long moments. His big mouth was closed, for once, but it worked as if he had a hot coal riding around in there. "All right, all right! But this here's a trial week!" He wagged a big finger in Mack's face.

"The last man who did that now goes by the name of Nub."

Again, the big fellow regarded him, then smiled broadly. "Oh, we're going to get along just fine, Mack Harrigan. Just fine." He stuck out his hand and they shook.

"By the way, who are you?"

The big fellow looked as if Mack had slapped him. "Me? Man, I guess you really are new in town. Name's Pardo. Pardo Zinski."

"Okay, Mr. Zinski. When do I start?"

The man looked up at the sky, squinted, then back to Mack. "Right now. Let's go."

"Now? Hold on a minute, Mr. Zinski."

"I could have given you ten minutes to do whatever you need to with your family here, but you been jawing the morning away!"

"I'll need a half hour or the deal's off."

"Five minutes."

"Fifteen."

"Ten."

"Okay, fine. Where do I meet you?"

"I'll swing by on my way out of town. Be ready or I'll charge you for every minute you waste. Might do that anyway, all this lip flapping." He stalked off shaking his head, muttering words such as mistake, going soft, and poor house.

Ell had been overhearing, she could not help it, and for a moment they looked at each other, then Mack said, "Ell, It's not too late. I can tell him I've changed my mind."

"No, you have to do it, Mack. We are down to almost nothing, except for what we have hidden away."

"No," he said, glancing about and thinking of the conversation he'd just had. "That hidden money stays that way. It's for land of our own, Ell."

"Okay, then you have to take this job."

"I understand," he said. "But we just arrived here in Devil's Creek."

"I can handle your load, Pa." Kane stepped up, puffing his chest a bit.

Mack nodded. "I know you can, son. That's not what I'm worried about."

"And I have Meghan to help me with the twins and Fitch," said Ell.

Again, Kane spoke. "I'll deal with Fitch. Meghan has enough to worry about with the twins and helping out with the food."

"Speaking of food," said Mack. "How are we set for stores? Do you have enough to get by on until I return?"

"Of course we do," said Ell. "And Kane can hunt."

Mack looked at the hills thereabouts. "I imagine this country is about hunted out."

Ell patted his chest. "Get your gear. I'll help. You'll need a blanket, an extra pair of socks, a shirt, and a sack of food. Hold on!" She bustled off to retrieve the items he needed while Mack fetched the shotgun and shells.

"Do you have matches? And flint and steel?" said Kane.

Mack nodded, patting the small buckskin possibles bag he wore about his neck. He'd gotten in the habit, as had Kane, of carrying the small items that might make a difference between survival and death when out in the wilds. It had been a strong and useful suggestion by Bearpaw Jones.

"Two knives? Pistol?" continued Kane, looking more like the concerned father than the concerned son.

"I'm fine, Kane. Look, take care of things here, okay? Be vigilant. I didn't ask for this to happen, but it seems a decent start. Help your mother, keep them all safe. I know it's a whole lot to ask of you, but I wouldn't go if I didn't think you could manage it." To his wife, he said, "Ell, you don't even know anyone here."

"Sure we do," said Fitch, walking up with Meghan and an older woman, red-faced and wiping her hands on a stained apron. "This here's Miss Sweeney!"

"How do," said the woman, holding out a red hand to Ell, and nodding to Mack. "Penelope Sweeney."

"Pardon me, ma'am, but I think I see Pardo Zinski coming."

"Oh, you his new jehu?"

"I think so, yes." Mack held up the shotgun and shouldered the sack of gear Ell handed him.

"He's a good sort. Honest, works hard, a bit rough around the edges, but you'll do all right with him."

Just hearing that brought relief to them all. Mack could tell by looking at Penelope Sweeney she wasn't the sort to brook nonsense, nor spin yarns.

He hugged the children, kissed the twins on the heads, patted Grinner, who bowed his head and offered up that odd grin of his, and then wrapped an arm about Ell and pulled her close. He whispered in her ear. "Just a week, my dear. I'll be back, safe and sound. You and the children stay safe, above all else."

"We will. It's a promise."

"If you're worried, Mr. Harrigan, no need to be. I've worked a pile of mine camps and this one's all right. Got ourselves a lawman of sorts, town officers, the works."

Again, Mack was grateful for the unbidden assurances from the brusque, but friendly woman. "Thank you, ma'am."

Pardo Zinski rolled up, his two-brace team of low, solid, work-thick horses pulling a wagon half-freighted with ore. He was shouting, and not quite slowing. "Get on, man! Daylight's costing us!"

Mack nodded to his family once more, kissed Ell on the cheek, and clambered aboard the rolling wagon, choking back a lump rising in his throat. Then they were off, somewhat slow, steady. The Harrigans and Penelope Sweeney watched the wagon roll on out of the northwest road out of town, and soon it was gone from Devil's Creek.

The apron-clad woman looked back to Ell. "You may have noticed there ain't too many ladies in camp. But there are lots of hungry menfolk. Most of them have enough money from their diggin's that they choose to eat, and eat well. And most of them eat at my place, yonder," she jerked her head behind her.

A the far end of the bustling street sat a large, tidy canvas tent, open fronted, with two long rows of tables stretching from inside to outside, benches flanking them.

"Oh, that must be nice for you."

"You bet it is, especially since I'm the only eatery in town. But I'm in a bind."

"Oh?" said Ell. "Is there anything I can do to help?"

"According to your little firecracker of a boy here—"

"That's me!" Fitch stepped up and jerked a thumb to his chest.

Meghan hooked an arm around him, pulled him back a step, and smiled. "They guessed that, you little monster."

"And your daughter, Meghan, I hear tell you are the best cook to ever have crossed the Rockies."

Ell blushed. "I don't think that's even possible. I'm sure you're a wonder, Mrs. Sweeney."

"Miss, not Mrs. Never got hitched. Too homely and I don't have patience for menfolk lingering past mealtime, if you know what I mean. But back to my purpose. I'm in need of help in the kitchen, Mrs. Harrigan."

"Oh, I . . . well, I'm sure Meghan could lend a hand. She's learned what she knows from me, for what that's worth."

"No offense, Miss Meghan, but I need an expert. A mother who's used to dishing up for such a brood as this is bound to have the skills and the speed I need in the kitchen."

"Oh, I . . . I don't know. The twins and Fitch."

"I'll take care of the twins, Mama."

"And I'll take care of Fitch," said Kane, imitating their father and wagging a finger at the little rogue, who stuck out his tongue . . . until his mother saw him.

"Tell you what, Mrs. Harrigan."

"Ell, please."

"Okay, Ell. We'll try it out for a day or two, see how it goes, if we get along. Might be you grow weary of me." Miss Sweeney smiled. "I can offer you a weekly pay and I expect we can make enough extra food to feed this brood of yours a meal or two a day, to boot."

"Aw, go ahead, Ma. If you want to, that is," said Kane, turning red.

Ell looked at Meghan, who smiled and nodded, knowing as they both did that she was quite capable of handling the twins for long hours at a stretch.

"Oh, I don't know. We haven't even found a place to set ourselves up."

"Bah, I own that entire empty stretch behind my place yonder. Follow me on up there and we'll find you a private corner all your own to camp on. What do you say?" Miss Sweeney looked back at her tent. "The smoke's thinning in my stove. I need an answer, Mrs. Harrigan. I used up my day's free time talking with you all. Time to bake!"

"Oh, all right. I'll do it. I'll give it a try, that is. If I'm not up to scratch, you promise to let me know . . . Penelope."

"Will do, Ell. Now, let's go!" With that, the large, red-faced, red-handed woman in the apron set off back up the street at a hard clip.

CHAPTER 19

By the afternoon of the second day out of Devil's Creek, Mack reckoned he had gambled, trusted his little voice, and made a decent choice in taking up Pardo Zinski on his offer. No, make that demand he work for him.

If anything, once Pardo got in the driver's seat, he was downright amiable. At times, he was too chatty. Mack, while not overly talkative, could hold his own in a conversation and reasoned he'd much prefer a trail mate who was prone to talking than a dour, somber fellow who wasn't.

By their fifth day on the trail, they'd visited two mine camps, one of them a grim place that reminded Mack of Sugartown, and the second little better. Neither had been given names, but once they'd unloaded and reloaded their wagon, Mack did his best to ask if anyone had heard of his uncle Zeke. He came away with nothing, save for confused looks and head shakes both times.

"Cheer up," said Pardo a while later, once they were back on the road. "Odds are if something foul happened to your uncle you would have found out by now. So not hearing is bound to be good news in itself, right?"

Mack grinned and said, "Yep," adjusted his boot and shifted the shotgun to cradle in his other arm.

It was Pardo's chance to drive and Mack didn't mind.

He'd spent the morning manning the lines. The horses were solid beasts, but young and full of vim and vigor, apt to get unruly now and again and kept the driver alert and honest. But it was tiring work.

"They ain't whip smart yet," Pardo had said about their occasional wild streaks.

"I haven't seen you touch them with the whip," said Mack.

"Course not! A man who'd strike a beast is no man at all, I tell you true!"

"I agree."

They rolled northward, on through a wide, slow curve flanked by a rock wall, then it straightened, the vista opening up once more to reveal more of the same gritty, grassy, rock-rubble terrain with foothills to both sides.

A thin, hunch-shouldered man stepped out from behind a boulder on the right side of the road. As the shotgun rider, Mack tensed, snugged the shotgun to his cheek, aimed it at the stranger, and made certain the gun was ready to fire.

As they rolled forward a few more yards, Mack scrutinized the fellow. The stranger wore a brown slouch hat, hole-riddled and flop-brimmed, and clothes that had seen better days years before. They were much mended and thready, and his lace-up work boots bore holes in the toes. Mack guessed the soles fared far worse.

The pinked-with-age bandana tied around his face allowed only his squinting eyes to be visible beneath the worried hat brim. That and the single-barrel shotgun aimed in their direction revealed without doubt what the fellow's intentions were.

Even from their distance of a dozen yards, the man's gun looked to be an ancient piece of weaponry. He held the forestock with his right hand and the left was curled near the trigger, with his left elbow wedged against his ribcage. He had as much meat on him as a birch sapling.

Mack noticed the man shook, either with fear or from the weight of the gun. Or both.

"Hold! Hold! Whoa, now!" Pardo tugged the lines, leaning back with the effort until, in a boil of dust, the team stomped to a halt and stood fidgeting and blowing. "Well?" he shouted, making no movement toward his side arm. "What's it going to be, man?"

The shaking fellow said something too low for them to hear.

"What?" bellowed Pardo, far too loud.

The fellow coughed, moved his trigger hand to wipe at his eyes. The gun slumped so he rammed the arm back in place. "I . . . I said you ought to throw down your money! Now!"

"Aww, I reckon not. I'm far too busy working for my money to give it to a useless mess such as you!" Pardo looked at Mack. In a loud voice as serious as Mack had heard the man speak, he said, "Shoot him."

"What?" said Mack.

"I said shoot him. Now."

"No." Mack stepped down out of the seat, keeping his shotgun pinned on the man. He walked up on the man from an angle so the fellow had to choose to aim either at Mack or the wagon. As he walked closer, he saw the fellow's shaking grew worse and his clothes were sopping. It was a warm day, but nothing that would warrant such sweat.

The man was a mess, as Pardo had said, but a nervous one.

No longer walking, Mack said, "What damage do you think you're going to do us at that range, and with that old gun?"

The man said nothing but backed up a pace. "Keep your distance," he said, his voice dry and cracking.

"I won't," said Mack, and he stepped slowly closer. It was then he noticed the man's eyes. They were wide, wide, wide. As if he'd seen something unspeakable. But Mack knew it as fear. For he'd felt the same, most recently in that awful attack on the Shoshone camp. He walked up to within a yard of the man, their barrels almost touching. "Why are you doing this, mister?"

"I-I got to have money. That's all. My business."

"Hard times?"

As if in response, from beyond the boulder came a thin, crying sound, a child's voice.

Hungry, thought Mack. "Your family?"

"Yeah." The man's response was a whisper. "Wife, two young'uns."

Mack saw those fear-filled eyes, and the fellow's arms trembling worse than ever. He kept his shotgun leveled on the fellow, his finger on the trigger, but with his other arm, he reached up and pushed the man's shotgun down. As he had suspected, the thing was ancient, rust-pocked, pitted, and poorly kept.

As the gun dropped low, the man's arms collapsed as if he'd been holding a boulder above his head.

Mack reached up and tugged down the bandana. The man would not look him in the eye, and his bony, whiskered face looked about to cry. Mack took the shotgun from him.

"It's just that we're stretched so thin, you see."

Mack nodded. "Wait right here. I have something for you." He walked back to the wagon with both shotguns in his hands and laid the old junker in the wagon. Snatching up his satchel, he rummaged for the food sack Ell had given him. The dozen squares of hard tack and that many strips of pemmican were the last of his stores he and Pardo had been nibbling on during the long days of travel.

His boss frowned. "What are you up to?"

"Making a business deal," said Mack, not looking at Pardo.

He walked back to the man, who looked ready to rabbit any moment, and handed him the cloth sack. "It's not much, but it's good, and it'll keep you and yours alive until you can get better."

The man didn't make a move to take the sack, so Mack shook it until the man grabbed it with a big-knuckled, working man's hand.

Holding the shotgun in the crook of his left arm, Mack dug into his inner pocket with his right hand. Pulling out his coin purse, he said, "You have a way to travel? We're still a few miles from a town, I think."

"Yeah," said the man. "Horse is still solid enough."

"Good."

He'd kept a couple of coins in his coin purse for an emergency, and another couple wedged tight in a slit in his leather gun-and-knife belt. Those in his coin purse he handed to the man. "The food will keep you alive, and the money should help you get better food and maybe partway home."

Again the man didn't raise his hand to accept, but stared at Mack, then at the coins, then at Mack's face again.

"Take it, please."

As the man reached, Mack held the coins over his palm, but before letting them go, he said, "Do me a favor, will you?"

"What's that?" said the man in a quiet voice.

"Take good care of your family. They're a gift that can't be replaced. And for the love of Pete, don't ever do anything like this again."

"I . . . I surely won't. I surely won't, mister. I . . . I don't know what to say."

"Say you promise."

"I promise. But this ain't right."

"What do you mean?" said Mack. "I bought your shot-gun from you, fair and square. I got a bargain, I'd say."

"But . . . it wasn't worth half of nothin'."

"Maybe not to you, but to me it's worth a whole lot. Trust me." Mack gave him a smile, shook his hand, and said, "Good luck."

"Oh, oh, thank you, mister. Thank you."

But Mack had already turned back to the wagon.

Pardo said nothing, but as soon as Mack settled into his seat, he slapped the lines and the team rolled forward. The man was still standing by the roadside, his big hand folded over the coins and the other clutching the meager sack of food.

Pardo nodded and smiled at Mack, who did the same. Dust boiled up and then they were gone from view.

As Mack had thought, it wasn't long before Pardo cut loose. "If I tell you to do a thing, as my employee, by gum, you will do that thing!"

Instead of being cowed by the big bellowing man on the seat beside him, Mack shook his head. "No sir. That's not how I operate. The only man who tells me to commit violence on another beast on this earth, be it man or deer or bird or plant, is me and me alone. You don't like that, I'll take my leave of you right now." Mack reached back behind the seat for his satchel.

"Hold on, hold on. For the love of all that's sane, I never said I'd fire you."

"You all but did."

"Yeah, but I never meant it."

Mack let it go as Pardo fidgeted with the lines and the horses kept rolling forward.

After a few minutes, Pardo said, "Tell me I didn't see

you give him money. Tell me I am wrong, at least about that!"

"I did." Mack would have to explain that to Ell, but the fellow needed help and that was all there was to it. "If I had been in his holey boots, and someday I just might, I'd want someone to show me a little kindness."

Pardo chuckled and shook his head. "You keep it up, you'll be there sooner than you think!"

A few more minutes of silence passed, then Pardo mumbled, "Just my luck. All the help out there and I had to choose one with a spine." He clucked the team onward.

Mack allowed himself a wedge of a smile. Spine, indeed. More like faith in his fellows. "Doling out a little human kindness never hurt anyone, you know."

"I know, I know. Heck, I reckon you did the right thing."

"I bet you would have done the same."

"Oh, now, don't go insulting Pardo Zinski!"

The man tried to keep a straight face, but he glanced at Mack and they both had a good laugh as they rumbled and rolled northward to the next town, a place Pardo had said Mack might like, an interesting town called Watts Corner.

CHAPTER 20

Bearpaw Jones stumped on into the little bustling mine camp of Devil's Creek about an hour past the midday rush for eats at Miss Penelope Sweeney's establishment. Though no sign hung out front, everybody knew well by smell and sound and sight the sprawling, half-tent, half-timbered construction anchoring the south end of the main and only street was an eating establishment.

Jones, leading his mule, Ol' Gravyfoot, and cradling Thunder, his mammoth muzzle-loader Hawken rifle in a fringed buckskin sleeve, trudged from the north end of the lane to the south. With each step his nostrils quivered and aromas such as the world had never smelled, or so he claimed in his feverishly hungry mind, tempted him and led him on like the slender fingers of a beckoning siren.

That feeling and ethereal image had cost him several fortunes at baize tables, whiskey kegs, and cleared patches on the earth, all throughout the emerging, vast, and barely settled West.

However, he had a few coins in his purse and an appetite that would put a herd of teamsters to shame. He'd been walking alongside his cantankerous trail mate, Ol' Gravyfoot, for weeks, moseying as they were wont to do in search of a new opportunity, a raw adventure, or a small or large fortune. They'd been short on the latter of late. But he had hopes.

"Hey, fella," he said to a man shambling by with a pick over one shoulder and a toothpick jutting from his beard. "Where be them heavenly smells coming from?"

"Oh." The man smiled. "You aren't from around here, otherwise you'd know the cooking at Penny's is the finest fare in the land."

"That tent there?"

"Yep, walk on in and she'll see you right. But there might be slim choosin's until supper time."

"Oh, I'll take my chances." Bearpaw sniffed the breeze once more. "Thanks, friend." He trudged on.

"Come on, Gravyfoot. We got to feed our flames before they go out."

The mule brayed low.

"I know, I know. I'll take care of you, don't you fret. Bound to be someone hereabouts who has critter feed. I'll see to it, but I have to make certain she don't run out of my sort of food, elsewise I might faint dead away. They'd haul me off thinking I was expired and not just in a food swoon, and then where would you be, huh?"

The mule blew slobber through her rubbery lips and shook her head with vigor.

"Oh sure, you laugh about it all you want, but if it weren't for me, you'd be dragging some starved home-steader's plow!"

The mule said nothing.

"Yeah, think on that, you ungrateful riggin'."

By then they'd arrived at the hitch rail out front of the tent the stranger had pointed out for him. Bearpaw looped Gravyfoot's lead line over the rail and wagged a finger in her face. "Now look you, see to it nobody takes a wrong-headed liking to our goods. Or that extra ration of oats won't be nothing to you but a memory."

She lowered her head.

"Now, you know I'm funning you, anyway. But just the same, take care." He leaned closer. "I can't lose you, Gravyfoot. Don't know what I'd do. Might have to up and settle down somewheres, and the very thought of it gives a man a bad case of the creeping shudders!" He stroked her long nose then strode on past two long, empty, mostly cleared tables and on into the open doors of the canvas-and-pole structure.

At the far end, with her back to him, bustled an amply sized woman muttering to herself, for he saw no one else about. She chucked pots and pans and skillets every which way, and made stacks out of everything she laid a red hand on.

Bearpaw swept his faded felt topper off his gleaming pate and smoothed the fringe of wispy gray hair. He walked forward, his rifle held in his left hand, his hat held before his chest with the other. Still, she didn't turn around. She was fearsome, what with her muttering and slamming, steam rising up out of a basin in front of her. He realized she was washing dishes and not cooking. Uh-oh, maybe it was too late.

He licked his lips and cleared his throat, and she spun on him, a wide carving blade held chest-high in her right hand. Her eyes gleamed narrow and fierce.

"Hold on there, ma'am. Nobody but ol' Bearpaw here!" He held up his hat in what he hoped would be taken as a friendly manner.

"What are you doing skulking up on a woman like that?"

"Skulking? No, no, stealth is my natural way. I'm fleet of foot and silent as a puma. It can't be helped, living as I do. But that's another story for another day. As to what

I am doing here, well ma'am, your fine establishment was recommended to me by a customer of yours as a place a fellow who hasn't seen a decent meal in a month or three might find."

She lowered the knife and looked him up and down. As she wiped stay hairs from her red brow with the back of her knife hand, she said, "You don't look as if you've missed too many meals lately, mister."

Before Bearpaw could voice a retort, she grinned and wagged the knife at a table to his right. "Set yourself down. I can only offer what's left over, though."

"Oh, that'd suit me just fine, just fine."

She slammed a few more dishes and pots out of her way and slid a skillet over on top of a massive black range.

"How'd you ever get that thing across the plains and mountains?" said Bearpaw, nodding toward the stove.

"Didn't."

"Huh?"

"Come by ship, then from Frisco to here!"

"Ah, well, if the food off that thing is half as good as it smells, I'm already a happy man."

"It'll fill you, anyway. But what you're smelling is the start of my stew for the supper crowd. Ain't ready yet."

"Oh." Bearpaw tried to hide his disappointment.

Not much more was said for the next few minutes while she heated up left over vittles from the lunch trade and piled them atop a tin plate. She carried it around the long work table and laid it in front of him. "Coffee? Tea?"

"I'd go for a cup of coffee, if you have it on the brew. Been weeks since I've had a proper cup. Been getting by on the last of my tea, with pine needles to top her off."

"That'll work."

He nodded and tucked under his beard the big red-and-white checked napkin she'd laid beside the plate of food. She'd wrapped a knife, fork, and spoon in it.

"Real steel utensils!" he said, holding them up. "I'm impressed. Been using my old wooden set, which are fine for the trail, but it's nice to pretend I'm civilized once in a while."

She smiled and set coffee before him. "I'd stay and chat but I have a mountain of dishes to work through."

"Soon as I gnaw my way through these vittles, I'll lend a hand if you'd like."

"A man in my kitchen? I think not. But I appreciate the offer. No, my help will be along shortly."

He nodded and chewed and slurped and smacked his lips and sliced and crammed, and before too long he'd cleared the platter of food. He'd barely had time to lean back and belch when she set two wedges of pie before him. His eyes boggled and she giggled as she fetched the coffee pot.

"As wolfish as you were on that plate full, I figured you could stuff in a little pie on top."

"Oh, yes, ma'am!"

"Apple, and a custard with raisins and spices. The recipe's a family secret and I'm sworn to secrecy."

The meat and potatoes and gravy and carrots and beans were more than passable fare, all dusted with cracked peppercorns. Lathered on top with butter had been two generous slices of toasted bread. But it was the pie, both flavors—he could not choose a favorite—that kept his eyes from doing anything but staying wide open. He savored each bite. When he thought she wasn't apt to turn around, he raised the plate and licked it clean. He lowered it to see her smiling at him, hands on her hips. and shaking her head.

"Oh, ah, ma'am. That was about the best meal I have ever had . . . and I have been all over this country, from way back East in Providence, where I dined with a skinny little man called himself the sultan of something or other, some place way off over two, three oceans. I'd saved him from stepping square in a fresh pile of green pony leavings in the street. He was wearing some sort of lady's slippers. I swear it's true."

He nodded his head with vigor. "By way of thanks, he treated me to a meal at a Hotel Diplomat, as I recall. It was delectable. I've et in Frisco at a grill on the docks. Fresh beefsteak with a mound of what the man called octopus or some such. It was an odd looking affair, but I'll try any-thing twice." He winked. "And to be fair, it was toothsome, I'll say that much."

He leaned back and stroked his belly, an impressive thing straining his buckskin tunic. "I've et in St. Louis, smack in the middle of this land. Place called Tupper's. More of a boarding house, but my word, that fat French fella who ran the kitchen knew his way around a fry pan, I tell you. And all those meals were what I'd call memory makers, yes, sir."

He nodded and sipped his coffee. "But this here?" He gestured with his two callused hands. "This fare beats them all and then some. And I'm not one prone to telling windies."

As he spoke he noticed Penelope Sweeney's already red color brightened to a crimson beneath her sweat-sheened cheeks. Soon she flapped her hands at him and left him to sip his freshly refilled coffee in peace. But he also noticed she kept looking over her shoulder at him.

Uh-oh, he thought. *Maybe I slathered it on a little thick.* He sipped the last of his coffee and looked again with sorrow at the empty, crumb-free plate that minutes before had held two slices of the best pie he had ever eaten. Some-thing about that custard piece was familiar.

He shrugged as it made no never mind. The pie was gone and he was full. No matter the woman's flittery eyes, they weren't going to keep him from returning for more pie. He felt certain he could keep her at arm's length and enjoy her culinary creations.

He shoved backward and stood, stretching and patting his belly once more. Snatching up his hat from the bench beside him and then his rifle, he walked to the front work table, digging out his coin purse. "Well now, Miss Sweeney. What's the tally on this fine feast?

"You know what?" she said, turning to face him.

"No, can't say I do. But I bet you're going to tell me!" He winked and tapped his nose.

"No charge today, Mr. Jones."

"But that's not right! Not fair to you!"

"Now, now, you don't worry about my business and I won't tell you how much a plew is worth come selling time." The entire time she spoke she was smiling.

Bearpaw felt gratitude and fear in equal measures. Time to skedaddle. "Well, I surely thank you , ma'am. I . . . I have to go tend my mule." He turned away, then half-regretting already, he turned back. "Eh, you wouldn't happen to know where a fellow can buy feed and some forage for a mule, would you?"

"Of course I do. Heck Whipple, down the lane to the left. Can't miss it. Big sign out front showing boot repair and such. He's also the closest thing we have to a feed seller. He'll fix you up."

"Oh, well that's right fine. Thank you, ma'am."

"Not at all. And if you need a place to graze your mule, I own the field out back. Only folks there now are in the back corner. A family with a passel of kids come on in last week or so."

"Well, that's doubly kind of you. I'll see how long I aim to be in town, but—" He edged to the open door behind him. "That's ah, mighty kind, ma'am." He made it through the flaps into the bright outdoors once more, then doffed his cap, and walking backward, nearly ran over a child standing in front of him.

"Hey, Mr. Jones!"

Bearpaw swung around, his fists balled and a fiery look in his eyes. "Who's tugging on my buckskins?"

"It's me, Shoshone Fitch Harrigan!" The lad looked up at the crusty old-timer.

Bearpaw held a hand to his eyes, visoring them, and scoped the surrounding terrain. "I don't see nothin' at all!"

"Down here!"

Bearpaw looked down and jumped back, his eyes wide. "Why . . . it can't be! I was expecting somebody, oh, about yay tall." He held a hand below Fitch's shoulder. "You can't be my old pal Fink!"

"Fitch! My name is Fitch, and yes I can, because I am him!"

Bearpaw bent down and rubbed knuckles in his eyes and then squinted right in Fitch's face. The boy stared back, not blinking.

"Well, I'll be a one-eared jackrabbit. If it ain't my old pal, Fippy!"

"Fitch! It's Fitch!"

"So it is, so it is." He hoisted the slight boy aloft. "How be ye, pardner? I hear tell you went native for a spell." He fingered the beads on the boy's tunic. "Mighty convincing, mighty convincing. I'd say you are near about the genuine article. You been keepin' well?" He set the lad down again.

"You bet I have." Fitch patted Bearpaw's gut. "Your belly got bigger since we saw you at the Shoshone camp."

"Oh, you notice that, too, huh?" Bearpaw rubbed both hands on it. "If I didn't know better, I'd say I was fixin' to whelp!" This struck him as a hot poker and he doubled over, smacking his thighs. Trail dust rose up from the man's buckskin trousers.

Meghan Harrigan stalked around the corner of the tent. "Fitch Harrigan! You're supposed to be— Mr. Jones!" she said, smiling.

He ambled forward and gave her a big hug, lifting her off her feet.

"You remember my bossy sister, Meg, don't you?"

"Naw, naw. I always hug strangers like I ain't seen them in forever! So what are you Harrigans doing here in"—he spun in a circle—"wherever here is?"

"Devil's Creek," said Meghan. "Papa got a job as a teamster and we're waiting for him to get back in a week or so. And Mama, well, she's cooking and baking and such."

"I don't doubt that, what with you Harrigans filling up every cranny on the frontier!!"

"No," said Fitch. "She means Mama's cooking here!" He pointed toward the interior of the tent Bearpaw had just emerged from.

"You don't say!" Bearpaw scratched his chin.

"Yes, I do say it." Fitch folded his arms.

"Miss Sweeney owns the place and needed help. So I'm taking care of the twins. Kane is supposed to be watching this one"—Meghan laid a hand on Fitch's head—"but he's gone off again looking at bugs or snakes or something. He's so odd."

"Your mama didn't happen to bake a pie in there lately, did she?"

"Sure she did!" shouted Fitch. "She bakes all Miss Sweeney's pies."

"Oh, I see. Now it's all less muddy than it was. Huh. Well, what say we go find a man about the price of a—" Bearpaw saw Fitch already over by Gravyfoot, the two of them staring at each other like they were communicating somehow. "Um, tell your mama I said howdy." Bearpaw winked at Meghan. "I'll drop back as soon as I have tended to Ol' Gravyfoot."

"Will do," she said, shouting to Fitch.

Bearpaw made his way over to the mule, who still didn't look pleased to be where she was, though she was showing interest in Fitch as the lad stroked her long nose.

Bearpaw grinned and chastised himself for feeling a little jealous that the boy had developed a bond with Ol' Gravyfoot.

CHAPTER 21

"Oh, you'll like this next town," said Pardo, over campfire coffee that night.

"Why is that?" said Mack, wiping out the last of the grease in the skillet. As the employee, he shouldered in an unspoken way more of the burden of camp chores. Which suited him just fine.

He was no great hand at cookery, but Pardo was downright awful at the task, something Mack found out early on in their travels. He didn't think it was an act on Pardo's part to get Mack to take on the task, but with Pardo Zinski, one never knew what was about to happen next.

It had been an interesting week. He'd seen a whole lot of the countryside, met folks—happy, surly, and lots in between—and most of all, he had gained a new friend in Zinski, despite their odd meeting.

"The town's a bustler, to be sure. Goes by the name of Watts Corner. I bet you don't know where they got the name, do you?" Pardo grinned and stretched his legs, wiggling his unbooted toes that were poking through the holes in his wool socks.

"Well, if I had to guess, I'd say someone named Watts settled there some time ago and it so happened to be at a cross roads. Perhaps he planted himself on what became a corner lot?"

"Ha! Wrong, I tell you. Wrong. See, here's how it happened. This fella Watts—"

"So I was partially right!"

"Okay, okay, but not by much! Now, are you going to let me get back to my story or am I going to have to leave you in suspense all night?"

"Oh, gosh, please don't do that," said Mack, grinning and settling down on his side of the fire.

"Good. So here's what happened. Watts—don't know his first name, not that it matters, it doesn't affect the story in any way."

"You remind me of someone," said Mack.

"Oh? Who's that?"

"A mountain man of our acquaintance named Bearpaw Jones."

"Huh. Never met the man. So this Watts fella, he camped there for the night and come morning decided he might as well do a little digging thereabouts before he went on his way. He got out his tools and stumped off into the hillside above his camp and saw what looked to be a promising vein of ore back behind a couple of boulders."

Zinski shook his head at the thought of it. "Instead of climbing around, which would have taken him a few minutes more, he ducked down and crawled down between those boulders. Why, he couldn't believe his eyes! Right before him was a fine vein of ore. So he reached back through the gap he'd crawled through and grabbed hold of his spade and pick and yarned them back to him.

"Well sir, here's where it gets interesting." Pardo leaned forward. "Watts, he somehow, and I know it don't make no sense but this is how it was told to me, he got his arm—it was his left—wedged. He dropped the tools and tugged and tugged, and made the situation worse by the second. After a fashion, not being all that stupid in the head, if you know what I mean, he caught on and shoved instead of pulling. That didn't help neither. He had himself a good think, then. And as he did, he noticed a sound behind him." Pardo paused and sipped his coffee, looking at Mack over the rim of the cup.

"Well? What happened?"

"Got you interested, didn't I?"

"Yep."

"Good. So anyway, ol' Watts, he wiped the sweat from his eyes and looked back behind him as best he could, given his situation. And he saw a rattler sliding out of the shadows just below that vein of ore. Almost as if it was protecting it." Pardo nodded. "He had left his rifle back at camp, which wasn't but a hundred feet down below him. Along with his donkey and all his supplies and goods. The one thing he did have on him was his knife. So he moved slow and easy and managed to slide that big ol' skinning blade out of its sheath. And he waited and waited. But do you know what that big bull snake did?"

"Nope."

"Well I'm about to tell you! It sat there, just out of Watts's reach . . . and it dozed off."

"How could he tell it was asleep?"

Pardo looked at Mack as if he had grown a second head. "On account of all the snoring!"

"Uh-huh." Mack didn't have all that much experienced with snakes, but he strongly suspected they did not snore. "Okay, then, what happened after that? Did Watts get his arm free?"

"Sure he did. It seems after a while, that snoozy snake caused Watts himself to relax. And when he did that, his arm sort of went to sleep, too, and he was able to jerk it on out of that crack. He kept his eyes on that snoring snake and backed on out of there, careful not to wake it. Then he grabbed up his tools and scampered down the hill to his camp. He snatched up his rifle and went back to the spot, his only thought was that vein of ore above the snake. But when he got there the snake was gone, never to be seen again. Then he did the thing he should have done in the first place and climbed up and around to get at the ore. Turns out it wasn't nothing special, after all."

"So then what happened?" said Mack.

"What do you mean? Ain't that enough for you?" Pardo shook his head. "Some folks are mighty hard to please, I tell ya."

Mack thought for a moment, then said, "So where did the word Corner come from?"

"Oh," Pardo drained the coffee in his cup. "No idea. You'll have to ask him."

"Ask him?"

"Yeah, we'll see him tomorrow. Watts is the assayer in town. 'Night." Pardo rolled over and tugged his blanket up over his shoulder.

Mack sat there staring at the last of the fire's flames and shaking his head. What an odd story, and what an odd man. He doubted he'd forget either for years to come.

The next day just before noon, found them rolling into a prosperous little scene Mack would say was more town than mine camp. Watts Corner was, on the face of it, a prosperous town with the intention of going in an even more prosperous direction. The numerous construction projects underway confirmed it.

It seemed all business types could be found on the modest but packed-to-the-rim main street—a dry goods store, a feed shop, a butcher, hardware, cobbler and leather goods maker, a tobacconist, and all manner of variations on a general mercantile theme. Mack even saw a shop with maps, writing utensils, and a one-sheet newspaper, all under the same roof.

Farther on, there were not one but three places of worship, and above it all floated the heavy, heady scents of food frying, broiling, and baking. Out of instinct, he rubbed his belly.

Pardo interrupted his reverie. "I take it from your silence it's been a while since you've been anywhere civilized. This is about as close as you'll get in these parts. Much of it is because of that man there," he nodded to their left and smiled.

Mack saw a slight returning nod from a tall, rangy fellow with an unflinching gaze emanating out of eyes the blue of river ice.

He watched the men and their wagon roll past as he stood on the wooden boardwalk, fingers hooked in his vest pockets, a tall black hat, neatly brushed, atop his silvered head. His face wore combed, voluminous dragoon moustaches. He was clad in a black frock coat and his long black trousers were tucked neatly into gleaming black stovepipe boots with dogear flaps.

And yet Mack found three things far more curious about the man's appearance than his general impressive overall look. The first was the gun belt he wore. It, too, was made of polished black leather, and visible beneath the parted coat was a plain silver buckle. Bullets were looped above in the belt itself. The bottom of a sheathed pistol hung below the coat's hem on the man's right side.

The second curious thing he noticed was the brass star on the man's left coat lapel. A law man. Somehow the occupation, and whatever attendant title it carried in the wee burg, suited the serious-gazed stranger. The third oddity, and the most surprising of all, was the white collar riding on the man's throat. A holy man.

A law man and a holy man. Mack had never seen the like.

Once they slowly rumbled past, he could still feel the man's steel gaze pinned to his back as if the man had a telescope trained on him.

Pardo seemed to know what Mack was thinking. He spoke without leaning over, as if he were afraid to speak while still in sight of the man. "His name's Pastor Rainey. He came along shortly after Watts established himself here and Rainey has been overseeing the growth of this place since. Some folks don't like him, say he's too hard, but there's no denying he keeps a tight lid on things. It's allowed Watts Corner to grow as clean and straight as it has.

"Anybody gets out of hand, he gives them fair warning and then he drops them. Interesting. They say he's a square dealer as long as you treat him the same. I expect in life we can't ask for more than that, eh, Mr. Harrigan?"

"That's a fact." Mack risked a look over his left shoulder, and though they'd traveled quite a ways up the street, he saw the preaching lawman still staring at them. It was unnerving.

"Okay. Enough cowering in the presence of the Almighty's earthly representative." Pardo smiled. "Or at least the one here in Watts Corner. We have a wagon to unload, then load up again. Then we find a meal. No offense, Harrigan. You're a solid trail cook, but I've had too many decent feeds in this town to ignore the possibility today."

"And after that?" said Mack.

"After that? Why, after that, we turn around and head back to Devil's Creek. Two quick stops on the route, but that's it. It's a lower roadway that loops eastward. We should be back in three, four days. How does that suit you?"

"Just fine," said Mack smiling. He'd been thinking they were going to return the same way they'd arrived. While it had been a pretty route, and offered a whole lot of time for him to learn about the world of freighting, it had been a long trip. He was ready to see Ell and the children. Ready to hug them all. "Any time for me to make a few inquiries?"

Pardo laughed and shook his head. "You don't give up, do you? I reckon if ever there was a town where they might have heard of this famous uncle Zeke, it will be here in Watts Corner. What say while I unload this"—he jerked a thumb over his shoulder at their laden tarped load—"you go on ahead and scout for sign of your long-lost uncle. We'll meet in an hour at Millie's Cafe, that place yonder." He nodded up a side street that ended with a wooden structure. Red curtains hung in windows flanking a red door.

"I know what you're thinking," continued Pardo. "It might look like a brothel, but it's a restaurant first, last, and in between. That woman makes the best, thickest, chunkiest, tastiest stew a man is ever likely to eat. With dumplings floating atop a big ol' bowl. Why, it's unforgettable. And cakes and pies . . . oh my, my."

"I look forward to that, Pardo, but I can't leave you to unload and then load the wagon on your own."

"Oh, didn't I tell you? Griff's depot has a couple of fellows who do all the work of lifting, unloading, and loading. I like to keep an eye to make sure nothing goes off kilter. They're Cuthbert Griffin's sons, Rupert and Dale. Not the sharpest knives, but they're muscled up and know enough to keep from damaging the goods and the wagons."

"Well, if you're certain, then that sounds great. Any place you suggest I begin?"

Pardo scratched his chin. "You could do worse than to ask over at the assay office."

"Oh, isn't that—"

"Yep, Watts himself. What he doesn't know about his town ain't worth knowing."

They negotiated around a side lane that led to a low warehouse with a loading dock out front. The sign atop the low porch to one side read, GRIFFIN AND SONS FREIGHT DEPOT. As if to emphasize the point, two broad-shouldered young men, perhaps in their early twenties, stepped out a door and onto the dock.

Mack saw why they were perfect for the task of loading and unloading wagons. They were indeed muscled, and looked at him with the placid but kind faces of grazing steers.

Behind them they were followed by a short, thin man whose hands moved at twice the speed of the rest of him, up and down, side to side, as if he did not know what to emphasize first, the boys, the dock, or the newcomers. He smiled. "Pardo Zinski! Welcome! Welcome back."

"Thanks, Griff. Mighty good to be back. This here's my new help, Mack Harrigan. Mack? This here's Cuthbert Griffin."

The birdlike man shoved his way between the two large young men, paused between them, and raised his arms as if he were about to hug them. "These here are my boys, Rupe and Dale."

Mack hopped from the wagon onto the dock and touched his hat brim. "It's a pleasure to make your acquaintance, Mr. Griffin, and you two, too, Rupert and Dale."

They all seemed impressed with Mack's manners.

"Well." After checking the wagon's brake and looping the lines around the long handle, Pardo followed suit in climbing onto the loading dock,. "Mack's got some inquiries to make while we get down to business here."

"Millie's, in an hour," Mack said to Pardo.

"Don't be late. I may eat the place clean!"

As he strode away, Mack heard Griffin say, "Can't go wrong with Millie's cooking!" That sounded good to him.

He asked one stout older woman the way to Watts assay office and she smiled, offered a quick bow with her head and shoulders, then nodded again and looked past Mack's left shoulder. He turned to see a sign telling him he'd found the very place.

"Thank you, ma'am." He returned her slight bow with one of his own and that blushed the woman. She smiled and bustled away.

Turning, Mack saw the preacher lawman, Pastor Rainey, eyeing him through narrowed lids from the other side of the road. Mack offered the man a smile and nod, but received nothing but more staring in reply.

Mack's smile slipped as he turned and entered the assay office.

"Oh, don't mind him," said Watts. "Rainey glares at everybody new in town. It's his way of putting his particular fear into you." He winked. "Has it worked?"

"I can't say I'm afraid of him, but I do feel odd being stared at by the man."

"Then he's accomplished what he wanted to, I guess." Watts chuckled. "Now, let's see, I haven't heard of any Ezekiel Harrigan or Zeke Harrigan, but I think I have heard the Harrigan name."

That sounded vaguely promising to Mack, though he was quick to point out it was not an uncommon name.

"It was in one of these ledgers." Watts ran a fingertip

down the spines of a stack of books, the top one wearing a light film of dust. "I had occasion to look in these a month or two back for someone and happened to see the name Harrigan, I think. Or something like it. Hmm." He pulled out book after book and ran that same finger down one long list of names after another.

"Are they all folks with claims?"

"Oh, some of them. Some of them just the same ones over and over. It's my way of keeping track of who gets what assayed and when. Ah . . ."

Mack felt a mild twinge of excitement.

"Nope. Not this one."

"Oh, I don't want you to go to any more trouble on my behalf, Mr. Watts."

"Pish posh. It's a quiet day. What else do I have to do?"

It was plain to Mack the man was snowed under with assaying work, as samples were stacked on every surface in the room, it seemed.

As Watts flicked through another book, he grunted, then without warning he spun the book around so Mack could read it. "See that name there?"

Mack squinted and bent close to the line. For a full-sun afternoon, he noticed how dark the office was. How on earth did the man get any work done in there?

Watts sensed his trouble, cranked the wheel on his oil lamp, and set it on the counter beside the book. There, on the page, Mack saw his own name.

He held his breath, confused and surprised, and traced his finger along the line. "But this . . . this is my name."

"What?" Watts craned his head and read it aloud. "Macknith? Macknith Harrison?"

"No, Mackworth. Mackworth Harrigan." Then an idea came to him. "Here, I'll show you." He tugged out his uncle's letters, bound by the same crossed wraps of twine that had held them all the way from Ohio, the same wraps he'd tied and untied too many times to count, looking for clues as to where his uncle Zeke might be.

"See? Right there, that's my name." He pointed to the name on the outside of one letter, where it had been folded in on itself, leaving the small blank square enough space to write Mack's name and address in Ohio. "Uncle Zeke sent this to me. And this one, and this—All these letters." He spread the wad of letters on the countertop.

Watts whistled. "Well look here. That's the same writing as on the line."

Mack looked and sure enough the hand was similar, and in some places, identical to his uncle's writing. Had to be him who wrote the line out. "Do all the folks lodging claims write their own particulars in here?"

"Sometimes. A while back I had an assistant. Before he caught gold fever himself. Anyway, he was lazy. I can't imagine that trait works too well while out prospecting." Watts shook his head and picked up one of Mack's letters. "Sure does look like his writing all right." He handed the letter back.

"What does it mean?"

"Well, it's plain what it means."

"It is?"

"Sure! Your uncle Zeke has filed a claim in your name. That's what it means."

"What?"

"Yep, makes sense to me, it does. It's not uncommon for folks to put claims in other folks's names. Usually family members. That way they can get more digging in."

"Oh, well, is it a good one? How do I find it? What do I do? Is there a fee?"

"Hold on, hold on. Let me look it up. See those numbers? That tells me the location, maps, all of it."

The pendulum clock on the wall chimed two and Mack said, "Uh-oh, I'm supposed to meet Pardo at Millie's Cafe. I'm late."

"You better get to it, son. Pardo won't wait. Once he's loaded up his belly as full as his wagon, he'll rumble on out of here. You wouldn't be the first of his side men to be stranded. Besides, Millie's food is too good to miss out on."

"So I've heard."

"I'll find the paper on this claim of yours and sketch out a crude map. Run back here before you leave town and I'll have it for you."

"Really? You'd do that?"

"Sure thing. Any friend of Pardo's is a friend of mine."

Mack turned to the door, then stopped. "A last question, Mr. Watts."

The man looked at him, eyebrows raised.

"Do snakes snore?"

The man tapped his nose with a long finger and bent back to the book.

Mack left the cluttered, dim assay office and as he closed the door behind him, he swore he heard a chuckle from within.

CHAPTER 22

All Mack's kind but persistent powers of conversational persuasion did not sway Pardo Zinski one smidgen from departing Watts Corner any later than he intended. And certainly not in spending an overnight in the town so Mack might be able to sniff around and find clues as to the possible whereabouts of his uncle Zeke.

Mack missed Ell's cooking, but Millie's was a close second, though he would not tell Ell so. He bolted down what was truly tasty fare, deserving of the praise it had received then left the eatery and ran back to Watts's assay office, where the man gave him a copy of the claim paper and a rough map. Watts told him the claim was but a few miles from town, in a wide ravine with a stream cutting through its base.

Beyond that, Watts couldn't recall, but he did say it sure was a likely spot for promising ore. "Keep in mind, I've never really struck a big lode myself. But I sure found a whole lot of likely spots!"

Mack shook the man's hand, thanked him, promised to return, then ran back to the depot, hoping Pardo wasn't in the act of abandoning him.

He was. In fact, Pardo had turned the team and was making for the main street proper when Mack churned up alongside. "Hey!" he said, half smiling. "You going to leave me here?"

Pardo shrugged. "Isn't that what you want?"

"Not like this, it isn't."

"Then hop on before you lose your wind!"

After a mile on the trail heading homeward, he gave up trying to persuade Pardo of sticking around town for a bit. It was unfair of him to ask, but after learning of the claim deeded to him, Mack hated to leave and not know more about it. Ideally, he'd be able to explore the region for a few days, but that was most definitely out of the question

A few miles later, they were making for a well-used cut road that led to their homeward route.

Ah well. At least I'm returning home to my heart's desire. Could be much worse, and has been at times, he mused.

The information, scant as it was, burned a hole in his inner coat pocket. But he didn't dare pull it out. His job was to ride shotgun. They'd swap driving duties in a few hours.

"Did Watts give you the papers you told me of at lunch?"

"Sure did," said Mack, patting his coat.

"Well, I bet good money you're aching to pull them out and give them a read." Pardo looked at him, smiling. "Go ahead. This is a quiet stretch. Still too close to town for anyone to dare risk getting on the preaching lawman's rough side."

"It can wait."

Pardo shrugged. "Suit yourself."

And Mack did try to wait. A full minute passed, then he said, "Oh, all right. I guess one little read-through can't hurt."

Much to his disappointment, other than a few numbers and compass bearing way marks, there wasn't much more information to be gleaned from the pages. The true test would be to visit the claim, naturally. He folded then stuffed the papers back into his pocket. "Not much to be learned from them."

"Oh." Pardo jiggled and jostled in the seat and that was all that was said for several hours.

Mack sensed it was time to cool the team and take a break. Pardo was fond of his coffee, as was Mack, and it had become a fine ritual. On the days they had the time, they kindled a small fire to heat whatever leftover food they had from the previous evening's fare, and brewed up a pot of strong, thick coffee, which stood them well for the remainder of the long, hot, dusty afternoon on the trail. Today, he hoped, would be no different.

Looking ahead, he saw one last decline to make for and leaned out as the roadway curved to the right between and beyond two massive boulders. It's almost like a gate. He hoped the land beyond it leveled off and wished for a source of clear water, perhaps a stream or small river. He glanced at Pardo, who wore his usual there-but-not-there look on his face, eyes open, but for all that the man could well have been asleep.

"Long hours on the trail do that to a man," Pardo had said more than once.

As they rounded the curve between the steep stone faces, Mack glanced up toward both sides, tensing for a possible ambush. It seemed a likely spot for such.

By the time they emerged from the short turn though the rock, the sun blasted down at them once more, luckily from behind. What he didn't expect was commotion down low on the road. Something had spooked the team.

The horses, usually steadfast and well settled in with a load by that time on a day's run, whinnied and jerked. Pardo half rose in his seat, trying to spy ahead to whatever had caused the commotion.

Ready to jump down to scout, Mack realized it was too tight a fit between the wagon and the last of the rock wall to his right. He might well get run over should he slip.

And in the next few seconds, he was glad he hadn't jumped down, for the horses, despite Pardo's sawing on the lines, grew even more agitated, then they lunged into a stomping gallop. Pardo barked orders and growled blue oaths at them, but nothing seemed to reach them. He jerked back hard on the lines, but it did nothing. The horses had bolted. They churned forward, dust boiling up around and before them in a great mass of choking clouds.

In the next instant, Mack saw a black blur race by his side of the wagon. And then he was swallowed by dust. Given the choking dust, it was impossible to see the roadway, narrow and pocked with holes and jags of half-buried rocks at the best of times.

"Hold on, Mack!" shouted Pardo as the horses broke into a full-bore gallop.

Mack did just that, his right hand gripping tight around the steel support of the armrest. Stuffing the shotgun by their feet, he reached with his left arm to help Pardo yank back on the lines.

"Won't do any good!" shouted Pardo. "They've gone mad!"

And then, Mack heard Pardo shout, "Oh no! No, no, no!"

He felt why. The wagon began tipping to the left. And it kept going.

Mack and Pardo leaned to the right to help slow the coming rollover. It didn't.

Though they were still barreling forward, their momentum was slowed by the new unforeseen catastrophe. So far they'd been sliding sideways down what felt like a long steep embankment. They saw flashes of pine trees and rocks; heard those same trees snapping as they slammed

into them; and heard the screams of horses. Some of them
pinched out as if silenced by a mighty giant's hand.
Moment by moment seemed to unspool as if time had
slowed.

In addition to the creaking and groaning, wood and
metal twisting, horses whinnying and thrashing, Mack
heard the sounds of the crates ripping apart and smashing
open and realized the wagon was about to roll over completely onto its left side, Pardo's side. They would be
thrown clear or crushed in the wreckage.

Pardo shouted, "Jump for it! Jump!"

Mack sensed his boss had somehow managed to take his
own advice. How, he knew not. But Pardo was no longer
beside him.

The wagon let out a crushing, cracking, shrieking groan
of wood and steel being twisted and ripped apart. Then it's
right side, Mack's side, rose up, up, up into the air.

Mack shoved himself up onto its top edge, once the
right side, and leapt what he hoped was uphill. He hit the
slope and smacked hard on his face. Something dropped
down with a mighty thud beside him, clouting him on the
head at the same time. Light and dust clouded his vision,
which begin to dim, in, out, in, out, then . . . blackness,
and out.

CHAPTER 23

"'Twas a stroke of luck your ma letting you accompany me to the rendezvous and all."

Kane nodded, looking once more at his traveling companion. He could scarcely believe it himself. Here he was, still sixteen years old, heading to a trapper's meet up with a genuine trapping mountain man, the likes of which he'd only heard of until they'd met Bearpaw Jones back in St. Louis on their way west. That seemed a hundred years before.

The two men, one young, lean, and barely able to call himself a man, and the other a round-bellied older fellow in buckskins and walking alongside his mule, were traveling northwest for a short jaunt into the mountains to meet with other mountain men of Bearpaw's acquaintance.

"It took some doing," said Kane. "But between you and Miss Sweeney, Mom was convinced. Mostly, though it was me who wasn't so sure. I was afraid of breaking the promise I made to Pa."

"How's that?" said Bearpaw.

"I told him I'd take care of Mom and the children."

"Oh, sure. I hear you. But I think they're safe. What with moving the wagon close to the rear of Miss Sweeney's tent and all. Why, your Ma's just out back of the kitchen now."

"And then there's Mr. Conroy," said Kane. "He's been helping with the clean up since the restaurant's gotten so busy. Plus, I think he's sweet on Miss Sweeney."

Bearpaw's eyes narrowed. When he spoke, his tone was darker. "And that's another thing. What a woman like Miss Penelope Sweeney sees in that one-legged, demented old swamp rat, I'll never know. Spends half his time exploring the innards of a bottle of corn liquor and the other half reeking of sweat and mewling about for vittles in exchange for paltry chores."

Kane smiled. "Oh, I don't think he's as bad as all that. He always seems sober enough when I see him."

The mountain man snorted, but said nothing.

"Plus, he's good with a gun. He was showing me and Fitch how to draw and fire in quick motion."

"Trickery, nothing but. I've seen more talented monkeys in circuses."

Kane said nothing, but knew that while it was true Mr. Conroy did like his gargle, as he called it, he was devoted to Miss Sweeney and protective of the womenfolk, as he referred to Ma, Meghan, and of course, Miss Sweeney.

Still, as helpful as that was, it was the fact that the rendezvous was only a minor one, more of a small gathering of old-timer trappers swapping stories more than anything else. And it was only going to be a one-day journey, one night spent there, and another day back.

Ell had pulled Kane aside and hinted that he might be doing Mr. Jones a favor, since he was older and not as nimble as he used to be. Kane doubted that, but appreciated this mother had tried to make his departure, even for so short a trip, as if it was going to be no great hardship to her.

"Mr. Jones?"

"Bearpaw."

"Oh, right. Um, Bearpaw?"

"Yes, Kane?"

"May I ask you why you walk beside Gravyfoot instead of ride her?"

The mountain man hid a smile and nodded. "You may ask, yes."

A moment passed, then Kane said, "Oh, right. Um, so why do you—?"

Bearpaw let out a belly laugh and smacked his thigh. "I'm just funnin' you, boy! I heard you the first time. Well, it's like this. Ol' Gravyfoot, I figure, is about my age, more or less, in mule years. Don't ask me how I know. I just know. Anyways, I figure that at my age I wouldn't much like anybody climbing aboard my back and digging their boots into my belly."

At that he rubbed a gnarled old hand over his drum-tight buckskin tunic as if he were a woman close to birthing. "No sir, Gravyfoot don't need the headache, nor the backache. Besides"—Bearpaw hopped in place into a short-lived, impromptu jig—"how else am I going to keep in such fine condition? Why, six nights a week, I can still dance the toes off any lassie who dares to try me!"

Kane grinned. "What do you do on the seventh?"

Bearpaw looked up at him and grinned, then tapped his nose. "A fella don't share all he's up to, now do he?"

Kane's cheeks bloomed red and Bearpaw let out another lusty bawl of laughter.

They rode and walked in silence for a while, then the mountain man said, "I expect you'll want to know a little about what we're headed for."

Kane nodded but kept his mouth closed. He didn't want to interrupt the man when he was about to tell him something secret and sacred.

"Well, son, a trapper's rendezvous is just what it sounds like."

Kane waited, but Bearpaw didn't continue. The youth almost cleared his throat when the man began chatting again.

"Truth is this ain't going to be like the rendezvous of old, where you'd have piles of folks, squaw men and such, their half-blood babies running around everywhere, everybody having a grand old time, trading plews for supplies, some money, mostly gear and food enough to head back into the hills.

"What money was left over, we'd wager on games of chance long into the nights, liquored up and such. Sometimes you'll get fellows who don't do so well when they're in that way, and they'll get to wrasslin'. Soon enough one of them pulls out a skinning knife, then the other does, and pretty soon they're cutting on each other. Women are screaming and babies are howling and critters are stamping and running loose. Oh, it's a mess. Usually somebody's dead by morning. The other soul's regretful, if he's still there."

"Where else would he be?" said Kane.

"Run off in the night! You gut a man, you sober up right quick, and you don't question the notion that come morning a whole lot of other folks are going to do the same for you, just to balance the scales. So you skedaddle."

"Did you ever do that?" Kane regretted saying it as soon as if fell out of his mouth.

If he was offended, Bearpaw didn't show it. "Naw, I never took to fighting like that. Oh, a brawl or two in my youth, but them who we're going to meet up with, my friends, they're all like me. We had sense enough in our younger years to keep our knives sheathed and keep our liquor to sipping and swapping lies, nothing more."

They were quiet awhile, then Kane said, "Can you tell me what it's like? To live out in the mountains alone? What sort of things did you see? I mean things we don't see hereabouts."

"Oh, so you want to know about the lonely camp, do you?" Bearpaw nodded and lit his clay pipe, which he'd been tamping a nugget of tobacco down into. He puffed and then said, "First thing you got to know is that it's not all that lonely . . . if you're the right sort of mind, that is." He tapped his temple with the pipe stem.

"And how do you know that?"

"Oh, you got to be happy being alone. No, it's more than that. You got to prefer being alone. And then it'll be all right. Also you got to not mind killing critters and skinning them out. It's gruesome work. Sometimes it's like skinning out little people, so human do some of them begin to look to you."

Kane sat tight-lipped. That was the part of the trapping lifestyle he didn't much care for—the trapping.

"I don't suppose there's any call for someone to be out in the wilderness just sort of—"

"Living out there, do you mean, son?" Bearpaw glanced at him, hiding a slight smile in his gray beard. "Well, now, there might be. There just might be. You know a whole lot of folks from the trapping line of work went into other lines. They've guided folks, travelers and such, through treacherous terrain. But that of course means they have had to scout that land themselves beforehand.

"And you got to know how to get along in the woods, the prairies, all of it. There's no hiding from Mama Nature. She will seek you out and she will find where your weakness is and she will burrow in there until you're froze to death or run naked and raving into the hills never to be heard from again!"

Kane swallowed and nodded.

"But don't let me scare you. There's plenty of room out there for a fella such as yourself."

"What do you mean?"

"I mean, I know you are the sort who goes around sketching and rummaging and trying to identify everything you see out on the trail. Am I wrong?"

"No sir."

"Darn right, I'm not wrong. Why, I bet you have been hankering to draw pictures of half the things we've seen while I've been limping along here and yammering. Am I wrong?"

"No sir."

"Darn right! And go ahead. I don't mind. Why, I think the talent you have is downright valuable."

"You do?"

"Sure I do. Without folks such as yourself, who'd be able to show folks back East and in foreign lands the wonders we get to enjoy seeing every day!"

Their conversation unraveled along those lines for a number of hours.

Before Kane knew it, and with plenty hours of light left of the day, they arrived at the rendezvous grounds. They heard it long before they saw it. And with each step, Bearpaw and Ol' Gravyfoot moved forward even quicker.

CHAPTER 24

It was the song of a bird, he knew not what sort, that aroused Mack from the darkness within his head. Kane would know what bird that was, Mack thought, then tasted gravel, sand, and dirt, as if he had been packed full of it. As if someone had jerked open his mouth and used a sugar scoop to fill his gullet with sand and grit and dirt and rocks. He coughed.

He remembered where he was, what had happened, the wreck of the wagon. Something had spooked the team, and Pardo had . . .

Pardo? Pardo! But he had jumped free, as had Mack, when the wagon began rolling down the embankment.

Hadn't he?

Even before he forced his eyes open, Mack tried to shout his friend's name, but nothing came out save for a croaking, gasping cough. It took all his strength to move his arms and legs. They didn't seem to want to do his bidding. He tried harder and felt his right arm move. It didn't feel broken. The left . . . the same.

He dragged them closer from their outflung positions and tried to get his palms beneath him. It worked, but it was slow-going. The entire time he kept trying to empty his mouth of gravel and sand and whatever else he'd swallowed. Then saying his friend's name, over and over, increasing in loudness as he could.

Finally, he was able to somewhat shout the name Pardo, and shoved himself up and over, onto his backside. The slope with the downhill edge beneath his heels told him he had jumped and landed uphill of the wreck.

What he next saw confirmed the worst that could have happened had indeed happened.

Twenty yards below him lay the overturned wagon. Or what was left of it. Mack's side of the wagon was dug into the far downhill slope. Only one of the four thick wheels was seemingly whole. The others had snapped in dozens of places, the spokes jutting like the fingers of a counting child.

No dust sullied the scene. To the right of the wagon Mack saw the huge shapes of grit-matted, unmoving horses. A tangle of harnesses and traces and the remnants of the bulky freighting wagon's tongue lay snarled and ripped and clotted, all at impossible angles.

The full and horrific predicament began to reveal itself to him. The foolish horses had been spooked by something, and they bolted. As they charged, blinded by fear, the trailing wagon swayed and skidded. The wheels must have caught, mired in softer soil too close, far too close to the steep edge of the ravine top.

And they were hours from a town or mine camp. His vision, which had been a blurred, wavery thing, slowly began to come back to him. How long had he been unconscious?

He shifted to look upslope, but did so too quickly. Again, his head thudded like a cannonade, his eyes felt as if they were about to be shoved outward, kicked from his skull by an angry, coarse little man wreaking menace in his skull.

Mack closed his eyes and waited for his aching head to settle down, then slit them open once more. The roadway was far above, perhaps a hundred feet, perhaps more. The embankment was steep, steeper than he could have imagined. It seemed obvious then, from his dizzying spot on the slope, that a heavy, fully laden freight wagon and four-horse team, could never survive such a tumble. Or could it?

The foolish folly of what he'd just thought came to him. Of course, they had not survived it. All about him, above and below, the wreckage lay strewn. The ripped planks of crates, the popped barrels of what looked to have been gunpowder, and slashed sacks of corn meal and flour, all of it and more lay in jagged tatters.

He slowly turned back to face downslope and knew he had to get down to the wagon, had to find Pardo. On his backside, he shoved himself downslope, raising dust and sending random bits of gravel and rock sliding down ahead of him.

Nothing in or around the wreckage below moved.

Though it ached his head, Mack resumed his shouts. "Pardo! Pardo!"

He shoved himself downslope, a yard or so at a time, pausing to let his reeling head settle before resuming his efforts. In one of the pauses, he saw something that confused him.

Below him, but still upslope of the wrecked wagon by twenty feet or so sat a dog-size hunch of brown-black hair. His mind began working up potential solutions. Perhaps it was some grisly part of one of the horses, ripped off in the fall.

Perhaps it was an entire horse, since he had only seen three of the four beasts, buried somehow in the sliding rubble? None of it made sense. He slid down farther and passed the thing well off to his right.

The closer he drew to the wagon, the more awed by the twisted mess he became. Still, he scooched closer and glanced back once at the dark, hairy thing. Then he saw it for what it was—a bear cub, perhaps the cause of the spooked horses—and recalled he had glimpsed something dark seeming to race by them, perhaps away from them, just before they were about to depart the roadway.

The thing was perhaps a few months old, certainly born that spring, but it would never see a second spring, nor another day. Its head lay at an odd angle, its snout open and crushed, and blood and tongue and bone lay exposed. The sight gripped Mack's innards in a fierce, cold fist.

His renewed thought was for Pardo. If this could happen to a bear cub, there was no telling what might happen to a man caught in the wreckage. He hastened as quickly as the landscape and his throbbing head allowed, calling his friend's name over and over.

He had to believe Pardo had somehow leapt free of the tumbling mess, just as Mack had done. Pardo was no fool. He was an experienced teamster and might even have been in wrecks before. Mack held to any thought with a hopeful edge.

To the left lay the wagon's tailgate, long since ripped free. Only one chain of it remained, hanging limp from a shard of wood. The bottom of the wagon faced upward and away from him, held in the leaning pose by a cluster of two stout pines. As he approached the wagon, he also noticed that beyond the wreck, the downslope led steep for what looked to be hundreds of feet, the trees growing thicker the farther down he looked.

He bet a creek was splashing away down at the bottom. What he wouldn't give for a dunk in a clear, cold stream just then.

As he slid closer, more cautious lest he lose his footing

and begin tumbling toward certain doom, he kept up with shouting his friend's name, pausing and cocking an ear, only to hear little more than stones and gravel continue on their way downward.

One more slide down and he was even with the end of the wagon. Mack reached up and grasped the hanging chain to help guide him around the wagon's corner. The entire thing shifted. Wood and steel squawked and the trees against which the wagon had lodged shuddered.

He held still and waited to see what would happen next. Nothing. He carefully let go of the chain and waited. It appeared to have settled more solidly against the trees. Or perhaps that was in his mind, wishing for more than what was before his eyes.

Looking up at the wreck above him, he whispered, "Okay," and scuttled around the wagon. With the bulk of the thing above him, Mack did his best to ignore it and kept up his loud, urgent whispering of "Pardo! Pardo?"

Carefully he crab walked sideways to his left, along the length of the wagon. There, in the half shade, he saw Pardo Zinski. The man was wedged beneath part of the seat and part of the side of the wagon, planking that had cracked and sprung. His legs poked out and downhill and he lay faceup, his arms by his side.

Even from several feet away Mack saw that something bad had happened to the man. A barrel-chested fellow, his robust breast and rib cage looked to be half its height.

Mack scuttled close and peered in. To his great relief, the planks he'd assumed pressed tight to Pardo's body were somehow not touching him. As far as Mack could see, no part of the wagon was resting heavily on the man. He might be able to get him out of there.

He leaned even closer in when one of the planks moved.

Mack raised it and gently lifted the plank. It came free and sunlight angled in, lighting his friend's face.

"Pardo? Pardo!" Mack gently patted the man's bloody cheek. A cut to the forehead had caused blood to trail down the right side of his upturned face. Mack did not expect him to be alive, but a thin, slight wheeze trickled from Pardo's mouth.

"Pardo!" Mack smoothed the man's brow with a grimy hand. "Pardo, can you hear me?"

"Uh . . ." Again, the response was so quiet.

Mack looked into the wreckage and saw that the wooden canteen they'd carried behind the seat was in there. "Hang on, Pardo. I'm going to get you a cool drink. Hang on." His fingertips brushed it, then it rolled away from him. Unlacing his sheath knife, he reached in and jammed the point into its wooden side. Coaxing it over a jag of jutting wood, his relief when the canteen rested in his hand was short lived.

The canteen had been popped open along one side, fortunately along the top, but Mack could tell by its heft there was still water in it. The wood was wet and would soon leach out. With care he peeled apart the damaged wood and saw enough water to wet Pardo's lips and give him a trickle of a drink.

Holding it over the man's mouth, he gently poured. "Pardo, a cool drink for you. Easy now, easy."

The touch of the water on his lips revived the teamster enough that his eyelids flicked.

"Yes, that's it. Try a little drink, Pardo. It'll do you good." Mack risked a bit more water, but it pooled and ran off the man's mouth. Then Pardo moved his mouth but not to drink.

Mack leaned close. "What's that, Pardo?"

The voice was a thin, quiet whisper. "Sell what you can, if you can . . ."

Mack was confused but he agreed, promising he would.

"Send money to Mama. My mama, Box Ankle, Missouri. Cleo Zinski. I'm all she's got, her only baby. Now she ain't got me, nor money." As he spoke Pardo's voice grew stronger, though still never rising above a hoarse whisper.

"Cleo Zinski. I hear you, but Pardo, you're going to be fine. I promise. I . . . I'm going to get you to help."

"Tell Mama I thought of her at my end, and I was smiling. Will you?"

"Of course, Pardo, but I tell you, I can get you to help, I know it."

"Not me, Mack. But you need to. Pretty wife and family. Lucky man . . ." Pardo's eyes closed. He stiffened and a grimace of pain whitened his face. It passed and then he sighed, a smile once more spread on his mouth. "Bye-bye, Mama."

As Mack watched, the vital parts inside the body that was Pardo Zinski flickered and drifted off and away. Mack was left with his friend's dead body, eyes closed and a quiet smile on his big, gruff face.

Never been one to give over to emotion, Mack preferred to keep his head calm in a situation of hardship and challenge. But everything that had happened—the pleasurable times he'd had with this man who had been a stranger to him, such good times, genuinely enjoyable times—landed hard on Mack. Pardo was gone, taken from this life because of an accident. A foolish accident.

"I am so sorry, Pardo. This was no way for a mighty fellow such as yourself to bow out." Tears welled in Mack's eyes and he sighed a deep sigh and let it out.

After a few silent moments, he set about to figure out what he had to do next.

He still held the shattered canteen and he looked into the pried-apart mouth of the thing. Less than a teaspoon of water, but it was better than none. He tipped it up and let the tepid, gritty water slide into his mouth. A paltry amount, but never had water tasted so fine.

"Okay," he said, knowing he had to make decisions and do it fast. He had to get up to the road before the wrecked mess decided it was not satisfied with clinging to the steep, scree-riddled slope for much longer.

Someone had to pass by at some point. How long that might take he had no idea. He chose to believe it would be no less than a day, perhaps two. But he was not going to be able to go anywhere until he dragged Pardo out of there and gave him at least a make-shift burial under a rock mound up the hill.

He had promised himself he would, and Mack Harrigan never backed out on a promise—to himself or anyone else. He also had to rescue useful items from the wreck . . . if he could do so safely. Once more, he reached into the little dark hollow beyond Pardo's head. His left hand scrabbled blindly in the space behind the seat, or where the seat had been, hoping to feel something, anything that might be of use to him. His battered fingertips brushed something softer than wood and rock and metal, something that gave a little. He risked another, deeper grope and was rewarded with what felt like cloth. Could it be what he hoped it might be?

His fingers pawed, clawed, and managed to snag the thing. He dragged it toward the hole and could not pull it through. He risked digging the rim of the hole out from below, then tugged out the sack. The very thing he wished for—the sack Pardo had had Millie stuff with fresh-baked

biscuits at the cafe before they departed Watts Corner—
was still full.

This was luck in droves. Now, if he could find a water
skin that had not burst. Luck again was with him, albeit in
smaller doses. Still wrapped about the hook where Pardo
always kept it, he saw a small goatskin of water. The two
discoveries might well keep Mack alive long enough to—.

The wagon began to shift again. He'd jostled it too
much.

"Hang on . . . hang on." He whispered the plea over and
over until it sounded like one word. Still on the downhill
side, with no idea how to get around it and out of its treacherous potential path he whispered it to the bent, cracked
trees holding the entire mess in place.

He had to make decisions and fast. He snatched up the
bag of biscuits, the top still cinched tight with a drawstring
and tied, and swung it backward, then threw it upslope. It
arced high and he heard it hit, then tumble, then stop. He
could not see it through the wreck, but trusted, hoped, it
was out of the way should the worst happen.

Tempted to gurgle a cool drink, he realized two things:
there was no time and the skin of water would surely puncture if it hit something sharp. Thus he hastily drew its strap
about his neck and swung it over his shoulder.

"Pardo," he said, sliding back to his right and to his
wedged, dead friend. "I'm going to try, but I cannot die
in the attempt, do you hear me? I have to get back to Ell
and the children. That said, I'll do my best, friend." Like a
digging rodent, he scooped gravel and soil out from beneath each side of the big, crumpled man. It was slow
work. After each drag of dirt he paused, listening for the
tell-tale creaking of the wreck.

Once he'd cleared what he felt was enough to slide
Pardo out from beneath the pinning wood, he wasted no

time, and tugged from the man's thighs. The big body inched downslope, and Mack had to adjust his own footing each time, digging in with his toes and the sides of his boots to prevent himself from sliding free of his friend and task.

He'd pulled Pardo roughly halfway out of the divot he'd trenched, and figured he needed another six inches or so of dragging. Then the dead man would be clear enough of the twisted wreck that Mack could drag him to his right, and with as much haste as he was able, back the way he'd angled around the rear of the wagon.

But that was not to be.

The pines, which had grown from a single stump, shuddered. He looked up at them to his left and watched as another, deeper crack racked right up the trunk of the near tree. They weren't big to begin with, perhaps four or five inches across, but they had to be rooted into something within the bank, in some robust way. Still, they looked to have reached their holding limit.

When that crack reaches the top, he thought, *that tree will give way.* And without it, the second will be unable to continue this last task.

He still had to get Pardo out from beneath the wreck, then drag him to the left and out away from danger. It was not a possibility. "Sorry, Pardo," he whispered, and scrabbled with all his strength and speed to his left, away from the wagon.

He barely made it before the trees cracked, exploded, and collapsed all at once, succumbing to the pressure of the heavily timbered wagon and the remainder of its lashed-in load.

Mere feet from where he clung to the steep slope, Mack watched as the wagon, unimpeded by the trees, tipped over.

It looked as though it might come to rest upright once more, but the slope was far too steep.

As the dust slowly dissipated, Mack took it all in with a sweeping glance and a few stunned, silent seconds. Divots appeared in the graveled bank where the dead horses had been. They had not gone far, heavier in their dead weight than even that determined wagon could drag.

The traces and harness had snapped, but not before dragging the beasts from their initial spots of repose in death. They had been bent at odd angles and he had assumed they had died of broken necks or soon after of injuries to their insides, unable to grasp anything in their last moments but great pain.

Arrayed in various poses down the slope, two were still tethered to each other by their harness leather, another below, and still the fourth, which he had not seen earlier, even farther below and east along the bank.

Only half a wagon, its sacrificed half was a snapped spew of wreckage along the slope.

Even if it had had great value, Mack doubted it would ever move again from that spot, so treacherous was the slope and the great distance down there. Thinking of Pardo, he scrabbled back to where the wagon had been and glanced upslope, knowing he'd have to climb back up to the roadway at some point. And felt his strength slowly leaving him.

He seemed to recall the roadway was wide up there. Even in the tumult of the accident that had struck him as odd. The horses should have not strayed so far to the edge of the road. Then he remembered the little dead bear. Yes, that's right, he thought, chiding himself for forgetting the little bear had spooked the horses and driven them over the road's edge, and thus to their deaths. For all of them.

Still, he hoped the spot above, not far from where they'd

left the road, was visible from both directions and well away from any intruding boulders that might prevent travelers from seeing the blaze he intended to create. A grim sense of hope to have a plan flickered deep inside him, no matter how impossible to accomplish some of it seemed.

The first trip, he reasoned, had best contain the heaviest item he needed to fetch to the top. That was Pardo Zinski. No way was he going to leave his dead friend exposed for all the roving creatures of the night to sniff out and perhaps feast on. No, he thought, dispelling the gruesome notion from his mind. That would not stand.

If the man's body was still there.

If he had strength after that, Mack would fetch whatever gear he might find, and then trek to— Where? Back to Watts Corner? Onward, east-southeast toward home?

Hadn't Pardo said home was still a three-day-ride? What about on foot? And addled in the head? Would he even make it?

His thoughts, unbidden, flickered back to his family. They might never know what became of him should he succumb out there. "No, no," he mumbled. "Can't think like that."

"You'll stay on the roadway," he told himself. He knew Watts Corner was a popular and growing town. It would require steady visitations from all directions. He had to believe that someone would come along.

Pardo lay untouched, save for a few shards of planking atop him and a renewed layer of dust. Mack scrambled to Pardo and cleared away the wood and grit from his face. He still wore the same slight childlike smile, unaware in death of what had just passed over him, leaving him untouched.

How he was going to get the big man up the slope Mack

did not know. He looked about for something, anything that might be useful. Perhaps if he had any rope, he could rig up a shoulder harness to—

"Harness," he said aloud, looking once more toward where the horses had been. Scraps of harness or some such were snagged about the base of the tree stump, a ragged mess to the other side of Pardo.

He reached past his friend and cleared away grit to reveal what was part of the lines ripped from Pardo's hands, no doubt, in the accident. Both lines were there, somehow whipped around the base of the tree. The far ends were buried in gravel.

Mack tugged on them and they popped loose with ease, their ends stretched and raw where they had snapped free of the harnesses. "Good," he said, still uncertain how he was going to use them to haul his friend upslope.

A tumble of gravel from above forced his gaze upward. And for the second time that day his heart was chilled to the core by what he saw.

A big bear—a grizzly, he thought—had walked cross-slope to the scene and had just discovered the young bear. It growled low in its throat and sniffed and sniffed at the thing, nosing the ruined snout, hunched away from it, then pawed at it, all the while making soft grunting, almost whimpering sounds.

Mack knew then it was no male, no boar bear as Bearpaw called them, but a sow, a mother bear. And she was aggrieved. He knew that as fact by the very sounds she made. The sounds mothers make the world over, be they human or not, at such a discovery.

He kept still, but the loose gravel gave him away as a fresh tiny runnel of sand and grit dislodged beneath his right boot. He stiffened and did not move, his left arm grasping the lines which were still jumbled about the ragged raw stump of the snapped tree. He prayed they held. He did not want trouble with this mama bear.

But the trickle of gravel was enough—she swung her big face toward him, sniffed once, twice, then opened her mighty maw and forced a deep, hollow roaring sound straight at him. A threat, a defiant oath from bear to man that her offspring was dead and he must be the cause.

Then she charged.

CHAPTER 25

The big she-bear's attack was a false charge, but Mack only learned that when she came to a skidding, gravel-spraying halt a half-dozen feet upslope of him. She popped her jaw with menace, spraying spittle and the waft of foul breath as she offered Mack her full rage by way of a wide-mouth roar. Her yellow teeth were among the few most frightening sights Mack had ever seen.

With a shaking hand he managed to lay his fingertips on the hilt of his hip knife. It came to him he might fare better with his pistol. He reached for it—and it wasn't there.

Without taking his eyes from the bear, though he did try to not look directly into her squinty, piggy eyes, for he knew bears considered that a challenge to fight, Mack realized his side gun had somehow fallen from its holster in the accident and its aftermath. He'd look for it later. If he was allowed a later.

She raked the gravel with a front paw, spraying him with grit. Her beefy size seemed far more menacing as she was uphill of him. Because of the slope, her huge shoulders and rump stood firm and wide, massive in proportion to the rest of her sizable girth.

He unlaced the blade and worked it out of the sheath, trying not to make any move the bear might take as a sign of aggression. She stared at him, growling and chuffing, her big muscled head flexing with her snapping jaws. Foam and slather stringed and pooled from her mouth. Then, as if she just remembered it, she swung back upslope a few feet behind her and resumed sniffing and snuffling her dead baby.

As frightened as Mack was, she was at least turning her attention away from him, however short that might be. She made low, grunting whimpers, not at all sounding like an angry mother. But Mack knew better. He held still, wondering what might happen.

It was obvious she had no problem with her footing on the gravel slope. If he had tried to run cross-slope in either direction, she would have been on him, bowled him over, and still somehow managed to save herself.

He, on the other hand, would likely be battered, torn open, and bleeding, and then would flail and tumble all the way down the slope to the river he heard far below. By then he would probably be dead or beyond help and caring.

No, he thought. *Best to wait it out, see what she was going to do.*

And that was trouble. The mother bear seemed to have no intention of leaving her dead baby. Soon Mack had no choice but to shift his footing. He was sliding and cramping. As carefully as he might, he moved his right leg, raising the sore knee and straightening it and then quietly wedging it back into gravel.

Halfway through doing the same with his left leg, he dislodged a fist-size rock. It rolled and rolled, knocking into other, larger rocks. That was all it took to snatch the bear's attention from her dead offspring once more.

She rushed him again. In a full-bore wave of gravel and bear rage she didn't stop. She lunged at Mack and he leapt over Pardo to his left, toward the shattered tree stump. He crouched low, clutching the ragged, splayed stump, and followed the big bear's slow, galloping progress.

She landed with all four massive feet on the spot he'd been, and was already turning her body to her right to get at him when she lost her footing. The momentum of her downhill charge warred with her intention to lunge to her side. Her weight kept her body going, rolling her downslope in a jerking, staggering lurch as she tried to correct for the unexpected loose, sliding slope. All the while she growled and howled, roared and bit at the air, at the gravel, at anything that offended her rage-filled mind.

Apparently that was just about everything in sight, including Mack. She churned gravel, her big body grabbing at the slope in frantic, pawing moves that seemed to be futile.

He looked upslope, wondering if he could make the road, however far it seemed.

And then what, Mack? he thought. *Run along the roadway until you lose strength to move?* It was a plan, but he didn't think he'd make it. She might be having trouble on the slope at that moment, but she could recover faster than him.

She finally came to a stop far, far below him on the slope. He estimated she'd slid and rolled and pawed in futility a good eighty to one hundred feet below.

If ever there was a time to save his sorry hide, it was then.

As he backed up the slope and moved higher, he muttered, "Okay, Pardo. I'll be back."

Staying in a crouch was an awkward way to climb, but he had to keep her in his sights. She looked angrier and more determined than ever to get at him. And then he realized why. His boot had bumped into something. He looked down and there was the dead baby bear behind him, slightly upset from where he'd found it earlier because its mother had pawed and prodded the corpse.

Mack looked back downslope, and though he knew a bear's eyesight was not nearly as keen as its sense of smell, he saw that his proximity to the baby was seen by the mother, and she did not like it one bit.

If the baby was truly what she wanted, maybe he could accommodate her. It was a quick thought, but in life Mack had learned that often the first idea that came to him in a situation was the best idea. Not always, but he had to try something. She was making progress up the slope at him, switchbacking a few feet at a time. And from her chuffing and growling, her rage was on the increase.

He jammed the knife back in its sheath. With a mutter of "Sorry, little one, for the coming indignity," he bent to the body on the uphill side, scooped beneath it, and rolled the dead bear downslope toward its mother.

He had hoped it would keep rolling and distract the mother enough that he could reach the roadway. The dead baby bear didn't comply. It rolled four feet and then slopped to a stop. He looked to the mother, and her rage had only grown.

Mack skidded down to the dead bear to give it one more shot, angling the body so it might tuck and roll. Just past the point where the wagon had initially rested against the tree, the slope, already steep, became even more treacherous. It was why the mother bear had such a rough time getting back up the hill, and why the little bear, now that he gave it a mighty shove, kept on rolling downslope, slopping, flopping, to be sure, but also gaining speed slowly and surely. It continued on, passing by its roaring, struggling mother, and continued at an even greater clip.

The big bear paused and saw her lifeless offspring roll on by, suddenly gifted with renewed life.

Mack took advantage of her confusion. Taking a cue from her, he switchbacked his way upslope. Staggering, he dug in and slid a good half-dozen feet and saw something that gave him a weak moment of hopefulness—the cloth sack he'd tossed before the wagon had continued on its way. It was filled with biscuits from Millie's diner.

He snatched it up, a glimmer of hope flickering in his chest that somehow he might live through the mess. He had a sack of food, a meager little goat skin of water still slopping about on his back, and a knife. And still around his neck—he patted there to confirm it—the possibles bag he and Kane each kept. In it he had a flint, steel, char cloth, and even matches, scarce as they were. He'd also managed to wedge into each of their modest pouches a couple of fish hooks and a decent length of gut line.

Yes, he reasoned, as long as the mother bear kept her distance, he might make it through all right. How he was going to keep Pardo's body from desecration by beasts from up there was another matter.

"Ell, I'm coming. First, I have to figure out how to deal with Pardo."

If worse came to worst, he could always hoof it to some settlement—the closest he knew being Watts Corner—and get someone to ferry him back in a wagon. But he'd still have to cover Pardo's body, likely with rocks.

That meant waiting the bear out. And in that there were no guarantees about anything the bear might or might not do.

As he rummaged through those thoughts, he picked his way upslope as quickly as he was able. Still mighty sore from the battering he took in jumping free in the wreck, and sore as the dickens in his head, but at least he was no longer seeing double of everything.

The late afternoon sun had begun to cook his head, and he realized for the first time that he'd lost his hat. He glanced about for it on the slope but saw no sign of it.

He did see the mother bear far downslope. She had given up trying to follow him and had turned instead to follow her rolling baby. It had fetched up on something, likely a jutting rock, and the mother was once more nosing it and pawing it. How long would it be before she gave up on the lifeless thing and refocused her killing intentions back on him?

"No time to wait around to find out, Mack."

Not far from the top lay two wooden crates, both smashed, but so close to the roadway, they gave Mack ideas. If the bear wasn't going to seek him out, and that was a lot to assume, he could use the wood for a meager fire, there being few trees along that stretch of roadway. But he'd know better when he gained the road's edge.

As he passed the crates, threading his path between them, he caught sight of the scattered remnants of each. One held cloth, for he spied bundled stacks of folded, bright fabrics in bold patterns of green and red and blue and yellow, in flowers and stripes and checked patterns—all what women might make dresses of. They poked from beneath gravel where they'd been jammed into the earth, no doubt, by the rolling wagon before it continued on its brutal path.

The other crate held, of all things, tinware—gray with black and gray flecks all over it. Plates, cups, and fry pans were scattered here and there about the slope. Some pieces had slid quite far to either side, skittering on their flat surfaces like a child's sled on a snowy hill back home in Ohio.

They might not be as much use to him as the cloth, particularly useful when it grew cold at night, which he knew it would in a matter of hours, but the wooden crates housing each shipment of products would burn nicely.

He gathered what he could of the wood corners and panels, all heavily planked and mostly ripped apart, saving him from having to stomp much of it into useable lengths.

CHAPTER 26

"Go ahead, Kane. Show Jim your sketchbook, as you call it."

Kane turned red.

"Don't be bashful," said Bearpaw. "Toot your horn. Ain't nobody else is gonna do it for you."

Kane dug out his book and with a trembling hand, offered it to the one and only Jim Bridger, then stuffed his hands into his coat pockets to keep them from shaking. He wasn't sure why he felt so nervous. Perhaps because he'd never handed it over to anyone to let them look inside . . . unless Meghan or Fitch had sneaked peeks at it . . . and certainly not one of the most famous folks Kane had ever heard of, let alone met.

Bridger glanced at him and nodded, sensing the sketchbook was important to the boy, then cracked it open. With calloused fingers, he thumbed through the pages, gingerly tweezering each paper before turning it. After long moments of doing little more than nod his head now and again, Bridger closed the book and handed it back to Kane. "Son, those are flat-out impressive. As Bearpaw can tell you, I don't lie."

Kane's portly friend coughed and hid his face behind a

cupped hand, but his rolling eyes told Kane to take whatever Bridger said with a pinch of salt.

Bridger went on. "In fact"—he scratched his chin—"I got a couple of folks I'd like you to meet. Come on." With that, Bridger turned and walked away from them.

Kane glanced at Bearpaw, who nodded then nudged him into action.

They threaded their way through a couple of vendors and passed one loud fur company buyer arguing with an Indian who kept shaking his head and stroking the fine pelt—a wolf, Kane thought—he had brought to trade.

The fur company man was growing red in the face and the Indian was as calm as a man could be. In fact, he almost looked as though he was enjoying making the white man squirm.

Bridger kept walking, leading Kane and Bearpaw along a narrow trail up to a plateau partially hidden by a tumble of boulders. At the top of the low rise, a scatter of trees offered shade.

In two folding wooden chairs beneath the shade, sat a man and a woman watching their approach. Behind them, four canvas tents were arrayed neat as you please, with a well-appointed cook camp set up in the midst of it all. The fire slowly puffed smoke into the clear blue sky. Horses were picketed and grazing off to one side, and a wagon flanked the other end.

As Bridger and his guests approached, the man rose and held a hand out to help the woman stand as well. She shooed him off and popped up out of the chair.

Bridger swept off his felt topper and bowed, a hand to his waist. "Sir and ma'am, I would like to introduce you to my old friend, Bearpaw Jones and his . . . apprentice."

Bearpaw's eyebrows rose at the mention of the word but said nothing. Kane wanted to ask just what Bridger meant.

It sounded as if someone had gotten the wrong end of the stick on this one, and Kane didn't want to get on Bearpaw's wrong side.

Bridger looked at Kane. He'd lapsed into silence, lost for the moment in the pretty face of the woman in the fancy dress, wondering how a woman so pretty could be out in the wild.

Bearpaw shoved him from behind, knocking him out of his reverie. "Boy's name is Kane Harrigan, sir, ma'am." The crusty mountain man also nodded, and, like Bridger, held his hat before him. "He don't get out much."

"Oh, yes, ma'am," said Kane, shaking his head. "My apologies." Quickly tugging off his cap and feeling his ears and cheeks and neck burn up in crimson shame, he nodded and bent at the waist. He backed up until he was nearly behind Bearpaw, who elbowed him.

Out of the side of his mouth, he said, "What's wrong with you, boy? Settle yerself!"

Instead of being bothered by Kane's unintended foolishness, the man stepped forward with his hand extended and shook hands with Bearpaw. "Please to meet you Mr. Jones. I'm Viscount Reginald Smithwick." His accent was English and his tone formal. He stepped before Kane and also shook his hand, but held onto it. Half turning, he faced the woman and the other men and smiled. "Not a worry, young man. I felt the same way when I first made the acquaintance of"—he nodded and smiled to the woman— "my fiancée, miss Lady Teal."

The pretty woman stepped forward, blushing slightly, and waved a hanky at Smithwick. "Oh, stop, Reginald. You're embarrassing the boy."

She held out a hand to Bearpaw and he gingerly held her fingers and bowed slightly, then glared at Kane, who understood and did the same when she proffered her hand to him.

"You can call me Iris."

"Or Lady Teal," said Smithwick, arching an eyebrow at her.

"Or that." She sighed. "Yes."

They then invited the trio to take tea with them. The viscount raised a hand and motioned lightly. Within moments, a tall, lean man with neatly oiled hair and wearing a short white coat and white gloves carried a tray with a teapot and cups and set it in their midst on a low table.

"I'll pour, Thomas, thank you," said Lady Teal.

The gloved man nodded and backed away, then returned to the array of tents from which he had emerged.

"Our man, Thomas," said Smithwick. "Don't know what we'd do without him."

Kane glanced at Bridger and Bearpaw, who were hiding their mouths behind their teacups. Kane did the same.

"So, Bridger, what brings you here? I thought you had the day free from our little caravan."

"Yes, sir," said Bridger, setting down his cup. "I wanted you to meet this young fellow here"—he nodded toward Kane—"and take a look at what he can do."

"Oh?"

Kane felt his insides turn to ice. What was this all about? He had no skills he could think of. Why was Jim Bridger saying that?

"Your pictures, boy," said Bearpaw, his bushy eyebrows raised once again in Kane's direction.

"Oh." Kane suddenly felt as if he were being swept under a tremendous swell in a river.

"Oh, for heaven's sake." Bearpaw reached for Kane's open-topped satchel and slipped the leather-bound journal free and handed it to the viscount before Kane could stop him.

"Oh, no. I . . . no . . . it's . . ."

But it was too late. The Englishman had already untied the leather thong binding it and opened the book. His reaction was much the same as Bridger's had been.

Lady Teal also looked at it with him, occasionally reaching out and tapping a page with a fingertip, then exchanging a glance with Smithwick and nodding.

Finally, they reached the end. Smithwick closed the book and handed it back to Kane. "Well spotted, Mr. Bridger." He turned to Kane. "Now, young Mr. Harrigan, we are on this grand tour of the frontier of this untamed—"

"Lovely, wild, free, exciting place!" exclaimed Lady Teal.

"Indeed," said Smithwick, not suppressing a smile. "All those things, too, in fact. As members of the British Naturalist Society, we are helping document unknown species of flora and fauna. Through collection, naturally, but also through mapping, scientific cataloguing, and painting and sketching. Crucial skills we thought adequate in those two latter pursuits are admittedly not as we wish them to be." He paused and looked at Kane.

An awkward long moment passed and then, because it felt as though he needed to say something, Kane said, "Ah, I see. Yes," though in truth he saw little and understood even less.

"What my dear intended means to say and has failed to do so," said Lady Teal, lacing a slim arm through Smithwick's, "is that we realize our expedition would benefit greatly from the skills of someone such as yourself. Yourself, in fact."

"Oh . . . what?"

She laughed and Kane found himself once more drifting

into a place in which he and the fair lady were alone on a small boat in the middle of a shoreless lake, in the sun, she gazing at him . . .

Once again, a prod from Bearpaw roused him in time to hear Smithwick ask, in a lowered tone, "He is all right, is he not?"

"Oh yeah, sir. He's right as spring rain. Just a little shy on food and sleep this last day or so." To the side, Bearpaw glared at Kane.

"What we would like," said Smithwick, suppressing a grin, apparently accepting Bearpaw's explanation. "is for you to consider a position in our band of traveling exploration. We can offer you a modest sum, food . . . and sleeping arrangements." He smiled. "In exchange for you sketching and painting and helping us document our discoveries. We expect to take the summer to complete the mapped tour Mr. Bridger has kindly detailed for us. What say you, young man?"

The import of what had been offered to him bloomed quick and bright. Kane could not help being overwhelmed by the sudden and unexpected opportunity and the possibilities it presented. For the first time, it gave shape to the very thing he had been trying to identify in his life.

"Well, what do you say, boy?" said Bearpaw.

"I . . . I thank you very kindly for the . . . kind offer. If it would be all right with you, that is to say if you don't mind, I should like to think about this. I . . . it's my parents, you see. I promised . . . I . . . might I tell you in—"

"Of course," cut in Smithwick. "You have a week from today, and then we commence our journey. Hopefully, with an official artist in tow."

"Thank you, sir." Kane bowed, then turned to the pretty woman. "And Lady Teal, I thank you."

Again, her light, musical laughter brought a smile to all

their faces. "But of course, Kane Harrigan. We do hope you will take us up on the offer. It will be a memorable trip and your skills will help bring to life so much that would have otherwise been adequate at best."

"And even on that point we are doubtful," said the viscount.

"Indeed," said Lady Teal.

Jim Bridger stood, gave his employers a nod and a smile, and the viscount stood as well and shook his hand. "Thank you, Mr. Bridger. You have a keen eye for what we need. I have a feeling this will be a fruitful excursion. And Mr. Jones, as you are a friend of Mr. Bridger, perhaps you might be of use to us as well. That is, if you are free and are interested."

"Well now, I thank you kindly, Mister Viscount Smith-wick, but Bearpaw works for himself, always has. So as fun as it would be, I bet, I'll have to decline your kind offer and continue on my way. Me and Ol' Gravyfoot have lots of miles to cover yet. Lots of miles."

"Very good, sir. I understand and respect your dedication to your task."

"Okay, then," said Bridger, clapping his hands together. "We best get back to the rendezvous. I have a couple of deals yet to make on behalf of the excursion to get us outfitted proper-like, and there's the matter of getting young Kane here familiar with how things are done at a rendezvous." He winked theatrically at Bearpaw, who offered a solemn nod in response.

"Come along, Kane," said Bearpaw, wrapping an arm about the young man's shoulder and steering him on out of there. "Time to get your ears wet."

Kane looked back once at his potential new employers and offered them a smile. "Thank you. It was a pleasure to meet you. Both."

They nodded and smiled in return.

As the three men walked away, Kane heard Lady Teal say to her fiancé, "What a polite young man. He was raised well, I believe."

Hearing that put a jaunty lift in his step. "Mr. Jones, what's this you mentioned about getting my ears wet? Is there a swimming hole nearby?"

Kane thought that sounded like a decent idea. It had been a long, hot day and a cooling swim would be most welcome. Then a good meal.

"Oh, in a manner of speaking, you bet." Bearpaw licked his lips and giggled as they descended the plateau and made their long route back to the rendezvous grounds.

Before they got there they could already hear the beginnings of a whoop-up, with fiddle music and shouts, a few random gunshots, and lots and lots of voices gabbling, shot through with bursts of laughter and shouts.

They threaded their way into the throngs of folks. Kane noted at least double the amount of people compared with how many had been there when they left for the plateaus earlier. Then Bearpaw was gone, as was Jim Bridger. Tall for his age, Kane managed to see over the heads of most of the folks around him and held his satchel close to his coat. Then he felt a tug on his left sleeve.

"Hey."

Kane looked down and it was Bearpaw, holding two horn cups filled with an amber liquid, one in each hand. He looked up at Kane.

"You're how old?"

"I'm seventeen—well, sixteen—but I'll be seventeen pretty soon, Mr. Jones. Why?"

The mountain man squinted, bit his top lip, and looked to the sky. "Well, I'm wondering . . . just wondering. Okay, then." He thrust one cup at Kane. "Happy Birthday, boy. Don't never say that ol' Uncle Bearpaw never gave you nothin', okay?"

"Oh, well, okay." Kane lifted the cup and sniffed. "What is this?"

"Never you mind. You get it inside you and then we'll visit a few more friends."

Kane watched Bearpaw upend his cup, sip, then swallow it all down. He pulled the cup away from his face, grinned wide, and shook his head, making a blubbing noise.

Kane shrugged his shoulders. Since he was thirsty—the tea didn't count, as he'd barely tasted it—he slugged the drink back, not testing it first . . . and regretted it right away.

Something happened to his windpipe. It tightened as if he were being squeezed about the neck with a brute, gripping hand. He gasped, fought for air, and felt a thin whisker of a trickle of it wheeze into his throat. He'd barely pulled in a half breath, then he coughed.

At the same time a seeping warmth crept into his chest and rose up his throat, warming his mouth and nose, leaving them numb. By that time he was able to breathe without the aid of gulping breaths, though he required a few thumps on the back administered by a grinning Bearpaw. "Is this whiskey, Mr. Jones?"

"You bet it is. Not just any. I sprung for the tasty stuff. Made by my friend, Norbert. He's a talented fella. I dare say you agree."

Kane was pretty certain it was not an experience he needed to repeat.

Bearpaw, on the other hand, looked to be in a hurry to give it another go.

Kane had not been raised in a household in which strong drink of any sort was any more common than as a

Christmastime toast. The hijinks and hoots and howls of the increasingly rowdy crowd he found himself in, coupled with the interesting, warming effects of the whiskey, left him inclined to cut loose and let happen what will happen.

But a voice in the back of his head told him he should use caution. "Keep a keen eye" as his father would say when in the woods stalking game. "Pause a lot, look much, listen more, and wait."

But it was almighty difficult to do that when everywhere he looked people were having what appeared to be one whale of a time. The other thing—the biggest reason Kane could ever think of to celebrate—he had been offered a position by an English lord, or some such, and his lady. She was by far the prettiest lady Kane had ever laid eyes on, and that included Bright Owl's younger sister, Blue Dawn. That was saying something.

He had really been asked to accompany them on their expedition.

No, that's not right. Their excursion is what they'd called it. And to do the very thing he loved doing—exploring and discovering and sketching new plants and animals, or what they'd called *flora* and *fauna.* He'd only ever read those terms in books,

If that wasn't enough, the famous tracker and trapper and mountain man, Jim Bridger, was leading the trip!

Kane shook his head once more at the incredible turn the last few hours had put in his life. It was, of course, an opportunity he wasn't at all certain he could take advantage of. He had promised his father he was going to look after the family. And a Harrigan never backed out on a promise.

That was all the time Kane had for thinking such thoughts. Bearpaw showed up with another cup, the very one Kane had held before, making him wonder when had it been taken from his grasp.

Handing the cup to Kane, Bearpaw said the most perfect thing. "We should celebrate your good fortune, son. The world awaits you."

Knowing he could not be rude and decline the drink, for that would be declining the very well wishes accompanying the cup full of cheer, Kane grinned and nodded. "Why, thank you, Mr. Jones."

"I tell you again, son, it's Bearpaw to my friends." The old man winked and they knocked back their libations.

As the fire bubbled and burbled and sparked in his chest, Kane realized he could breathe a whole lot easier than he could following that earlier drink. *Must be a new batch,* he thought. *And it sure does go down smooth.*

CHAPTER 27

Mack woke early the next morning, following a night of very little sleep and a whole lot of eyeballing the darkness. He'd kept his ears perked for any little sound that might well be an angry she-bear looking to peel his limbs from his body. As dawn was finally imminent, Mack sighed in cautious relief at the first hints of gray dimness tickling the eastern skyline.

He was more sore than he could ever recall feeling, even after the brutal beating from the trading post skunks back on their trek westward, even after the brutal, close-in fighting during the kill-crazy rogue Piegan attack on the Shoshone camp. And the accident had tumbled him from topknot to toes and slammed him into every rock on the slope before he had come to a sprawled, sloppy stop.

Spying the long, cloth-shrouded shape of his dead friend, Pardo Zinski, Mack knew he had no right to complain . . . for he had survived the rolling of the wagon.

Pardo would never again know the dull, throbbing pain of sore muscles, either from a beating or from an honest day's labor. He would never again know the love of a woman such as Ell. Or the shining trust and hope and goodness he saw whenever he looked into the eyes of his children.

Mack shoved to his feet. "Enough of the thinking," he mumbled as he pushed his knees into place and rubbed them. He felt cold and mighty stiff all over. He glanced again at the sun, or the place on the horizon where the sun would be. "Come on, old friend. Warm me up. Lots to do today."

Mack swigged lightly from the water skin and patted his hip for the reassuring feel of the big knife he carried. *Still there.* Nothing had made off with it in the night. He shook his head at his silliness and gave thought to the mental list of tasks he had composed in the night, in the long hours of his lonely, cold, fear-filled watch. His first task of the day was to cover Pardo with stones to help prevent critters from getting at him.

Once that was in hand, Mack intended to proceed with the second item on his short list— walk back toward Watts Corner to fetch help. Then he would return to the spot in a wagon loaded with a pine box and he would retrieve Pardo's body.

Following that, if possible, he would drive to Devil's Creek, which seemed to be Pardo's home base, and he had friends there. Heck, Pardo seemed to have friends everywhere.

"First things first, Mack," he told himself, looking about to verify the place he'd chosen to lay out Pardo. Well off to the side of the naturally wide spot in the road, it served as Pardo's temporary resting spot.

Even in the dim morning light, he verified that, yes, it had been a decent choice of the night before. He'd been so exhausted he wouldn't have been surprised if he'd imagined the flat place off to the side of the roadway. Assured it was real, Pardo still lay where he'd dragged him up the slope.

It had been quite a labor. The harness lines had proved

effective, if painful. He'd gone back to the pile of wrecked cloth once to retrieve wads of it to use as padding beneath the strapping. He'd lashed it over his shoulders and crossed it over his chest and back in bandolier fashion. The cloth had helped, but the weight of the dead man's body flopping and snagging on every slight rock jutting from the slope turned the trek into a task of many hours.

Never one for giving up, giving in, and admitting defeat, Mack had tugged Pardo's body up the slope. After what had seemed like an eternity, he'd looked up to the top for the first time in many, many long minutes.

Seeing the great distance still to go had quivered his *heart and given rise to a voice in his head. Aw, go ahead and leave him be. You gave it your top effort, but nobody could do finer. You'll never make it, so admit it now and leave him here.* But that voice was a *false* one, self-serving and not to be trusted. Even if he knew it to be true, he might find it difficult not to follow through with it.

With the top of the slope at the roadway so very far away, and with the afternoon sun drawing stinging sweat into his eyes, and with his shoulders feeling as if they were about to be sliced clean off his body by the straps, continuing the task had seemed impossible . . . so he'd rested. Lying there on the slope, an arm over his eyes, Pardo's last wishes had come back to him in the man's own distinctive, gruff voice.

No way could Mack give up on him.

He'd looked back downslope for sign of the mother bear, but she was gone. The humped form of the dead baby bear was also gone, and he'd detected a trail beyond where it had snagged on a jutting stone. Perhaps it had continued on downslope into the stunty trees that had begun clawing their way upslope.

Thoughts of the angry mother bear eyeing him had

prompted him to roll over, shove up to his knees, and
readjust the make-shift harness into as comfortable a
position as possible—or at least a less painful one.

Three, perhaps four hours later, he had made it to the top
of the slope. To get Pardo up over the last angling of the
road's shoulder proved the most difficult. It meant a final,
mighty heave. His first attempt did not take. The momentum and the steepness conspired to pull Pardo downslope
once more. Only by shoving his heels into the slope had
Mack been able to keep the body from pulling him with it.
Even at that, Pardo's dead weight was winning.

Mack had felt the ramrod stiffened body sliding downslope, losing precious inches he'd fought for long, grueling
hours to gain.

"Gaah!" he'd shouted, doubling his efforts to hang on,
feeling the little strength he had left ebb from him. His
arms were locked in a half-bent position, his elbows
jammed as hard into the slope as were his heels.

Far downslope beyond small trees, he'd seen a big black
shape pacing back and forth with restless energy. He'd
heard her snorting and chuffing, bawling in a mix of rage
and grief for her dead offspring. She kept returning to the
spot, half-hidden from his sight, nosed there, then pivoted
back out in the open. It had looked as if she were looking
upslope, in Mack's direction.

He'd watched her repeat the sad dance twice more, then
a feeling of renewed strength and calm had seeped into
him. With Ell and the children never far from his mind, he
knew he'd been given the precious gift of surviving a hor-
rible situation yet again, and had best make the most of it.

Once more, he'd turned his left side into the slope, and
inch by inch, tug by precious tug, managed to get his own
body back on the flat at the top. Within reach, a rounded
stone jutted six inches up from the earth. It looked solid.

Risking an arm's reach, Mack had quickly grasped it and pulled. It felt solid enough. He'd wasted no time looping one, then the other strap about it. Keeping the other ends wrapped about his fingers, swelling with their efforts, he'd used the stone as a capstan to help him hoist Pardo up the last few feet to the top.

It had taken long, long minutes, perhaps the better part of an hour. At that point, Mack had lost all sense of time and could only guess at it by the position of the sun in the clear blue sky. Finally, the biggest part of Pardo, his torso, lay flopped beside Mack on the flat.

Mack had groaned and rested for long minutes.

With the coming of dawn, he went through Pardo's pockets. The button flap on the breast pocket had survived and was still buttoned. On quick glance, it contained folded papers detailing Pardo's accounts of who owed what, which was a surprisingly low number given that Pardo had many clients and customers.

Mack also knew Pardo had kept his money in a leather folding wallet in a front trouser pocket. This, too, had made it through the wreck. Mack lifted it free and thumbed through the contents quickly. Two papers told of his identifications, and verified the name of his home place of Box Ankle, Missouri, as well as a substantial wad of cash and two promissory notes written to him from merchants. Mack vowed he would ensure they were paid up, and then he'd send all the money to Pardo's mother.

There would be no measurable profit from salvaging the wreck. Indeed, he doubted much of anything would be worth rummaging down that deadly slope.

With that difficult task behind him, Mack built a crude

frame of snapped crate planking over Pardo's face. He knew the man was beyond caring, but the thought of laying something heavy right on his friend's face, no matter how gently, made him wince.

He then proceeded with placing the rocks from the boots up. He wasn't worried about running out of rocks, just about unearthing a snake, and prodded each clutter of rocks thoroughly before lugging them off.

Nearly an hour of steady lugging passed before he realized he'd not need many more to complete the task, and finished in a few more dedicated minutes. His arms and legs were aching for rest, and his tongue, swollen from lack of water, could no longer lick his cracking lips. He hefted the water skin, felt it to be less than half full, and rewarded himself with two brief swigs. And though he knew a biscuit would likely cause him to feel dry in the mouth once more, he tucked into one. As Bearpaw put it often, Mack was sore peckish, and so he indulged in a second. They were likely the best biscuits he'd ever had, though he would never tell Ell such a thing.

Mack was about ready to depart when he thought of one more thing. What if for some reason he was unable to make it back to fetch Pardo's body? He slid back downslope a dozen feet eastward and lodged against a jutting rock. Beside it lay more flayed remains of a wooden crate. He wrested three lengths from it and tossed them back up to the top.

As he turned to claw his way back upslope, he glanced about the slope once more for sign of his pistol, which had become lost in the accident. Of it or any other useful items, he saw nothing.

He looked back down toward the trees where he'd seen the dark, restless shape of the mother bear roving back and forth the evening before. He saw nothing save for the trees and hoped she was gone for good.

"Go have a new life. Raise new babies, Mother Bear," whispered Mack as he turned and made his way back up to the top once more.

Using the planks he'd tossed up and strips of leather sliced from the harness lines, he fashioned a cross by lashing a horizontal arm to a vertical piece. On the arm piece he carved PARDO ZINSKI/TEAMSTER, FRIEND/JULY 1850. Getting the cross good and secure took some doing, but he managed to wedge a half-dozen sizable rocks about its base to prevent it from wobbling and toppling easily. He hoped it would last until he could return.

With that last task completed, Mack took to the road. Pardo had said they were a few days from Devil's Creek, if he recalled the teamster's words correctly. What if he came to no other settlements heading toward Devil's Creek? He reconfirmed his earlier decision was better—to make for the known location, that being Watts Corner. It also helped that it was a bustling, busy town and not a degraded, run-down mine camp like so many they had visited in the past couple of weeks.

Over one shoulder he carried the water skin, and over the other the satchel holding the biscuits. His steps were light for long minutes, reflecting that he had somehow left behind an immense burden. Though armed only with his hip knife and a stout, five-foot slender length of planking he'd hacked a handhold into one end, Mack trekked a backward route. In his entire life, he'd never intentionally gone back to a place he'd just left. Not something he liked in the least, it felt as if giving up, taking the easy route in any situation.

But then again, he'd never been in a situation like that before.

He walked on for an hour or so, then stopped in a spot of shade cast from an overhanging sandstone ledge. As he swung the water skin around to his front, he thought he caught a glimpse of something far behind along the roadway. He kept still and watched, not moving his eyes, but sipping and savoring the few precious drops he tasted.

He saw nothing and rested in the blessed shade another few minutes, then resumed his slow, steady way northwestward. Not for the last time, and not for the first that day, Mack wondered about the likelihood of someone passing by.

It seemed a possibility, perhaps a probability, but so far there had been no sign of a soul other than himself, a few eagles and hawks, and one stringy rabbit that crossed the road far ahead of him, moving about as lame as Mack felt.

During one of his increasingly frequent pauses, Mack stood still in the middle of the narrow roadway and cocked an ear forward, hearing little but his own breath. Then from behind he heard a far-off clatter of small rocks and spun around. Again in the far distance, he saw something, a quick flash low and dark. He waited to see if whatever it was came into sight once more.

He rubbed his eyes with the thumb and forefinger of his left hand and squinted as he opened his eyes to look behind him. He saw nothing save for the roadway and the vestiges of little black points from the harsh rubbing he'd given his eyes. *Maybe that was it,* he thought. *Rub too hard, see things that aren't there.*

He resumed his walking and, despite trying to convince himself he was alone on the road, he kept turning back to look behind. After three or four such attempts and seeing nothing, he laughed at himself and kept walking.

Sorely needing rest, he decided to call it a day when he

reached what looked to be a well-used campsite alongside the trail, even though it was still only late in the afternoon. He had a bit of water, enough to keep him trudging into the next day, and he had ample biscuits. The spot offered shade and he hunkered down beneath yet another visor of sandstone large enough to keep most of the sun off him for a spell. Perhaps he would rest long enough to drift away to much-needed sleep and wake early, refreshed and ready to walk. If so, he would get up as early as possible, well before dawn to walk in the cool of the day.

He knew he should have scouted up wood and made a fire, no matter how knackered he felt. And yet . . . he sat too soon, sinking into a relaxed pose and telling himself he was just going to indulge in a quick nap. Before dark and the cold off the desert-like region at night set in, he would fetch whatever burnable items he was able to find.

But it did not work out that way. Within moments of slumping down and sighing, Mack Harrigan sank into a deep, heavy-breathed slumber.

He awoke to find it had grown dark. He also awoke to find he was not alone in the camp.

Something huffed and snuffled, drawing closer to him— too close for him to make any sudden movements, save for his snapped-open eyelids. He swallowed once, and even that sounded too loud. Although darker than dark, once his eyes adjusted to the lack of light, it was still going to be too dark to see much of anything.

But he wouldn't need to see. Soon he was going to be attacked. He knew it surely . . . as if he had heard the story as a boy. The low sound increased in intensity and in proximity. Along with it came the smell of the inside of a deer carcass greening in the sun.

Whatever it was, seemed to his left, not but three, four feet from his outstretched legs.

Unlacing the top of the knife sheath, he let the rawhide thong flop and his fingers scrabble, gipping the handle tightly, ready to draw it out in a moment.

The stranger in camp sounded as if it had shuffled to a stop. It offered a low, deep, raspy, shuddering moan that tapered off in a blast of stinking hot breath. And he knew what it was—the mother bear. She had tracked him all day long. He'd glimpsed her far behind, always far enough back that she could dart out of sight. Were bears that clever? Why not? And who cared?

At that point, Mack knew several things with more clarity than he'd ever felt about anything in his life. He was alone with an angry, wronged mother bear who had stalked him all day. It was full dark, and there she was. He was seated and armed only with a knife. He had a stick but what had he done with it when he sat down?

Never mind. A stick will only provide something for her to swat away.

And then, once again, she closed in on him.

CHAPTER 28

Kane awoke to a smell so foul he knew he was about to empty the contents of his belly. He didn't even make it to his knees before whatever was in there began boiling up in his gullet. He shoved to his feet, legged it over to a stand of nearby trees, and there his gut and chest spasmed over and over until it felt as though he had managed to disgorge his innards.

The stink of curdled food wafted in his face. He wasn't even certain he could open his eyes. And so he remained bent over the meager pool of offerings he'd spewed to the graveled forest duff. He heard soft footsteps beside him and looked to the side—Bearpaw Jones's moccasins.

The man laid a hand on Kane's shoulder. "Not about to ask you how you feel, son, but I will say I am heartily sorry."

Kane tried to speak, but the thudding, lancing pain in his head prevented it. He licked his lips and tried again. "Why apologize?"

"I am afraid I got you in the state you're in."

It was all coming back to Kane—the visit with the fancy folks from England and the promise of an exciting trip with them, then the general camp-wide celebrations, and that fiery liquid Bearpaw had given him to celebrate. Kane was pretty certain it was whiskey of some sort—something he'd not had much experience with. He didn't think he ever wanted that experience again.

Bearpaw Jones held a horn cup out to him. It looked suspiciously similar to the same horn cup that got him into that state.

"Oh no, not that again."

"Now, now, this ain't what you think it is." Bearpaw raised the cup a little closer to Kane.

"What's in it?" said Kane, hesitant to even take hold of the offered cup, recalling with a wince what happened the last time he did.

"Oh, gunpowder, brimstone shavings, and a few other things I can't recall at the moment." He winked. "Ol' Bearpaw wouldn't steer you wrong, would I?"

Kane's eyebrows rose.

"Okay, okay, but I wouldn't do it twice in a row, I promise. I also promised I'd get you back to your mama safe and sound, and this here is the first step to do that."

"Okay, if you say so."

"'Course I do! Why, I was feeling and looking the same way you do not but half an hour ago, and now look at me." He thumped his chest with a fist and let out a wheeze.

Kane had to admit the old mountain man didn't look all that bad. He took the cup and made to sniff it.

"Don't do that!" Bearpaw shook his head and waved his hands. "No, no, it's better just to have at it all in one go. Pinch your nose—it helps— and swallow it down."

Kane nodded and, in no mood to put up a fuss, did as he was told. For a moment the cup full of thick liquid seemed to want to go the way of everything else he'd had in his gullet, but then it settled down.

"Good. Now the thing you need to do is sit still right

under that tree. Trust me. It helps, too, if you close your eyes and wait for the tincture to have its way with you."

The next thing Kane knew he was being jostled about the shoulder again. He awoke and focused his eyes to see Bearpaw's big hairy face leaning in close.

"Um, Kane, you have visitors."

That didn't make any sense. Oh well, he thought. Nothing makes sense anymore, so why not have visitors in a place where I know no one.

Kane opened his eyes and looked up from his seated position leaning against the tree. Bearpaw moved to one side and there stood Lady Teal and Viscount Smithwick, looking down at him, their eyebrows arched high. Lady Teal held a gloved hand before her mouth.

"He got hisself a touch of the camp-wide jangles," said Bearpaw. "It usually lasts into the next day, then it's gone."

Kane barely heard him, so stunned was he to see those two esteemed people standing before him.

"Ahem. Young Mr. Harrigan," said the Englishman, "we, ah . . . were about to move on to relocate our camp to a promising location several miles from here, and wished to bid you goodbye, for now. We still are in hope that we will see you again in a week. Mr. Bridger will let you know the location."

Kane felt himself nodding, then realized he should not be sitting in their presence. He struggled to stand.

"No, no!" said the viscount. "No need to trouble yourself. We're leaving. Come, Lady Teal, we'll let Mr. Harrigan cope with what appears to be quite a severe case of . . . the jangles." He touched his hat brim. As he turned, he held out his hand to escort Lady Teal.

Kane saw the man smirk, and fancied he saw the same look on the pretty lady's face.

After they left, Kane looked at Bearpaw. "Do I look that bad?"

Instead of rushing to reassure him he was fine, the mountain man said, "Well, son, truth is . . . I've seen you look a whole lot better. 'Course, I've seen men with your affliction look a whole lot worse, too." He turned away, mumbling, "Most of them was dead, though."

"What?" said Kane.

"Oh, nothing. Now, how'd that concoction work for you?"

Using the tree as support, Kane stood up, surprised that he felt better. Much better, actually. "I . . . I feel much improved, thanks."

The mountain man beamed. "See? Ol' Bearpaw never did steer a fellow so far wrong he couldn't be yarned back onto the right and true path again."

"In fact," said Kane. "I think I could eat some breakfast."

"Well that's not the best idea you've ever had, for two reasons. One, it's nearly midday. And two—trust me on this—you should have cold water and more of it. Then a cup or two of coffee. Best let the tincture do its work." He tapped the side of his nose and nodded.

"Okay, Mr. Jones." Kane was in no fit state to disagree with anyone.

The day passed in much the same fashion, slow and uneventful. As he followed Bearpaw about the rendezvous grounds, making the rounds and chatting about every topic Kane could think of, it was soon apparent the old mountain man knew everyone.

And he wasn't shy about introducing Kane to everyone, either. To a person, they were smiling, friendly, and welcoming, offering him sips of their own remedies. As much as Kane was tempted, for the very tonic Bearpaw had given him had indeed worked wonders, whenever he caught the old trapper's eye, Bearpaw would quietly tell him to decline such offers.

Later, he asked him why, and Bearpaw said, "Because most of them were just offering you the hair of the beast that bit you. You'll end up tumbling down the same old hole you were in last night!"

"Oh, no. I don't want that."

"I know you don't!"

By nightfall, Kane was feeling much more himself, and tucked into a hot meal of beaver stew and biscuits. It was his first time tasting the rodent and he found it succulent and tender.

"I lament the passing of the plews," said Bearpaw when they had finished. Each was stretched out with their feet to the flames of their small but serviceable fire. Like everyone else, they had set up a modest camp away from others, though not necessarily out of sight.

"What do you mean?" said Kane.

"Oh, the fur trade is still booming here and there, to be sure, but the future's plain as the beard on your face." Bearpaw winked. It was a mild joke between them.

Kane was still young enough his whiskers weren't much yet.

"It's all dependent on fashion, you see. Folks such as the viscount and the Lady Teal, well, they decide to wear a beaver hat one season"—Bearpaw shrugged—"then a hand-knitted cap the next. And that's that. All these folks here are out looking for other ways to make cash money."

"What else can they do?"

"Oh, the buffalo trade's looking promising."

"Buffalo? Is there much call for buffalo hides?"

"You'd be surprised. Not just the skins but the meat as well. And the horns. In fact, most tribes will use nearly every little bit of a buff. That's a notion I admire. No wasting that critter's most precious gift so we can fill our bellies and shod our feet."

Kane nodded. "Maybe so, but I can't imagine killing a big, slow-witted beast is much of a challenge."

"You'd be surprised. And skinning them is another game altogether!"

They were silent awhile, then Kane said, "There must be some other way to get along in the world while still exploring all this beauty out here." He held his hands up as if weighing unseen items.

"Oh, you got it bad, ain't you?"

"Got what bad?"

"A love. For this place, I mean." Bearpaw smiled. "I've seen it before, you know. Had it myself. Still do! This pretty land winks at you once and you never forget it. Why do you think I keep roving and roving with Ol' Gravyfoot? Can't get enough. Just like anything that's good in life, the more you see, the more you want to see. And just like life itself, the more you see and learn, the more you realize you don't know a blamed thing." He shook his head, nursing the last of the coffee in his tin cup, which he'd laced with whiskey from his battered pewter hip flask.

"What do you think will happen if I show up late to meet with the viscount and Lady Teal?"

"And Bridger. Don't forget Jim."

"Yes, him, too."

"Well, I expect they have a lot of ground to cover, and if you're not there, you'll be left behind."

Kane grew silent once again, musing on how he was going to ask his parents. Tell his parents. He had to convince them the offer was something he needed to do.

"It don't mean they won't be disappointed, though."

"Who?" Kane asked.

"Boy, climb back down out of those clouds. The count, or whatever he is, and his lady. They took a shine to you, and they see promise in you. Maybe more than you even see in yourself. They are quality folks, elsewise Jim wouldn't have dragged us up there to introduce you to them."

"I appreciate you letting me go meet them."

"Let you? Heck, son, you're a grown man as far as I'm concerned. Otherwise I never would have let you sample the popskull last night. It was a hard lesson, but I hope it taught you to keep your wits about you. Whiskey's nice, but in sippin' doses. I lost track of you after that second drink, and from the state of you this morning, you didn't stop at two cups full." Bearpaw smiled and shook his head.

"You really think I'm a grown man?"

Bearpaw chuckled. "In most ways, sure. But in lots of ways, life ways, you got plenty of growing to do. Don't be in a rush. It all happens as it needs to. And then it happens too fast. Enjoy the journey."

"Pa told me the same thing."

"Wise man is your Pa. Speaking of, you decide how you're going to tell them, yet?"

"No, not yet."

"Well, we have a tidy little journey ahead of us tomorrow back to Devil's Creek. It'll give you time to mull it over. Your pa might well be there by then."

They sat for a while longer, the whoops and shouts of the previous night sounding as if they might be slowly commencing once again.

Finally, Bearpaw yawned and stretched. "Not sure about you, but I ain't half the man I was when I was your age. Well, except for this"—he smacked his belly and chuckled—"so I am going to call it a night. Let those fools have at it. You do as you please."

Kane nodded. A moment later, he, too, stretched out and pulled his blanket over him. "Good night, Mr. Jones."

"Good night to you, Mr. Harrigan."

Mr. Harrigan, thought Kane.

He liked that. It had a ring to it. Downright adult sounding, it was.

CHAPTER 29

The thought that he should have worked harder to find his gun, any gun—they'd had several with them on the wagon—gnawed at Mack's mind while the bear sniffed and pawed and closed in for the attack.

He still could not see the bear but did not need to. He knew it was the same she-bear who had lost her cub in the accident. The same shadowy presence had followed him all day, never quite in sight. It was too late to do anything but fight her to the death with his knife. For he had nothing else save his fists and feet. His own teeth were no match for the bear. The make-do staff he'd carried all day lay in the dirt beside him but would be useless anyway.

Then she was on him, bellowing hot, stinking breath in his face. The sound of her deep huffing rasping bawl mingled with the sickening stench rolling off her as if she stood upwind of him.

Her outline, skylined against the night sky, was visible enough to show she had grown! No, no, Mack. He cursed himself, freeing the knife and trying to roll to his right.

She drew back, growing taller before dropping straight on him, her big, wide maw leading the way for the rest of her death-dealing attack. A massive paw landed on his left shoulder, pinning him breathless while she bellowed and snapped her teeth.

It was going to be a close-quarters fight, and felt as if it would be short and painful, especially for him.

As if to confirm those suspicions, she raked Mack's chest from high up on the left side to below the bottom of his ribs on his right. He felt the hot seepage of blood weeping and oozing out. Overwhelmed by her speed, he finally thought to jerk upward the knife firmly gripped in his right hand.

He didn't know if he landed a blow that pained her, but he did feel grimy fur writhing about his gripping hand. As soon as he shoved the knife toward her writhing bulk again, she swatted at it as a man might an irksome fly. He kept his grip on the knife, but his arm swung away to his right, slamming his knuckles into the boulder against which he'd sat.

Her big face and big, stinking mouth bellowed without ceasing. She seemed intent on shoving her face into his, as if she intended to scare him beyond thought before she swatted his head with a mighty paw and sent him sprawling dead or, at best, never to regain his wits.

In the scant slivers of moments before that happened, Mack Harrigan struggled to renew his grim, tight-mouthed demeanor. He felt the hot stickiness of blood on him and didn't know if all of it was his, or if he had landed a wounding strike to her big, hairy body.

But she was more worked up than ever, and still held him down, pinned at the left shoulder. She pulled her head back, preparing for another savage blow. Mack was as ready as he could be and brought his right arm and knife around just as she lunged.

He heard nothing but bear rage, smelled nothing but the

rotted-flesh stink of her hair and breath, and felt her mass pressing down on him once more. He positioned the big knife up high, risking another swat from her large, dismissive limb, but she was moving fast and the blade evaded the blow.

As she descended on him, the hilt of the knife pushed down at him. He kept it upright and felt the deadly tip of the wide blade pierce something. Her skin?

It must have been the force of her attack, thought Mack, that enabled him to puncture her hide. Unless he was wrong.

Her rage increased as she flailed. Mack refused to let go of the knife handle. It was his only hope.

She jerked backward and off the knife blade. Mack had no way of telling if he had landed a critical blow, but it had been somewhat effective. She spun and flopped to her right side, clawing at her exposed chest.

Mack jerked hard to his right. On his second attempt, he freed his shoulder from beneath her pinning paw while visions of his pistol and his shotgun swam in his mind. Using one would be so easy, so simple, but he had neither.

He did have that brief moment of respite as she'd jerked away from him. But for how long?

Long enough to roll away, Mack. Get the rock, any rock, between you and her.

She was no longer skylined against the purpling sky, but he heard her constant low, growling, thundering rumble from deep in her body. A thought he should have known earlier came to him. *She won't give up until I am dead or she is dead.*

That was not what he wanted for himself, and it was not what he wanted for her, but her mothering instinct was too much within her. She couldn't think of anything but killing the still-breathing thing she associated with causing the death of her cub.

All this and more Mack thought as he scrambled backward to get around the big rock, knowing she was but feet away, swaying and chuffing, popping her teeth and sounding beyond enraged.

Gripping the knife as tight as he was able to hold it in his sweat-slick hand, he continued backward. Gasping but wishing he could keep as quiet as possible, he felt the stickiness of blood leaching down his raised arm.

When she attacked again, any second now, she would stop playing with him. She would sink her fangs into him, close her big, yellow-toothed mouth on his head and crush his skull right there, and then rip him apart for other creatures to devour, leaving little trace of him. Ell would perhaps never know what became of him.

He shook off those grim thoughts and continued to slam his shoulders and the back of his head into the boulder. Big and cold it had to have an end. There had to be a way to get around it.

And then it was there. If it was low enough for him to climb, it would be low enough for her to do the same. Still, perhaps he could climb it. Perhaps he could reach a higher spot than she could.

And then what, Mack? Wait her out? It's a long ol' time until morning shows itself.

She would not give up on him.

As if to prove the point, he heard her growling and huffing draw closer once more. At best he figured he'd only managed to get a dozen feet from her. He shoved upright. However, with his shaky legs beneath him and the boulder to his back, he was on the backside of it. The roadway was somewhere before him, perhaps twenty feet away.

And then, once more, she was rushing at him, barreling at him on all fours.

How could I know that? he wondered as he sidestepped, feeling as though he were evading an ordinary billy goat. The partial moon was beginning to light the landscape from low on the horizon to his left high enough to wink out from behind thick, fast-moving clouds. He wasn't so certain it was a good or useful thing, for the beast driving at him was smeared in something wet and shining—blood, yes, but whose?

Hers or mine?

It matted her chest and was smeared on her snout and bared, snatching, flashing teeth. Her eyes might well have been made of blood and fire, for all the rage in them.

Five feet from him, she jerked to a halt as if yanked by a rope. Then she shoved upright, taller than him once more, and advanced on him, walking like a man on her hind legs, her front legs pawing at him.

Just as this bloodied demon reached him, Mack made one of those decisions in life you don't have time to mull over. Only in hindsight are you able to determine if it was a good call or not. By then it was far too late, of course, if you'd made the wrong choice.

Mack covered the remaining few feet, propelling himself forward, his right boot sole shoving hard away from the rocky face behind him. He bent low, but she was already surging forward and dropping down into a crouch herself, her head lower than he expected.

His free left arm he held close to his chest, hoping to keep it between his tender, damaged chest and her seeking jaws and clawing foreleg. With his knife hand, he sought her chest.

Man and bear met, the man with his one great, deadly

hand poised, but not raised high. Instinct told him that would only result in her swatting his arm away, perhaps ripping it off his body.

It did not work out the way he had planned. Not that he'd had much time to think his attack through.

She knocked him back, slamming him from his feet as if he were a child new to walking. And then she descended on him once more, this time for good.

The only thing that he thought might save him was that knife, but though he held it before his chest, blade out like a ship's prow, her face reached him first.

Her mouth, stinking and wet and bloody and growling and huffing her death breath on him, closed over his face and he felt the teeth squeezing together. All the while her claws from both paws sought to puncture him through his wool and leather garments.

He jammed upward harder than ever, doubling the strength reserves he'd dragged up from somewhere to lug the dead Pardo up the steep slope.

Once more Mack felt the sickening thick wetness that is only ever blood. It comes with the fading warmth of life itself, and with it also the only thing in all the world that smells as it does. It is the thing beasts the world over share, hot blood pumping inside. But when you smell it, that means something has gone wrong and it is outside of its intended vessel.

And is even worse if it is your own precious blood.

Mack smelled it and gagged as it filled his mouth and poured over his face. He thrashed, bucked, and flailed, but the big bear bore down on him, rushing him with her deadly bulk and cloying, stinking, matted fur.

As his mouth and nose and eyes filled with blood—hers or his or both,—he knew not. As his strength ebbed, it occurred to him the same might be happening to the bear as well.

Either that or he was dying, fading from life and losing his ability to detect movement. Already sound was gone, for he no longer heard her growling.

And then Mack Harrigan knew no more.

CHAPTER 30

It took Mack many long minutes the next morning—at least he thought it was the next day—before he was able to stand. Even at that, the most he could muster was a bent over, swaying hunch in the roadway. With his hands on his knees, he worked slowly and steadily to draw breath back into his lungs—big improvements over the whistling trickle of sweet air he'd managed when he first dragged himself out from beneath the dead bear.

If ever a man felt worse than death and still drew breath, he reckoned he was that man.

He massaged his chest and wondered if the weight of the bear had somehow crushed something vital as she lay across him, but he felt none of the tell-tale sharp stabs of pain he'd felt a few times when he'd damaged a rib bone. And his breathing, while poor, seemed to be getting better.

Oh, how on earth do I manage to get dragged into such scrapes?

The wry answer came to him as he pulled in air, gaining a bit more with each wheeze and pull, wheeze and pull. Despite his situation or perhaps because of it, the answer caused him to pull a weak grin. He dragged himself into such scrapes. He and nobody else. It was a mad world he'd entered into willingly, a world he'd dragged his family into despite the dangers to them all. The raw frontier was everything he had thought, had hoped it would be.

Not the deadly encounters with bears and kill-crazy warring tribes, but all the rest of it, the good, the bad, and the in-between. It represented a life he had yearned for beyond the time worn borders of Harrigan Falls. It was fine for some, for most, actually. But all his life, Mack had been different from most other people. He had always hungered for adventure. Ell knew that about him, and had agreed to join him in life anyway.

And his uncle Zeke had dangled the real possibility of an extraordinary life every time one of those letters came.

The letters. Did he still have them?

Mack half straightened and patted his inner pocket, where he kept them tied and tucked away. They were there. Not that he needed them. He knew everything in them by heart, having read them over and over for years.

Suddenly hearing a heavy breathing sound, like an animal huffing, he thought, *Oh no. Not again.* He staggered backward a few steps to look behind the boulder, but the big mother bear was still there, still slumped, still as dead as she'd been a few minutes before.

His hand sought the knife in his sheath once more, his fingertips dragging through the thick, slick gore covering his body. Touching the knife, he lifted it free with a shaky hand and thought, *What's that sound?*

If it wasn't the mother bear . . . maybe it was another one. Maybe it was its mate.

Oh, it didn't work that way. Did it?

Coming from the road, from the direction of the wreck, the same route he'd walked, the sound grew louder. He leaned forward to see what made the sound, but the sun hammered down on him, causing him to squint. Filled with sweat and heat, his eyesight wavered, then he felt as though the earth had decided to trade places with the sky.

Once more his mind began to darken. Though he fought the coming cloud of unconsciousness, he knew that's what it was. He was far too weak to struggle. As the sounds grew louder, he saw less and less, heard his own heartbeat thudding in his ears, and then he lost the fight. Before his knees buckled, Mack Harrigan was out.

"Hey. Hey, mister!"

Somebody was shouting. The voice came to Mack as an echo, louder and louder. Then he was hit.

Feeling the sting on his face, he forced open an eye. "You look familiar . . ." Mack squinted at the face peering down at him.

"Harrigan. Harrigan? That you? Mother, it's that Harrigan fella from the trail. Them Shoshone folks, you remember!"

Mack felt cold all over, and his eyesight began to blur around the edges. He staggered but somehow didn't fall. Maybe he was dying. It wasn't so bad, except he'd never see Ell again or the children. "Ell?"

"Mother, quick!" a voice close by him said. "We got to get him warm! We'll camp here. Children, help your mother . . ."

That was all Mack heard, for once again, along with his fading eyesight, his hearing pinched out, too.

Mack awoke to darkness and the smell of wood smoke and the crack and pop of dry wood succumbing to flame.

"Papa . . . he's awake!"

The voice Mack heard was a woman's, and it sounded like a whisper. He tried to speak, but his mouth was dry as an old hunk of sun-bleached leather. He ran his tongue over his lips and tried again. "Who . . . where am . . ." That was all he could manage before a dry, wracking cough coursed like a hot lance from his chest up through his throat. It hurt like the devil himself was in there waving a hot brand about.

"Easy now, easy, Harrigan." It was a man's voice. "You're okay now. Rest easy. You don't talk, I'll fill you in, okay?"

Despite the man's directive, Mack managed a croaking attempt at speech. "Who are you?"

"Old friends, okay? Just rest. Ethel, hurry up with that water."

"I'm coming, I'm coming."

As the man shifted position, Mack saw his face in full and knew who it was. "Judd Newcomb?"

"That's right, that's right! How-dee-do, Mr. Mack Harrigan?"

Just then the man's wife bent over him, elbowing her husband out of her way.

"Mrs. Newcomb," said Mack. "But how? How did you find me?"

"We come from Devil's Creek, saw your wife and all them child critters of yourn."

"Ell!" said Mack, shoving his elbows beneath him.

"Now, now," said Judd Newcomb. "Everybody's fine, just fine. Why, we even met that wild old mountain man you told us of on the trail some months back. Nice fella. They all said to keep an eye out for you, as they expected you any time."

"How far is it to Devil's Creek?"

"Oh, no more than . . . what would you say, Mother? A day, two?"

"If that, yeah," said Ethel.

"I . . . I need to get back there. I promised Pardo I'd see him buried properly there." Mack let that hang. He didn't know what to do next, but he did not expect his saviors, his hosts, his friends, the Newcombs, to do what they did.

Judd exchanged a quick glance with his wife, who nodded once, then freshened their coffee cups.

"Mack . . . me and Mother, we'd be more than happy to fetch you back to Devil's Creek. Truth is, we're sort of partial to the place ourselves. Even left our goods there in a little spot outside of town proper that came up empty before we got there. Only reason we were roving on toward this Watts Corner was because I had an itch to see it. But we ain't in no rush to see it, are we, Mother?"

She shook her head, her kind eyes smiling.

"I'm glad you came along."

"I bet you are!" Newcomb laughed and, in a move reminiscent of Bearpaw, he smacked his trouser leg.

"What about my friend, Pardo?"

"What about him?" said Judd. "Oh, we'll see him right enough. Got a tarpaulin in the back, in case we bought goods that needed covering. I expect our two-horse team can lug us all back to Devil's Creek, and him, too. Lighter than when we come West. Though if he's getting whiffy, we'll have to wrap him up and keep him downwind of us. Won't be for long, anyway."

A long pause was followed by Mack clearing his throat. "I don't know how to thank you for this, for your help. For all of it."

"But?" said Judd, smiling and shaking his head. "There's something else, ain't there?"

"How did you know?"

"He's like that," said Ethel. "Always has been. Sees ha'nts and whatnot, too."

Judd nodded with his eyes closed, his head bowed as if by a heavy weight. "Too true."

"I see," said Mack, willing to believe anything at all about those people who'd showed up at such a time and who'd agreed to anything he'd asked. *Up until now,* he thought. *I have nothing to lose.* He cleared his throat. "It's about the bear."

"I was going to ask you about it," said Judd. "Just didn't know how. Some folks are sensitive about such."

"Oh?"

"Yeah, my first thought was that you'd want it as a rug, then as you spoke I thought, 'No, this fellow has spent time with Indians. I bet he has other notions.'"

"As a matter of fact, I do. But you'll think I've gone odd in the head."

Judd laughed. "A man who wrassles bears? Nah, from what I've seen out here, you're about average."

Mack smiled, too. "You see, the accident took this mother bear's cub from her. She was mighty worked up about it."

"I'll say," said Ethel, looking at the tattered man.

"So if you're game, I'd like to use that tarpaulin of yours, flop her on it, cinch her in, and drag her back to the accident site. That's where her baby is, somewhere down that slope."

Judd rasped a big hand over the back of his neck. "Aw, heck, why not? I'm game, if the tarpaulin holds out. Rough dragging, you know."

"Yes, I realize that. I'll buy you a new one, for certain."

Judd scratched his chin then glanced at his wagon. "I ain't worried about that. It's the loading and the lugging that'll challenge us. Might be with the two of us we could manage to hoist the bundle up enough that she'd hang instead of drag."

"You think?"

"Worth a try."

Their conversation went on like that for a while longer, with Mrs. Newcomb shaking her head at them and tending to supper and the three children.

The next morning, though Mack was stiffer than ever, between him, Judd, Ethel, and even the three Newcomb tots, they bundled the mother bear's body as they'd hoped and made the journey at a slowed pace back to the accident site.

Mack was relieved to see Pardo's make-do burial mound had not been disturbed.

Mrs. Newcomb rummaged in the strewn wreckage and squirreled up a few bundles of cloth and other goods splayed out on the slope. "I don't imagine anybody would think ill of us for laying claim to a little of this, do you?"

"No, ma'am," said Mack, though he suspected the goods were strictly speaking, the property of whoever it was Pardo had been hauling for. Likely a merchant in Devil's Creek. He'd worry about it later, but he was not about to tell his rescuers they weren't entitled to a share of what battered spoils they found appealing.

They dragged the bear to the edge of the slope and lifted the tarp. She flopped and nearly stopped, then gained momentum enough that she continued on down the slope.

She rolled past the place where the wagon had first come to a rest, and kept going. And then beyond, right about where he'd last seen the baby bear's body. At the end of her last journey, Mack and Judd could only see a distant downslope black patch.

Then they turned their attention to uncovering Pardo, used the same tarp they'd used for the bear, and managed to get Pardo's body lashed and cinched good and tight at the rear of the wagon.

During the journey back to Devil's Creek, the children sat up front with their parents, and Mack rode in the back with Pardo. It was a quiet, jumbling ride that took them less time than anyone had supposed, a fact that didn't come to him until before noon on the second day, when they drew within sight of Devil's Creek.

CHAPTER 31

Mack's homecoming elicited much in the way of shock to everyone in Devil's Creek, relief to Ell and the children and to Bearpaw. Kane, Meghan, Fitch, and the twins, Henry and Hattie, who had changed quite a lot in the days since his absence, were so very happy to see him, though not nearly as much as was he to hug them, all at once.

Ell, dear, sweet Ell's reaction mirrored his own the most. She held his torn coat and shirt in both hands and looked up into his face for long moments, her eyes glistening. Then she leaned her head on his chest and they stood in an embrace he hoped would never end, for a long, long time.

Until Fitch complained that he was hungry.

While they ate, Mack told Ell all about the claim his uncle Zeke had staked for him, but she had very little to say about it. She smiled and dabbed salve on his wounds. "Time enough to talk about all that when you're well again."

Other than his wife's quiet reaction to what he considered to be wonderful news, the only thing that seemed off to Mack about his family was the obvious fact that Kane had something to tell him and Ell.

The day after the Newcombs fetched him back, a day of rest and mourning was called for and the entire town turned out to see Pardo Zinski buried in the new town cemetery. The death and burial of the much-liked man was marked town-wide with many hung heads and toasts of whiskey to his kindness and friendship, and to his odd, seemingly gruff ways.

Mack was to learn the man he'd come to know as a friend was highly regarded by most everyone in town who knew him. All commended Mack for fetching Pardo back to the town he'd called home.

The next day, a contingent of men from the town agreed to take an empty work wagon and ropes and see what they might be able to recover from the wreck, cargo-wise. Mack set about attending to Pardo's business affairs, assisted by Penelope Sweeney, who, Mack learned, had always helped Pardo with his accounts books.

Other than that, upon his return to Devil's Creek, Mack had no desire to do much of anything except rest up, heal up, and bask in the loving glow of his family.

Several days after his return, Mack set out to walk early one morning, as was his custom. It felt good to stretch the knots and kinks in his body and finger the various slowly healing gouges and lashes from the bear. He beckoned to Kane, and they each took a cup of hot coffee from the campfire and walked off together.

"What is it, Kane, that you need to tell us that you aren't telling us?"

The young man shrugged. "I'm not so sure it matters anymore."

"Well, try. You never know."

"Okay." He scratched his chin and Mack noticed the young man standing before him was no longer a boy. Sure, he'd always be a boy, his boy, his son, his first born, but he was a man now. With chin hairs and everything.

"You know I went to the trappers rendezvous with Bearpaw, right?"

Mack nodded. "He said you had a rip-roaring good time."

Kane blushed and nodded. "Well, something else happened there, too."

"Oh? What's that?" Mack sipped his coffee.

"I . . . I—" Kane sighed, then blurted out, "I was offered . . . the opportunity of a lifetime, Pa." He looked at his father then, his face bright, his eyes wide, and with a true look of excitement. And a smile spread wide on his face.

Seeing Kane's excitement, Mack said, "Tell me all about it."

"Well, there might still be time, if I tell it quick. Then I'll have to go."

"Go?"

Kane nodded.

Mack smiled and put his arm around Kane's shoulders and steered him back to camp. "Then you'd best tell it once, to your mother and to me. And then you'd best pack."

"Pack?"

"Sure, son. If it's as you say, the opportunity of a lifetime, you can't very well miss out on it, can you?"

"But—"

"You don't need our consent. You're a man now, Kane. Near enough, anyway."

As they neared the camp, Kane looked at Mack. "Funny, that's what Bearpaw said."

"Well, he's a wise man," said Mack.

A voice from the shadows spoke up. "Darn right he is!" Bearpaw Jones walked into the light, holding his own steaming cup of coffee. As he sipped, he winked at Kane over the rim of the cup.